The Lottery

A NOVEL

THE LOTTERY

A NOVEL

D. K. WALL

Conjuring
Reality

All inquiries should be addressed to:

Conjuring Reality LLC
PO Box 2231
Murrells Inlet SC 29576-2231

ISBN 978-1-950293-00-1 (Paperback)
ISBN 978-1-950293-01-8 (eBook)

Library of Congress Control Number: 2019901422

This book is a work of fiction. The story incorporates real locations and entities, but all are used in a fictitious manner. The events of the story, the characters, and Millerton itself are products of the author's imagination and purely fictional. Any resemblance to actual persons, living or dead, is coincidental.

Cover designed by Glendon S. Haddix of Streetlight Graphics

CONTENTS

PART I

FOOTBALL FRIDAY NIGHT

Fourteen Years Ago

1

The four best friends stood shoulder to shoulder in the cold, driving rain. The future stretched only one second ahead in their minds. The hulking man screaming in their faces prevented them from thinking of anything else.

"Your choice. Right here. Right now. Are you winners?"

"Yes, Coach!"

Coach Tommy Burleson stood in the center of the huddle of uniformed teenagers as rain dripped from his navy-blue ball cap, the white-stitched MHS logo a waterlogged gray. Fog puffed from his mouth and hung in the chilled air with each shouted word. "One second on the clock. One play left to run. That's it. This is all about pride. Ain't nothing means more than pride, right, gentlemen?"

"Yes, Coach!"

Nathan Thomas bounced on the toes of his cleats, burning nervous energy and keeping his muscles loose in the frigid November air. His shoulder pads clacked against the pads of his teammates crowded beside him. The coach thumped him in the chest with a meaty fist and waved at the three boys closest to him, their dark-blue jerseys covered in mud. "We'll do it for these four right here. The Fearsome Foursome. Our defensive seniors. They are about to walk onto that field for the very last time as Millerton High School football players. They'll never again suit up in the blue and white. And we owe it to them to bring this victory home. We'll do this for our seniors, right?"

"Seniors, Coach!" The surrounding underclassmen slapped the backs of their seniors, a thunderous smack against their soaked jerseys.

The steady downpour and drifting fog obscured the scoreboard at the far end of the field. The speckling of burned-out light bulbs made it difficult to read, but Nathan knew what it said: one second to go, Home 14, Visitors 10.

One second. With a single tick of the clock, his football career would end. Holding on for a victory in their final game, especially against their hated rival who had beaten them every year, would take some of the sting away.

The Fearsome Foursome had first put on uniforms together as five-year-olds in a Pop Warner league in the town's park. They hadn't become fearsome yet—barely able to run the length of the field without tripping over their feet—but that was a big step up from the chaotic, muddy backyard tackle fests before that.

Ever since, they'd been a team both on and off the field though football was their uniting passion. But in the blink of an eye, that would come to an end. Charlie Mills, Hank Saunders, and Danny Morgan would join him in walking off the field for the last time. He would never intercept another pass. Never slam an opponent to the ground again. Never play side by side with the boys he considered brothers.

Last play ever. Contemplating that was difficult. Nathan thought nothing mattered more than being on the field, surrounded by his teammates.

The coach wrapped his beefy fingers around Hank's face

mask and pulled the muscular teenager forward, bouncing him off Nathan's shoulder. Burleson leaned until his head touched Hank's helmet. Spittle flew from his lips. "Your little brother has run his heart out tonight. Two touchdowns! Has us up by four. Do you want to win this game for your family, son?"

Hank swiveled his head and beamed with pride at his younger brother, Matt, standing a few feet away with the offense, their season already over. No matter the outcome of this last play, they would not take the field again. They were relaxed and loose, celebrating the taste of victory just a second away by leaping in the air and butting chests while whooping in delight.

Matt stood to the side of the chaos, his attention focused on a cheerleader shivering in her skimpy outfit. Colette Morgan blushed and smiled back.

Shorter and thinner than his older brother, Matt possessed the natural speed and grace of a running back. While Hank liked the collisions of defense, his younger brother loved tucking the ball close to his gut and eluding defenders.

The coach used the brothers' differences to motivate each of them, constantly comparing the success of one with the weakness of the other. Weight-room workouts turned into battles. Locker-room pranks raged. During practice, Matt's quick feet outmaneuvered his brother in one play, but in the next play, Hank would slam his brother to the ground and stand over him to gloat. At least once a week, a fistfight broke out between the two, stopping practice as the coaches separated them and dispatched them to run punishment laps. Even those laps turned competitive as Matt would taunt his slower, older brother by running circles around him or by jogging backward. More than once, to the exasperation of the coaching staff, they came to blows in the middle of being disciplined.

But as competitive as they were with each other, they

shared a familial loyalty and would come to each other's aid without hesitation. Hank might enjoy crushing his smaller sibling in a tackle, but anyone else who hurt Matt had to answer to a fiercely protective big brother. Tonight, the Roosevelt Rough Riders felt Hank's furious response to every hit they placed on Matt.

Not that the blows bothered Matt. Their defenders—and they always needed more than one—dragged him to the soaked ground repeatedly, but as the referees untangled the pile of bodies, he would spring to his feet with a flashy grin across his muddy face. Nothing made a boy tougher than a bigger brother's constant harassment, and none of the Roosevelt players walloped him as hard as Hank did.

Burleson released Hank's helmet and gestured toward Matt and his offensive teammates. "That whole offense has pounded it out all night long. Played our style, yard by yard. Left their blood on that field. Put points on the board. Given us the lead. With heart, gentlemen. They've played with heart."

"Heart, Coach."

"And so has this defense. You've slugged away all night long. You're cold. You're wet. You're tired. But you're winners, and winners don't care about cold, wet, and tired, right?"

"Right, Coach!"

Nathan hadn't thought of the weather since jogging onto the field with pregame jitters. But he felt like a winner every time he donned the uniform. With all the adrenaline coursing through his body, he would run through fire for his team, so a frigid, soaked field was a picnic.

Burleson dropped to a knee and lowered his volume as though sharing a secret he wanted no one else to hear—a private message just for this team—forcing the boys to lean forward, low into the huddle. "We know their play. Too many yards to run, too little time on the clock. They have to go to their stars—Michael Jenkins's magic arm to Ricky Ward's outstretched hands. One last Hail Mary pass."

He gestured at Hank and Danny. "If Jenkins gets time to set up, he can make that ball sail. So you two will make sure he doesn't have the time. Force him to scramble and throw off-balance in this rain and wind."

Hank and Danny gathered a fistful of fabric of each other's uniforms as they hopped with eagerness. "Yes, sir."

Burleson waved his arms wide at the seven sophomores and juniors lined up behind their senior stars. "This line will be impenetrable. A solid wall that will not yield. You will tie up their line so bad they can't peel off and block Hank or Danny."

Bouncing on their toes, the boys hooted their ascent. "Yes, Coach."

"And you two"—Burleson stood tall, his ample abdomen jiggling under his soaked sweatshirt, and pointed at Nathan and Charlie—"will make sure neither receiver has an inch of air. Not one inch."

Nathan and Charlie. Their names had been spoken together as one since long before they could walk. Born just weeks apart to fathers who had always been best friends, they had shared cribs, toys, meals, games, and lives. Nathan's first real fight had come in the first grade when Toby Gearson had pointed out they couldn't be brothers since Charlie was black —though Toby had used a much nastier word—and Nathan was white. Nathan bloodied Toby's nose and stood over the crying boy with his arm around Charlie until Toby agreed they were brothers.

On the football field, they shared the bond of playing the backfield, intercepting receivers or burying them in the turf. They had played together so long that they knew, without asking, what the other was thinking or what he would do. They grinned at each other as they responded to their coach. "Not an inch, sir."

Burleson cupped his hand around the back of Nathan's helmet and looked up at the clouded skies. "Your old man is watching. You know that? He's proud of you. Proud of you on this field tonight. Proud of how you handled yourself every day since he left. Do you hear me, son?"

An ache exploded in his chest as it had so many times since that highway patrolman sat in front of him just over a year earlier, hat in hand, explaining how his father was never coming home. A heroic effort to avoid a broken-down car on a curvy mountain road had ended with his crumpled semi at the bottom of a ravine.

Nathan glanced toward the crowded stands, at the front-row seats his dad and Ronnie Mills had shared for so many years, but Ronnie was sitting alone, with an empty spot beside him on the aluminum bleachers, just as he had all this season and most of last. Nathan closed his eyes to hold back the tears.

Not trusting his voice, he could only nod. Charlie threw an arm around his shoulder pads and squeezed him tightly. Hank and Danny rested their hands on his helmet.

Don't worry, Dad. I've got this. I'll make you proud.

Burleson pulled Nathan and Charlie in close. "Don't you dare let Ricky Ward get his hands on that ball. I don't want to hear his name again until he's in the NFL. No one has kept him out of the end zone for an entire game until tonight. Years from now, you can sit around on barstools, bragging how you held the great Ricky Ward scoreless in his last high school football game. You'll have that memory forever, you hear me?"

Nathan joined his shaky voice with Charlie's steadier one. "Yes, Coach."

His own eyes misting over, Burleson patted Nathan's helmet and turned his attention to all eleven defensive players. His breath formed clouds in the cold air. "Boys, no matter what, after this play, we've finished our season. I'm proud of all of you."

The boys threw their arms over each other's shoulders and howled. The pounding rain splattered against Nathan's face and hid his unbidden tears. Friends. Brothers. The only family he had.

Burleson stretched his arms wide and challenged the team with his booming voice. "How about one more story for our seniors right now? Stop these sons of bitches from scoring, and you end Roosevelt's season. They expected to come in here for an easy win and be in the playoffs next week. Ricky Ward might be playing college ball this time next year, but you'll make sure his last high school game ever is a big fat loss."

The referee approached to signal the end of the timeout as Burleson stoked the flame of his team. "You've said no all night. And with this last play, you have the chance to change their history. To send them back to Charlotte and their glowing skyscrapers, all quiet in their fancy buses. Back to their shiny locker rooms. Back to watching everyone else in the playoffs. I'm tired of losing to them year after year. I'm tired of watching Ricky Ward score touchdowns. And I know you're tired of it. So change it. The future is in your hands. It's your choice. You control your destiny, gentlemen."

THE RAIN-SOAKED home crowd rose to their feet, stomped on the metal bleachers, and roared their encouragement to their gladiators as the team broke the huddle and swarmed onto the field. Friday night in the small North Carolina mountain town of Millerton was high school football night, and the town turned out, no matter what the win-loss record and no matter what the weather. No opponent inspired the fans as much as Roosevelt High School, the hated rival from Charlotte, the sparkling city rising while small manufacturing towns like Millerton declined.

Charlie trotted through the muck beside Nathan. "You good?"

Nathan grinned and pointed at the sky. "I have to be. My old man is watching, right?"

Charlie gestured toward the stands where Ronnie stood among the crowd and screamed his support. "Yeah, well, my old man is watching, and he'll kick both our asses if we let Roosevelt win this thing again. I can't stand another night of hearing him talk about how they beat them every year."

"Don't even think it. Ricky Ward ain't getting into that end zone. Not tonight." He tried to sound confident, but the butterflies in his stomach churned.

Ricky Ward was being recruited by a dozen colleges though rumors were strong that he was University of Georgia bound. Nathan and Charlie were being recruited by none. No matter what happened in the next second, the superstar would play football again—in college and likely in the NFL—while the two Millerton boys would be relegated to the stands for the rest of their lives.

The hype around Ricky Ward—and everyone used both his names as though he were already some superstar—grew each season as he danced and twisted around every defender who challenged him, scoring repeated touchdowns and dazzling the crowds. No one stopped him. Defenders might get a few tackles, even a rare interception, but no one had kept him out of the end zone an entire game since his sophomore year.

Millerton High School had been no exception. For three years, late in November, Nathan and Charlie faced Ricky on the field, and each year, his speed and footwork proved too difficult to contain.

The Roosevelt game was always the last of the regular season, taking on a festive atmosphere though they went to playoffs each year and Millerton did not. Since the schools alternated hosting, the Millerton Mountaineers traveled to Charlotte every other year and played with the skyscrapers gleaming against the night sky, an intimidating sight for boys from a small town. Their field was manicured, well drained, smooth, and used only on game nights. In the shadow of their fancy concrete stadium, their practice fields glistened with thick green grass nicer than Millerton's game field.

For last year's game in Charlotte, reporters and recruiters had packed the glass-enclosed press box to watch Ricky elude his defenders time after time under those glaring stadium lights. Nathan, stinging from the death of his father, hadn't played well in weeks. Sensing the weakness, Roosevelt sent Ricky to Nathan's side of the field play after play, and he racked up four touchdowns. The ride home to Millerton in that creaky school bus was miserable after the season-ending drubbing by their hated rival.

They played this year's game at Millerton on the pitted field used by soccer and football teams, JV and varsity, practice and games. The constant wear left ruts and large dirt patches absent of grass, an uneven field that slowed the all-star receiver in the best of conditions. But tonight's nasty weather, a remnant of a late-season tropical storm that came farther inland than expected, gave Nathan an additional advantage.

He had practiced so many hours on this field that he knew where each hole and divot lay hidden in the standing water. Nights in deer stands had acclimated his body to the freezing temperatures. Days of trout fishing in frigid waters had kept his cold, taped hands as nimble in tackling as in removing fish-hooks. Endless childhood games in the creeks and hills around Millerton had prepared him for the muck of tonight's battle, making the mud-soaked uniform a badge of honor.

Roosevelt started the night by sending Ricky toward Nathan, hoping for a repeat of last year, but their quarterback struggled to deliver the ball in the miserable weather. With the sloppy passing, Nathan contained the star receiver and dragged him down in the sludge, keeping him scoreless. Each play, they fell together into the cold water standing on the field, Nathan smiling and Ricky shivering. When the frustrated quarterback attempted a pass to their other receiver, Charlie intercepted, setting up Matt Saunders for a touchdown a few plays later.

Roosevelt flipped their receivers in hopes of igniting the game, but Jenkins continued to struggle, and Charlie covered Ricky just as well. When the quarterback again tried to engage their second receiver, Nathan got his own interception. Matt waltzed into their end zone just four plays later.

Ricky grew frustrated at his failure to get the ball. Gone was the confident receiver who had taunted and delivered last year, replaced by a dispirited boy not accustomed to losing. He pushed and shoved against his opponents, but that only fired them up to smother him.

With the passing game shut down, Roosevelt relied on running to grind out the yards, keeping the score as close as they could. But with only one second on the clock, too many yards to run, and a playoff season slipping away from their grasp, they would be forced to let Michael Jenkins throw one last pass to his star receiver.

The Mountaineers were one hit, one tackle, away from sending their nemesis on a quiet bus ride back to Charlotte with his fellow Rough Riders, their playoff hopes spoiled by a sub-.500 team that everyone had expected to just fold.

The deafening roar of the crowd reached their ears over the pounding rain. Playoffs and conference championship dreams for Millerton had died weeks before, if not before the season ever started, but beating the rich Roosevelt kids was its own championship, a unifying passion to end the season.

Ricky lined up on the far side of the field against Charlie. Disappointed he would not get the last hit on his nemesis,

Nathan concentrated on closing down his own man in the event they tried a pass to him.

The center snapped the ball to the tall, lanky quarterback. Jenkins dropped back and searched for his target. Millerton's fired-up defense pushed hard, and Roosevelt's line collapsed on the slick field. Hank and Danny fought toward Jenkins from the two corners, threatening to pull him down on the field in a humiliating ending to the game. The quarterback scrambled toward the sidelines, gripping the wet ball and desperately scanning down the field for an open receiver.

Ricky faked a burst deep along the left field line before hooking toward the center of the field, showing the speed the University of Georgia Bulldogs wanted on their own field the next fall. As so many other defenders had, Charlie fell for the fake and found himself several steps behind his target.

The second receiver sprinted right, trying to draw Nathan out of the center of the field and down the sidelines. If he followed and the pass went to Ricky, he would have an open field for a quick sprint to the end zone. But if Nathan covered their star instead, he would leave his own man open for a pass.

Nathan asked himself, with playoff hopes at stake, which play would Roosevelt make? A long last-chance pass to their star, of course. They wanted to drop the ball into his hands, counting on his height and speed advantage to outmaneuver his opponents.

Nathan watched Jenkins scramble away from Hank and Danny's outstretched hands, the quarterback's eyes focused down the field. In the chaos, he didn't have time to find the other receiver nor notice he had been left open. He could only see his star, the preferred target.

Jenkins abandoned any planned fake and heaved an off-balance pass high into the air as he stumbled out of bounds. Nathan broke toward the center of the field, zeroing in on the wide-open receiver. The poorly thrown ball floated through the air, hit its peak, and descended much shorter than planned. Ricky had to slow his run to be under it. Charlie was closing the gap but too far to catch the faster receiver.

Ricky opened his arms for the catch, but with his attention on Charlie, he never saw Nathan coming. He probably wondered why his opponent was grinning despite being out of position.

In the split second he had, Nathan weighed his options. He could attempt to step in front of Ricky and catch the ball, but an interception was pointless and dangerous to attempt, leaving nothing between the speedy receiver and the end zone if he failed. An incomplete pass was ideal, but even a completed pass was fine as long as they dropped him to the ground as time expired. The only thing that mattered was keeping him from scoring, so Nathan concentrated on a well-timed, solid hit.

But this was more than winning a game. This was payback for three years of humiliation. Three years of running up the score. Three years of eluding Nathan's tackles.

The ball fell into Ricky's outstretched hands as Nathan aimed his body right at the point that the ball and the receiver met. He dug his cleats into the soaked turf and launched his body through the rain. As the ball touched his fingertips, Ricky spun to aim for the open field but was surprised to see a flying torpedo only a foot away. Nathan's arms wrapped around Ricky's body as his shoulder rammed into his chest pads. The boy's feet continued to run forward, but his body slammed backward. The noise of the collision reached the crowd, and a chorus of "oooh" floated across the field.

Ricky rocked backward and splashed onto the soaked field, Nathan's body falling on top of him and knocking his breath out of his lungs. Their bodies intertwined and slid through a lake of muddy, cold water.

Charlie pounced on the loose, bouncing football and slid to

a stop beside them, smiling behind his mask as mud dripped across his face.

The referees' whistles shrilled, signaling the end of the game. The crowd erupted in celebration.

Ricky lay on his back, half submerged in the water, writhing in pain from the hit and gasping for air.

Lying on top of him, Nathan raised his head, mud caked on his face, and grinned. "Got you."

2

Showered and dressed in street clothes, Nathan and Charlie left the warmth and celebration of the locker room for the brisk breeze of the parking lot. Only half the scattered lights were on, reflecting off puddles of water on the cracked asphalt but doing little to illuminate the cars. Pools of shadows covered most of the sprawling lot.

Small crowds of people huddled and chattered, insulated by the warmth of the win. Some gathered around cars, making plans with friends for unexpected but hoped-for postgame celebrations. Others waited near the building to congratulate exiting players. Clouds of cigarette smoke hovered over most of the clusters.

Everyone exchanged excited stories of their favorite plays, the last, punishing hit on the star from the city being the best of the best. A small cheer erupted as Nathan emerged from the locker room. He waved his hand in acknowledgment as he strutted past.

Charlie slapped Nathan on the shoulder and pointed at the buses parked in the far corner near the visitors' locker room. The logo of a charging horse covered most of the side. A large panel truck stood beside it with its door open as trainers loaded equipment.

Their transportation was a far cry from Millerton's beat-up old school buses, which spewed smoke as they sputtered down the highway, windows forced open to fight the stench of sweaty equipment piled in the aisles.

Most of the opposing fans had slipped out of the visitor stands as the home crowd celebrated. They had already left for the long ride home, leaving only a small knot of parents and friends to greet the dejected players as they trudged out. Even the nicest bus was miserable after a loss, just like torn bench seats seemed like heaven after a win.

"Shall we go wish them safe travels and a happy off-season?"

Nathan beamed at the idea. "Maybe I should see if Ricky enjoyed tonight's game."

"After that last hit you laid on him, bet he doesn't even know where he is."

"Well, let's go remind him."

"I think that's about the dumbest idea I ever heard." Ronnie Mills's voice boomed as he emerged from the shadows near the building. His dark-blue mechanic's uniform and dark skin had camouflaged his wait in the shadows. Despite his clothes being soaked from sitting for hours in the rain, he didn't appear cold or tired. He walked tall and strong, his work boots splashing through puddles, and exuded a quiet authority that the two boys respected.

"Come on, Dad. It would be fun," Charlie protested half-heartedly, a mischievous grin plastered on his face.

"Fun would be staying out of trouble, graduating in a few months, and then starting community college. Doesn't that sound like a better idea than getting into a fight over a football game?"

Danny exited the locker room and walked past them, his

car keys jangling in his hands. "No way, Mr. Mills. A fight would be much more fun."

Ronnie's eyes followed the muscular teen. "Don't you derail my boys from college, Danny Morgan."

Though smart enough to keep walking out of reach, Danny widened his cocky grin as he called over his shoulder, "College? They should join the Marines with Hank and me. We're gonna see the world and kick ass!"

"See the desert is more like it. I believed all of that crap when I signed up for the Navy too. These two are going to college. And so should you."

"Oorah!" Danny pumped his fist into the air as he strutted toward his car.

Nathan wiped his rain-soaked hair out of his eyes as Ronnie's attention returned to them. "I still don't know if I can handle any more school. Gonna be hard enough just getting to graduation day."

Ronnie fixed his glare on Nathan. "Never known you to shy away from work. You'll be fine in college. And you're not going into the Marines."

"Oh, no, sir. No Marines. I'll leave that to Hank and Danny. I'm just thinking I should work full-time and make cash."

Ronnie crossed his arms over his chest and drew himself to full height. "We've talked about this. You will work for me part-time at the plant, keeping equipment running, which will give you more than enough money. The biggest employer in town, lots of machinery, lots to learn. Danny's dad taught you all about fixing cars. Your dad taught you how to repair big diesel trucks. And now I will show you how to keep factory equipment running. A man who can fix stuff can always make money. Add a college degree to that, and you can manage other people doing the work."

This was the lecture Nathan had heard over and over, first

from his own father and now from Ronnie. "I appreciate it, sir, but part-time won't cover the rent."

"What rent? Ain't no rent in my house. And you're going to college. Period. The money you make working at the plant will pay for tuition and books. I made a deal with your dad, and I'm keeping the deal."

"But—"

"I ain't taking your money. That's your college money. And that's what you're going to spend it on. You pay me by getting this knucklehead"—Ronnie nodded toward Charlie—"through math."

"I get him through math because he gets me through English. I never would have figured out Shakespeare without him."

"Good, then the deal doesn't change when you graduate high school. You live at the house, work part-time, go to community college, don't worry about rent. That's what your dad would want. If he were standing here, he would say the same thing."

"Yes, sir, but—"

Ronnie held up his hand, spreading his long fingers wide. "Your dad would have taken Charlie in if something happened to me. You know it's true, so we ain't talking about it anymore."

"You know I don't want to be a burden."

"Boy, you were at the house half the time before your dad died. Now it's just full-time. You ain't no burden and never have been, so stop it. All this rent talk is just because you want a place to yourself where no one is checking to make sure no girl is in your bed." Ronnie dismissed the debate with a wave of his arms, eyed the two boys, and changed the topic. "So, when should I expect you two home tonight?"

After the boys exchanged glances, Charlie took the lead. "We're going over to Hank's for a bit and then we'll be home."

Ronnie crossed his arms and looked down his nose. "Uh-huh. You two and Hank and Matt? And Danny, too, right? Mr. Mo-rine himself."

"Yes, sir."

"Anyone else?"

Charlie tried to hold Ronnie's stare but dropped his eyes to study a dark puddle in the pavement instead. He mumbled, "And some others."

"Some others. Like half the school?"

Charlie squirmed. "Just some friends, Dad. I don't know how many are coming. Celebrating our last football game. Come on, you remember what it was like."

"Oh, I remember exactly what it was like. Why do you think I'm asking? Girls will be there, right? Girls swooning over their football stars?" Ronnie turned his attention to Nathan. "Donna?"

Nathan gulped but couldn't deny it. "Yes, sir."

"Hank's mom is still working third shift, right?" He held up a hand to cut off the reply. "Don't answer, because I know it's true. So that means no adults at Hank's after midnight?"

Charlie and Nathan looked at each other. They might fail to volunteer information, but neither would lie to him. They knew better and confirmed the lack of supervision with a slight shake of their heads.

Ronnie opened his arms wide and smiled at the boys. "Here's the deal. I'm feeling good because you boys finally beat Roosevelt. Took you long enough, but you did it. You can go to Hank's, but I'm not interested in being a grandpa yet, so get your butts home by midnight." When both boys opened their mouths to protest, he cut them off. "Midnight and not a minute later. Or you can come home right now. Those are the only two options. Which one do you want?"

The boys threw their hands up in defeat. Trying to argue

would only result in them going straight home, and they knew it.

"That's what I thought. I know Hank and Danny well enough to know a keg is involved though I sure don't want to know how they got it. Season is over, and Coach Burleson won't be riding you about drinking anymore, so now that's my job. If I smell any beer on you when you get home, I'll ground you through New Year's, got it?"

The boys looked at their shoes and glumly nodded.

"So I'll see you at midnight, right?"

Nathan could only shrug. "Midnight it is."

Satisfied, Ronnie turned and walked to his truck, shouting over his shoulder. "You know your dads beat Roosevelt every year we played them! I have told you that, right?"

The boys groaned as Ronnie climbed into his pickup truck and joined the line of traffic exiting the high school, taillights reflecting off the puddles.

NATHAN HEFTED his gym bag onto his shoulder. "Midnight? What are we, eleven years old?"

Charlie laughed and shoved Nathan's shoulder. "I'm pretty sure your old man said we had to be inside the house by the time the streetlights came on when we were eleven." His face grew serious as he stared at the taillights of his father's truck, idling in the traffic leaving the school. "We have to get an apartment or something when we graduate. I might be able to handle community college, but I can't deal with a curfew. College girls will not put up with curfews."

They talked about getting an apartment every night, stretched out in their beds on opposite walls in Charlie's bedroom, so Nathan didn't respond. Across the parking lot, Donna and Hank leaned against Danny's car, heads close and chatting conspiratorially. Donna laughed at something Hank said and playfully pushed against his chest. He returned a wolfish grin and sidled up closer to her.

Charlie followed Nathan's watchful stare. "Getting jealous, Mr. Possessive?"

Nathan shook his head but never took his eyes off his girlfriend. "Nah, nothing like that. Hank's my bro, and ain't none of you are going to cut in on a girl I'm dating any more than I would cut in on a girl any of y'all are dating."

"Oh, yeah, sure he wouldn't." Charlie rolled his eyes. "So, when are you going to stop dating her so he can? You've been telling me for two weeks you're going to break up with her."

"Can't." Nathan adjusted the gym bag on his shoulder. He licked his lips and drew in a deep breath. "Donna's pregnant."

Charlie's mouth fell open as he stared at his friend. "Wait. What? Are you sure?"

"Yeah. She told me this afternoon after school. She's been acting weird all week and said she wasn't going to tell me until tomorrow because she didn't want me distracted for the game. I found her crying outside the gym, so I kept asking her what was wrong until she spilled it."

"Whoa." Charlie wrapped a hand over Nathan's shoulder and squeezed. "You going to take her down to Charlotte and get it taken care of?"

Nathan shook his head again, a slow, defeated twist from side to side. "She got furious when I suggested it. Said her mom didn't abort her and she sure wouldn't abort her kid. Said I'd just have to deal with it."

"So that's why you pushed Dad again about working fulltime. Wondered what got that stirred up. You really do need the green to cover some serious child support."

"Worse." Nathan paused and cleared his throat. "I think my old man would tell me I got to marry her."

Charlie dropped his bag and stepped backward. "Wait. No.

What about love and all that stuff?" Because the boys spent most evenings in the twin beds sharing every detail of their days, especially about girls, Charlie knew all the sordid details.

Throughout high school, Nathan had almost always been in a relationship. But unlike a lot of his classmates, they were rarely intense. They would start slowly—hanging out at lunch, chatting in class, studying after school—and last for several months. Then, just like they started, he would slowly drift back out until one or the other of them decided that they should "just be friends." And he was friends with almost all his exes.

His pairing with Donna followed the pattern. They had been friends for years but had fallen into a relationship after hanging out together at a party over the summer. He liked her, had fun with her, and didn't want to hurt her feelings.

But liking someone and being in love with them was very different. He didn't go crazy thinking about her when they were apart. He never dreamed of them being old together. Never pictured their wedding. So he didn't think he really loved her. Though he sure did love sleeping with her. "What about duty and responsibility? I can't abandon her. That kid is half mine, so I sure can't abandon him. I know how hard it is to be a kid without your parents around."

When he tightened his grip on the handles of his bag and started toward the car, Charlie's hand grabbed his arm. "I get it, really, but you can be there for the kid without marrying her."

Nathan shrugged. "But ain't marrying her the right thing?"

"Honest answer? No. At least, I don't think so. Don't go rushing to get married until you're sure."

"I ain't in no rush. I just don't know what else to do."

"Talk to my dad about it before you do anything crazy." Charlie paused before continuing. "But please do me a favor and let me know when you're gonna tell him so I can be far away. He's going to kill you and then lock me in a basement so I don't get a girl pregnant too."

A grin grew across Nathan's face as he teased back. "Wow, way to back a friend."

"I ain't dying because you were an idiot and got a girl preggers."

Nathan sighed and looked toward Donna, still absorbed in her chat with Hank. "Sometimes, I wish I could join Danny and Hank in the Marines—room, food, and they even help pay for college."

"You forgot the part where people shoot at you. Just a minor detail."

"Might be safer than marriage." Nathan shuffled his feet. "You think Danny's dad would hire me as a mechanic in his shop? Then I wouldn't have to tell Ronnie."

"My dad would kill you twice, once for being stupid, and then he'd resurrect you just so he could kill you again for not telling him you were stupid." Charlie picked up his bag and shook the water off it. "If Danny stayed out of the Marines, he could take over the place and then hire you."

"Let's see you convince Danny of that. All he can think is Marines."

"He and Hank better not go over there and get themselves blown up." Charlie rolled his eyes. "Besides, what are you worried about? My dad'll be furious, but he'll still hire you at the plant. That way, he can keep a real close eye on you."

Nathan groaned as they walked through the puddles to Danny's car, the engine already running so that the heater could attack the chill inside.

Seeing their approach, Donna broke away from Hank, stood on her tiptoes, and gently kissed Nathan's lips. "You and Ricky Ward become best friends tonight?"

Placing his hands on her hips, Nathan laughed. "Yeah, we had a real bonding experience. He's coming to Hank's party as my guest. I'll introduce you." He pulled her body up against his own and held her tightly. "You *are* coming, right?"

Donna leaned back and opened the coat she was wearing to reveal a drenched cheerleader's outfit. "Maybe. Got to go home and change. I'm soaked to the bone and freezing."

He slid his arms around her waist under the coat, his best come-hither look on his face. "Want me to come help you change? I like getting you out of that uniform."

Donna playfully slapped his chest and pushed him away. "Yeah, sure. Mom would love that." She leaned back toward him and spoke quietly so that the others wouldn't overhear. "She was so sure you were hiding in my room last Saturday when she got home from work. Looked in the closet and under the bed and everything."

"Good thing she didn't look out the window."

"Yeah, she would have loved seeing your bare ass run across the yard."

He put on his best serious face, the one he thought got him out of trouble with teachers but really didn't, and shook his head. "No, ma'am. She would never have seen it. I got dressed in the bushes before I took off running." He leaned over and kissed her again before she pushed him back.

Hank moved to the front passenger door of the car, ready to climb inside. "Would you two mind not doing that while she's wearing my coat?"

Nathan studied the letter jacket for a moment and realized it was too big to be his own, a coat she had claimed shortly after they had started dating. "And why are you giving my girlfriend your coat?"

"Just being a gentleman, like always." Hank made a mock bow. "Your slow ass was still in the showers. She was freezing, and I always help a damsel in distress."

"Oh, please, only if you think you're going to get lucky."

"Then she would know yet another thing I do better than

you." Hank's eyes sparkled with mischief as he settled into the front passenger seat.

Donna blushed and shivered despite the coat, her lips almost as blue as her eyes. Nathan stroked the wet hair back over her ear. "You need a ride home?"

"Crammed into the car with your crew? No, thanks." She nodded her head at a car across the parking lot, toward her best friend and fellow cheerleader. "Colette is driving a couple of us back to her house."

Danny and his little sister, Colette, had cars to drive because their parents owned a small grocery and convenience store that had a multibay mechanic's garage in the back where Danny's dad did auto repairs and sold used cars. Nathan owned his father's pickup truck, popular on sunny, warm days when passengers could crowd into the open bed, but not in miserable weather, so Danny was the designated driver when it rained.

"Is she coming to Hank's?"

"Matt sure hopes so."

Matt was leaning through the driver's window of Colette's car, chatting and smiling. They had started dating over the summer and spent almost all of their time together, much to the consternation of their older, protective siblings. Hank and Danny bantered endlessly about it, exhausting everyone.

Donna tightened her arm around Nathan's waist. "You know us cheerleader types can fall under the sway of a football star."

"Star? He's a junior."

"He scored two touchdowns tonight and won the game for us."

"I'd like to think the defense—mostly me—stopping Ricky Ward won the game."

"Oh, I like it when you get jealous."

Red flushed across Nathan's face. "I'm not jealous. Just…"

"Just team and all that, huh, Mr. 'Mostly Me.' But you better hope little Matty gets Colette to come to the party so I have a ride. You know she doesn't like crazy parties. And she hates seeing Danny get drunk, and he always does. But she does think Matty is cute." She turned and grunted in satisfaction, staring at Matt's butt as he leaned through the car window. "And she's right. He ain't a little kid anymore. I would say he's growing up fine."

Most guys acted like jealous idiots when their girlfriends talked about other guys, but Nathan didn't. Maybe he just thought of it as harmless talk, or maybe he just didn't feel that possessive about Donna. "You know it's killing Danny that Hank's little brother is crushing on his sister."

"I don't think either one of them cares what Danny thinks."

Nathan tried to pull her close again for another kiss, but she shook her head and stepped back. "I've got to go. Maybe see you later."

"Tell Colette that Charlie and I have to be home by midnight anyway. That'll give her an excuse to leave before it gets rowdy. Come on to Hank's so we can hang out a bit, and then we can be gone before the crazy drinking starts."

Her face brightened. "Midnight? Ronnie's being harsh, but she'll be happy with that."

"Matt won't like it." Nathan pulled her forward and kissed her again as a horn blasted across the parking lot. He looked up to see Colette leaning on the horn and waving.

Matt had broken away, smiling and strutting toward them.

"Matty will live." She disengaged from him and tightened the coat around herself. "And so will you. I got to go. I'm freezing. See you in a bit." Donna took off across the parking lot, ruffling Matt's hair as they passed. As she climbed into the car, she yelled over her shoulder to Hank, "Thanks for the coat! I'll get it back to you."

Matt slid his fingers through his hair, settling the mess Donna had caused, as he walked past Nathan and threw open the back door. He slid across into the middle of the backseat beside Charlie. Nathan slid in behind Danny and closed the door.

Hank turned from the front seat and glared. "Typical. You didn't even get my coat back. Your girlfriend, and I'm the one freezing."

3

"Midnight? Are you kidding me?" Hank's face purpled as he scowled at Charlie.

"Sorry, dude. My old man was clear." Making an exaggerated gesture with his hands, Charlie mimicked his father's voice, "Midnight, boys. Not a minute later."

"And you're just going to do it?"

"Yeah, I like living."

Hank stared out the front windshield at the line of cars exiting the high school parking lot and drummed his fingers on the dashboard. He twisted again in his seat and focused on Nathan. "What about you? You partying with us? He ain't your old man."

Nathan held up his hands in surrender. "No way. He'll kick my butt just as fast. I get no slack from him."

Hank exhaled loudly as he slumped in the front passenger seat. "Man, you would think there would be *some* benefit to being an orphan."

As Charlie rapped his knuckles across Hank's head, Nathan muttered, "Funny thing. Hasn't worked out that way."

Rubbing his head, Hank turned back around, the glower in his downcast eyes gone. "Sorry, man. I…"

Always the peacemaker of the group, Danny draped his arm across the seat, creating a barrier between front and back. "So what's the problem, Hank? We just go get the keg started now."

"Mom's still home. Can't pull the keg out until she goes to work." Hank slumped in the front seat, crossed his arms, and stared out the window at the dwindling crowd.

Danny adjusted the knobs for the heat in the car, turning the defroster on high to chase the fog off the front windshield. "So let's go do a preparty. We can stop by the store and get a case of beer."

"And go where?"

"Up to the Point. No one will be there."

Hank rolled the window down and extended his arm, letting the rain splash in his upturned palm. "Of course no one will be at the Point. No one else is that dumb. They would freeze their butts off."

"I won't," Danny said. "I'm wearing a coat."

The trio in the backseat chimed in. "So are we."

"Oh, great. I'm sitting in the clown car." Hank turned around and pointed at Nathan. "If we're going to the Point, you're giving me your coat. That's your girlfriend wearing mine."

Nathan feigned innocence. "But she said she'd give it back to you."

"Oh, funny. And your fault we're even thinking like this with your stupid curfew."

Refusing to take the bait, Nathan leaned back in the seat and looked through the rain-coated side window.

Wanting to fight with someone, Hank turned his attention to his little brother in the middle of the back seat. "And you aren't going with us to the Point."

Matt leaned forward, always eager to battle his brother. "Not fair. Why not?"

Hank held up two fingers. "Two reasons, Matty. You ain't a senior, and you're my little brother."

Danny leaned over to Hank and spoke quietly. "Let him come. He played a great game tonight."

Hank crossed his arms and shook his head. "Nope, can't do it. Besides, he's got a job to do."

Matt's face crinkled in puzzlement. "What job?"

"Someone has to be home to make sure a bunch of crazies don't show up too early for the party. Mom will kill us if she finds out we're having another one. I told her just the usual crew."

"So why can't *you* do that?"

"Because I'm going up to the Point with my buddies to drink beer."

"So you guys are going out partying, and I'm staying home with Mom?"

"You got it, little bro."

Matt sat back in the seat and pouted. "Not fair."

Nathan leaned over and said softly to Matt, "You can help me, though. Colette is bringing Donna to the party, and Donna won't like it that I'm not there yet. So if you could be nice to them and keep them distracted, I would owe you."

Matt broke out a wolfish smile. "Colette? Sure. Glad to help."

Danny turned around and glared at Matt. "Watch yourself around my little sister. You better not get her pregnant, or I'll rip your balls off."

Hank laughed and hooked a thumb toward the backseat. "Don't worry, Danny. I'll let you know if the little twerp tries to get her into his room."

Red in the face, Matt leaned forward. "Oh yeah? Maybe

I'll just tell everyone which girl you've had in your room lately."

A chorus erupted from the other three. "Oh, this is getting good." "Who was she, Hank?" "She must have been ugly if he doesn't want us to know."

His face flushed red, Hank grabbed a handful of Matt's coat in his hand and dragged him until the brothers were nose to nose. "Nobody, right, Matty?"

Everyone laughed in the car except the two brothers as they glared at each other, neither blinking. To defuse the tension, Nathan put his hand on Matt's shoulder. "Come on, relax. We don't care who Hank is banging. I need you to help me with Donna. And you'll get to chat with Colette, right?"

The tension drained from Matt's face. Hank released his brother's coat from his hand, and Matt settled into the back seat, a smirk on his face. "Fine. I'll go home."

Danny stared into the rearview mirror and caught Matt's eyes. "And chatting with my sister means chatting. Out front with everyone else."

Matt smiled and winked. "Of course, sir. I'm a total gentleman."

Danny slipped the car into gear and drove across the now-empty parking lot. The headlights reflected in the falling rain as he turned onto the main road and accelerated. "Glad that's settled."

———

ABE'S MARKET was about as far from a modern-day convenience store as possible, and not just in distance though it was perched just outside the industrial zone, miles from Millerton's lone interstate exit that the brightly lit stores clustered around.

Different from its well-lit, glass-walled counterparts, Abe's was an older white clapboard building with few windows. The old gasoline pumps were turned on with a wave and a smile if Abe or Martha recognized customers. Otherwise, they had to trudge inside and lay a deposit on the counter.

Unlike the fast-food focus of his competitors, Abe's inventory leaned more to regular groceries—canned and packaged goods, bread, baking supplies, and locally grown fruits and vegetables from area farmers, depending on the season. The coolers along one wall carried beer and soft drinks but also stocked milk, orange juice, butter, cheese, and a freezer of ice cream.

The proprietors greeted regular customers by name and inquired about the health of their families. Martha would make sandwiches in the small deli or discuss the selection of fresh flowers cut from her own garden.

Abe spent his days in one of the mechanic's bays behind the store, working on customers' cars. When a car reached an age at which more repairs made little sense, he always had a small selection of used ones for sale.

Behind those bays stood their house, surrounded by the flower gardens Martha tended when not working in the store. Locals knew that, in an emergency, the couple could be persuaded to open the store after hours.

The passing truckers hauling freight to and from the factories sometimes stopped on the road in front of the store, hazard lights flashing while they rushed inside, even though the truck stop better accommodated their large vehicles. Locals crowded the small store for its diverse inventory. Cars and pickup trucks parked haphazardly throughout the day though traffic dwindled as the smaller second shifts took over the nearby plants.

Without the nighttime traffic to support the business, Abe's was only open fourteen hours a day, from six in the morning until eight at night, six days a week—never on Sundays. And never on football Friday nights.

Like much of Millerton, except those corporate gas stations and the fast-food chains by the interstate, Abe and Martha closed their store early on Fridays in the fall to go to the high school and watch their son play football and their daughter cheer. The rain and cold had not kept them away that night either.

Danny and Colette had grown up working in the store after school until closing, all day on Saturdays, and throughout the summers. They stocked shelves, made deli sandwiches, pumped gas, worked on cars, ran the cash register, and kept the inventory records—both preparing to one day run the store themselves if they chose.

Their friends envied that they had cars, albeit from the used-car inventory that Abe might sell at any moment. But long before that, their friends appreciated that they had keys to open the store on a hot summer Sunday for a soft drink or ice cream.

And those keys gave them another advantage.

If a teenager dared to waltz into the store and attempt to buy beer with a fake ID, no matter how carefully crafted, they would be denied. And, worse, Abe or Martha would pick up the telephone and dial the offender's parents, a common courtesy in a small town.

But a teenager with a key to the store was a secret weapon in the never-ending teenage quest for beer.

AFTER DROPPING Matt off to keep early party arrivals at bay, Danny drove them to his parents' store. He pulled his car off the main road, past the gas pumps, and around to the back before parking beside the dark garage bays surrounded by the cars waiting for repairs and the used cars with placards in their windows advertising their sale.

Nathan picked up a wet basketball from the concrete and drilled a shot through the hoop attached to the side of the shop. Grinning, Charlie scrambled for the rebound and drove past Nathan for a layup. A quick game broke out, with pushing and shoving and calling out fouls. Hank and Danny stood under a small roof over the back door, illuminated by a single bulb dangling from a metal fixture, and cheered them on.

When the ball bounced toward Hank, he grabbed it, tucked it under his arm, and charged the other two. They wrapped their arms around him to drag his bulk to the ground, but not before he ripped his arms free and tossed the ball into the air. It banged off the metal rim, skimmed the wall, and rolled through the net.

"Scooore!" Hank shouted as the others laughed.

Danny shook his head, unlocked the door, punched in the alarm code to disarm it, and led his teammates inside. After unlocking the storeroom, he flipped a switch illuminating a string of incandescent bulbs hanging from a wire stretching to the back wall. He waved his arm toward the stacked cases of beer. "Fresh shipment waiting for me to stock the coolers in the morning."

Hank ran his hands over the boxes and smiled. "This'll do."

Danny shook his head. "Nope, we are just taking *one* case. We don't need more. We have the keg waiting for us at your house."

Hank protested, "But we might need extra."

"One case. And everyone pony up cash so I can get it into the register tomorrow."

Nathan pulled his wallet out of his pants pocket and removed some bills. He studied the inventory stacked on the shelf. "Can we take chips? I'm starving."

"Yeah, sure, whatever you want."

Hank opened his wallet. "I got plenty of cash. Let's get two cases."

Danny rolled his eyes as he shook his head again. "Can't. Dad told me to be careful about taking too much beer because he could lose his license. I have to ring it up tomorrow just like it's a regular sale in case the ABC guys inspect."

Charlie handed over his own cash and grinned. "But munchies are no problem, right?"

Danny laughed. "No license needed for those. Take all you want."

Nathan picked up a package of chewing gum and couple of Mountain Dews. "And don't forget we have to pass the Ronnie breathalyzer."

Hank rolled his eyes. "You two might as well live in a prison."

The boys stacked bags of potato chips, boxes of donuts, and a case of beer on a table. Danny wrote it all down on an envelope and stuffed the collected cash inside. He slid the envelope under the open cash-register drawer, where it would be spotted upon opening Saturday morning.

Supplies in hand, the boys exited the back door. Danny reactivated the alarm and twisted the key in the lock. They walked back toward the car and spotted Abe Morgan spinning the basketball on his finger.

"Not bad, huh?" he said.

"Pretty decent for an old man." Danny grinned as Abe clasped his hand across his chest, faking pain from a wound.

"You boys headed out?"

"Yes, Dad. Headed to Hank's for a little after-game cele-bration."

"Good. You staying over there tonight?"

"Yes, sir."

"Perfect. I don't want you drinking and driving." He motioned toward the supplies in their hands. "Make sure you lock that beer in your trunk. Absolutely no driving around with open cans in the car."

"Yes, sir, of course not."

Danny opened the trunk, and Hank dutifully loaded the large box into it. They would have done the same even if Abe had not come upon them. They had plenty of time to drink up at the Point, a detail they omitted disclosing since Abe never asked if they were going anywhere else.

"I thought I heard you boys shooting hoops down here and saw the lights come on in the store. Figured you were getting some snacks for celebration. You deserve to have a little fun after that great win tonight." As they grinned in response, Abe focused on Nathan. "And that hit at the end of the game. Wow, I wouldn't have wanted to be on the receiving end of that. Bet your dad would've loved it."

"Thank you, Mr. Morgan."

"Why don't you boys plan to come over Sunday afternoon? I'll grill up some burgers. Martha will make her potato salad and one of her pies—I know none of you would refuse that. Charlie, ask Ronnie to come, and Hank, get your mom and Matt out here. Colette will be mad at me forever if I don't ask your brother."

Hank rolled his eyes in mock protest. "Sounded great right up to me having to put up with my little brother."

Abe rolled the ball across the wet concrete and onto the dirt behind the garage. "And after we eat, I'll show you how a real basketball player can handle you on a court."

"Really?" Hank asked. "What basketball player you inviting to join us?"

"Starting point guard right here for the Millerton conference champs. Including beating Roosevelt every year." The boys groaned at the reminder as Abe pointed at Hank. "I might just start with you, smart mouth, but you'll actually have to play basketball and not bang around like a football jock."

Hank hooted at the banter. "Ain't a real sport if you can't tackle."

"A real sport calls for finesse and skill, not just brute strength." As a second chorus of groans arose, Abe turned toward the house. "Sunday it is. You boys have fun and stay out of trouble. And, Danny, don't forget I need your help in the store tomorrow. Be home by opening."

"Yes, sir. Good night."

"Good night, and remember: no drinking and driving." Abe disappeared into the shadows as he walked toward the house.

Danny cranked the engine and left the parking lot.

4

A hundred years earlier, old-growth forests had blanketed the hills surrounding the original farming community. Timber companies swooped in and harvested the lumber. Once the large trees were nearly depleted, they abandoned the land but left a network of logging roads criss-crossing the rolling terrain. One of those abandoned roads led to a small, flat clearing that jutted out from the recovered forests several hundred feet above the town.

The Point, as the locals had dubbed it, offered a view of the entire park and the town in the distance. On a clear night, the lights from Charlotte glowed on the horizon, a distant beacon of economic prosperity.

Despite the spectacular view, few people ventured to the Point. The fading No Trespassing signs installed years before intimidated few, but the rough, twisting fire roads were the real barrier. They didn't appear on maps, so only local knowledge served as a guide through the many intersections and branches. Rutted from years of use by heavy logging trucks and overgrown by more years of neglect, only the hardiest of vehicles could navigate the labyrinth.

That isolation made the Point a popular teenage gathering spot on Friday and Saturday nights. Pickup trucks and Jeeps crept through the forest until they emerged in the opening. Music played, and laughter echoed. Beer was guzzled. Cigarettes and marijuana were smoked. Couples drifted to the shadows of the nearby trees. More than a few of the children of Millerton had been conceived at the Point.

But the dismal weather of that cold November night kept even young lust at bay. The Point hosted only the four boys sitting on the hood of Danny's car, drinking beer and eating snacks. Fog settled over the mountain, shrouding Millerton in a gloomy haze below them.

"Can you believe it's over? No more football. Ever." Danny tilted a beer over his head and drained the last drops down his throat.

He crushed the can and tossed it onto a large pile of empties at the edge of the clearing. Periodically, some enterprising—and broke—high school student gathered all the cans and recycled them for a few dollars, beer money to start things all over.

Danny popped open another beer. Hank swallowed from his own can and wiped his mouth with his jacket sleeve—actually Nathan's jacket sleeve since he carried through on his threat to confiscate the coat until Donna returned his own. "No more banging heads on the field. What are we going to do?"

Danny clanked his beer can against Hank's as the two boys shouted, "Mo-rines!"

"Morons is more like it." Nathan, coatless, shivered in the cold. "What are we doing up here tonight?"

"Celebrating victory over Roosevelt High!" whooped Hank as he tapped a cigarette out of his ever-present pack and lit it. "And if you'd stop sipping like a sissy and actually drink that beer, you might be in a better mood."

"You guys celebrate. I don't want Ronnie to kill me for drinking." With his arms wrapped around himself for warmth, Nathan headed for the back door of the car. "I'm getting in so I don't freeze."

Shouted insults questioning his manhood followed him as he settled into the backseat. The dome light flashed on again, and Charlie slid in the other back door. He shut it firmly, sipped his beer, and grimaced. "Why did we get warm beer when there were plenty of cold ones in the coolers?"

Hank and Danny leaned on the bumper and raced to see who could drain an entire beer first. Danny won by just a second, slammed the can on the hood of the car, and released an echoing burp.

From the backseat, Nathan gestured toward their friends. "Because those two will drink anything."

"Why are we up here freezing in the rain while the girls are all in town?"

"Because we're idiots."

"Yeah, well nothing personal, but being at the Point in the backseat with you is not the best plan I've ever had." Charlie shivered in his rain-soaked clothes, nodding at their two friends in front of the car. "You think they will really do it? The Marines?"

"Hank will for sure, and he'll be good at it. He's been talking about it since kindergarten. All I ever heard him say he wanted."

"And Danny?"

Nathan shrugged. "Probably. Though I don't know why he doesn't stay here and take over the family store. Sure sounds like an easier way to make a living."

Charlie watched through the window as Hank blew smoke rings and Danny broke into a drunken song. "You know what I have thought about doing?"

"Based on our last two thousand conversations, I guess writing great novels."

Charlie grinned. "Well, that too, but I meant what I am going to do for a couple of years *before* becoming a best-selling author."

"What?"

"Teach high school English."

Nathan looked at Charlie in surprise. "For real?"

"I know you think it's silly, but I love reading and books. Getting lost in some story. Teaching English would be fun."

"Man, I think the Marines would be easier than corralling a bunch of idiots like us to read Shakespeare."

"And yet, somehow, I got even you hooked on the Bard."

"Not sure I would call it hooked, but yeah, you made it make sense. And some lines are hilarious once you wade through the weird way he says it."

Charlie looked down at his hand wrapped around the beer can. "But that's what I mean. I have fun helping you see the jokes. And sometimes, the students are smart—like Colette."

"Gee, thanks. Smarter and prettier than us dumb jocks." Nathan waved off Charlie's protest. "Makes you wonder how she's related to Danny, huh?"

Charlie shrugged. "Matt's related to Hank. He's smart. *And* he's a jock, so anything is possible."

They sat in silence for a few minutes before Nathan spoke up again. "You would make a great teacher though even you can't make me like *Billy Budd*."

Charlie smiled at the thought. "What about you? You going to listen to my dad and go to college?"

"I really can't see it." Nathan opened his Mountain Dew bottle. "If Ronnie doesn't kill me when I tell him Donna's having my kid, I'll work at the plant. Learn how to fix that stuff while I pay for diapers and baby food and doctors. Besides, I ain't smart like you."

"Come on. You're smart. Especially in math. Go to college and be an engineer."

"Engineer? Ha! Four years of college. Can't imagine. Even without the kid, I couldn't handle all of that studying."

"Why not? What do you think fixing equipment and setting up manufacturing lines means? It's engineering. I know you could do it."

Nathan stared out the window at the lights from the town below as he fiddled with the bottle cap. "What makes you think that?"

"It's like how I can read a Robert Frost poem and get what he's saying, but I still suck at algebra. You might have trouble with Shakespeare, but you're a wiz with equations. I don't have a clue how you figure that stuff out, but the answers just come to you."

He cocked his head as he puzzled over his mind's workings. "I don't know why I can do that. It's like working in Mr. Morgan's shop, fixing cars in the summer—it feels natural. I just know how."

"It's not just you can solve equations. The freaky thing? I watch you working on cars, and you always grab the right wrench. Always know the part number without looking it up. Always know what will and won't fix something. I guarantee you on that last play tonight, you were calculating the arc and speed of that football in your head. It's the way you think."

He remembered how he knew where the ball would land the second it left the quarterback's hands. The trajectory was a clear image in his head. "Yeah, in a way. I could just see it." He studied the plastic bottle in his hands, peeling the label off in a single piece of paper for something to do. "It's more than just dreading the college work. I get a charge out of fixing stuff. Working with my hands. Making things come to life. I'm not sure I want to sit at a desk, shuffling papers."

"If I can handle grading papers, you can push a few."

They laughed at the visual and then settled into a comfortable silence in the car, both with visions of the future floating in their heads.

Charlie broke the quiet and asked, "You really thinking of marrying Donna?"

"Before she told me she was pregnant, never thought about it. I mean, we joked about it a little, but I think we both knew we weren't that serious." He turned to face his friend. "But how do I leave a kid out there without both parents to raise him? What I would give to still have my dad around. And to at least have known my mom."

"I get it. Really. I wish my mom was still alive too, but I think you can be there without having to get married." They sat quietly again, nursing their drinks, before Charlie continued, "It's just with football over and graduation this spring, it feels like the beginning of something really awesome, you know?"

Nathan had expected to feel regret with the end of the game. Football had been such a large part of his life, but turning in the equipment had been easier than he thought. He agreed with Charlie—it felt less like an ending than a beginning. In a few short months, they would have their diplomas and move on with their lives.

Also, he realized with some sadness, the Fearsome Foursome would probably drift apart in the years to come. Not he and Charlie, of course—they would be neighbors and best friends just as their dads had been. Danny would probably come back after a couple of tours overseas and take over the family business.

Hank, however, was a military lifer. It was all he had ever wanted to be—the only future that made any sense for him.

Charlie broke his reverie with another question. "How many beers have they had?"

"All of them."

"All? You think they're okay?"

Nathan leaned back in the seat and closed his eyes. "I've seen them drink more. And wait until they tap that keg tonight. They won't be able to stand by morning."

"Well, we won't be around for that. But maybe we should drop by real early tomorrow and make sure they're awake." They laughed together as Charlie cranked the window down and leaned his head out into the rain. "You guys ready to go yet?"

Danny drained the beer in his hand and belched. He crumpled the can and fired a hook shot, and the can clinked against other discarded metal. "What's the hurry?"

"Hank's little brother is alone with your sister."

Hank flicked his cigarette and ground it into the wet ground with the heel of his shoe. He lifted the empty box and shook it in the air. "Good for my li'l bro, but we're also out of beer. A much bigger crisis."

Danny crumpled the empty box and tucked it into a pile of cardboard on the edge of the clearing, saved for campfires in drier weather. "Well, that's two good reasons, so let's go party!"

Slimy mud oozed around Nathan, chilling his already freezing body. His head rang as he wiped debris out of his eyes and opened them. He couldn't make out any details from the shadows in the thick darkness.

Only muted sounds reached his ears. A river gurgled nearby as it meandered past rocks. Woodland creatures scurried through the forest. Trees swayed, and leaves rustled in the wind. An engine ticked as it cooled.

The smell of smoke tickled his nose. Mechanical smoke. And radiator fluid. And spilled gasoline. Nathan had hung out enough in Abe Morgan's shop to memorize those odors.

He wiped his eyes again, and objects came into focus in the darkness. Trees. The river. Boulders. Graffiti on the boulders.

Aiden was here
Tammy gives great head
Nathan + Donna

Aiden had been out there a few times, just like every other high school kid. Tammy wasn't that great, according to Hank, and he did claim a lot of comparison points. But that last, Nathan himself had painted a few weeks earlier, so he knew where he was. The Point. Or close to it. The old logging road that cut through the forest high above Millerton.

He lifted his head an inch off the ground and looked around. Danny's car lay on its driver side, the tires facing Nathan. Steam curled into the cold air.

"Danny?" His voice came out strained, water and mud caked in his throat. He coughed up debris, spat it onto the ground, and tried again, "Danny? Dude? You okay?"

Only the click of the cooling engine responded.

He gathered his arms under his body and pushed to sit up. Pain flared through his legs, and the world grayed and wobbled. He closed his eyes, breathed deeply, and waited for the motion to stop.

Praying he would not pass out, he reopened his eyes and examined his injuries. His left leg was twisted, the foot pointing the wrong way. A bone had erupted through the right leg of his jeans, inches above his ankle. Both legs were shattered. Walking would be impossible.

"Hang on, Danny. I'm coming." He dug his hands deep into the muck and tried to drag his body across the ground, his useless legs in the wake. He managed a yard, nearly two, before his left foot hooked on a rock and twisted. He screamed in agony and collapsed on the ground.

Hank's voice pierced the darkness. "That you, Nathan?"

Nathan struggled to raise his head, spat out dirty water, and answered, "Yeah. You okay?"

"Mostly. Hurt like hell, but I'm okay. You?"

"Not so good. I need some help here."

Hank materialized from the darkness and leaned over him. "Thank God. I thought…" He hesitated and decide not to vocalize what he had feared.

"I think both legs are broken."

"Yeah. And your left arm. Can't believe you're crawling on that."

Nathan looked at his twisted arm, shocked to see it was swollen and blue. "I didn't feel it. The legs... too much pain from them."

"Your head's gonna hurt too. You have a nasty gash."

With his right hand, Nathan swiped more gunk out of his left eye and forced the eye open. In the dark, the bright-red blood looked the same as the mud. He felt his skull and eye socket, but everything felt intact. "How's Danny?"

"Alive. Barely. He's trapped by the steering wheel, and I can't get him out. He's talking, sort of, but not making a lot of sense."

"And Charlie?"

Hank stared out into the darkness. "I can't find him. But I couldn't find you either until you called out. You two idiots were always too cool for seat belts. Can you hang on while I look again?"

Nathan waved Hank away with his good hand and settled back down, scared at how good the ice-cold ground felt on his swollen face. The chill eased the pain, making it bearable. He could just close his eyes. Rest. Sleep. So easy.

Coach Burleson flashed into his mind, rain dripping from that ever-present navy-blue Millerton High School cap. "Shake it off, son. Fight through the pain." Nathan pushed up again with his good right arm and shook his head to clear his brain.

Nathan listened as Hank crashed through the forest, walking in an arc and calling Charlie's name over and over, the panic growing in his voice. He stumbled over a fallen branch. Cursed it. Stomped through piled leaves. Splashed into the river.

"Jesus."

"What?"

"I found Charlie." Hank went silent.

"And?"

"He's…"

Nathan waited. Dreaded the answer. Prayed. "How is he?"

"Not good. Man, he looks awful. He's bleeding bad. His face is all smashed up. But he's alive."

Splashing sounds came as Hank sloshed through the river. "Had to move him, prop his head on a rock. Otherwise, he would…"

Nathan waited for more but realized nothing else was coming. "He would what?"

"Drown. His face was half in the river. But I've got his head up, and he's breathing… for now."

"Can't you get him out of there?"

"I don't know. He's all torn up. What if I paralyze him or something?" Hank waded back through the river and up the stony bank. He knelt beside Nathan. "He's okay, Nate. He and Danny both. You too. For now. But I got to go get help."

"What happened?"

"Danny didn't make the curve. Too many beers, I guess. I don't know—I'm wasted too." Hank looked around at the wreckage, steam rising from the twisted metal. Shattered glass glistened on the ground. "He was going too fast, and we slid coming around the curve, hit that giant boulder, and went airborne. When we landed, we rolled over and over and over. You and Charlie just flew out of the car. I almost… I had Charlie's leg in my hand for a split second as he flew over… but I couldn't hold on."

Hank sobbed quietly for a moment before he took a deep breath. "Then we hit that tree, and everything stopped. I blacked out a little, but when I came to, I could crawl out. I undid my seat belt and slid out where the front windshield used to be. I tried to get Danny out, but he's stuck. I mean, he's crushed in there."

Nathan shivered. "But he's alive?"

Hank slipped the coat off his back—Nathan's coat—and draped it over his prone body. "Yeah, they both are. But they won't be if I don't get help now. I'll run out to the main road. Get to the houses out there and bang on doors until I find someone."

"That'll take you an hour."

"You got a better plan?" Hank glanced at the car, lying on its side, then gazed out into the shadows of the river, Charlie's head above the surface somewhere in the darkness. "God, I hope they can last that long."

"Help me over to Charlie. I will keep his head up."

"No way. Your legs are broken. I could kill you trying."

Nathan collapsed onto the wet soil, sobbing against the pain and frustration.

Hank stood and shivered in the drizzling rain. "Are you going to be all right? I got to go."

"Got no choice. I'll make it. Just hurry."

"I will." Hank stared down the dark road before looking back. "You be alive when I get back, you hear me?"

"All three of us will be alive. I promise. Now go."

Hank leaned over and rested his hand on Nathan's good shoulder, tears streaming down his face. Then he stood and started half running down the road, a distinct limp with each stride. Nathan lay his head down on the cold ground and slipped back into unconsciousness.

HE WOKE with a start as filthy water flooded into his open mouth. Choking and spitting, he tried to lift his body, only to be greeted by flaring pain from his mangled arm. His vision grayed and swam, but he fought back to alertness.

And silence.

"Danny?"

A weak voice came from the car. "Here. Thought I had lost you. You weren't answering."

Nathan focused on the water flowing in the river. Through the murkiness, he could just make out the shape of Charlie's head balanced on a rock. The water swirled around his neck, bobbing his body in the rapids. "Have you heard from Charlie?"

"Not in a while. Just coughing. No words. I've tried."

Nathan studied the terrain to where Charlie lay—a dozen feet of flat ground with a thick layer of leaf-covered sticks and rocks that would snag his broken legs. Then down a rocky slope to the river, banging his legs as he dragged them down the hill. And if he hadn't passed out yet, twenty feet of frigid water would have to be crossed with only one good arm to paddle.

From years of trout fishing in the river, he knew the water was only knee-deep—if you were standing. And standing wasn't possible on his shattered legs. And if he couldn't stand, he couldn't walk. The doubts grew in his mind.

Can I drag myself through the river? If I reach Charlie, can I hold his head up? Would I drown trying to save him? Or would I freeze to death in the icy-cold rapids?

But as he stared across the darkness, only one answer came to him.

Have to try.

He reached forward with his right hand, sank his fingers deep into the muck, and pulled himself toward the river, his broken legs sliding over the hidden tree roots. He screamed at the effort and collapsed.

Danny's worried voice came from the shadows of the car. "Nathan?"

"Trying to get to Charlie. Don't worry." He took a deep breath and reached forward. Driving his numb fingers into the ground, he pulled himself forward a few inches, his legs shrieking in pain. He sucked in a lungful of air, his fingers grasped for purchase in the mud, and he pulled forward again. Inch by inch, foot by foot, he dragged his mangled body to the edge of the bank and looked at the slope to the river.

Rocks covered the bank, broken up only by twisted tree branches fallen from limbs above and pushed to the bank in a jumbled heap. The water raced by, white foam curling across the surface. The question was gone. Plunging into that water was certain death.

"Charlie?" Nathan asked.

He looked at the shadow of his friend lying in the swirling water, his head resting on the rock. The only sound that came to him across the flowing river was raspy breathing, shallow and weak.

"Can you hang on, brother? I can't get to you, so please hang on."

A weak cough answered, but no other movement came.

Nathan looked back toward the car and called out, "I can't get to him! It hurts too much."

Silence reigned for several minutes before Danny replied, "I wish I hurt. I can't... I can't feel my legs. At all. They aren't numb. It's more like they aren't there. I can touch them, but I can't feel myself touching them." The rain bounced off the leaves above and trickled into the river. When he spoke again, Danny's voice was barely above a whisper. "I'm scared."

Pushing himself back up on his right arm, Nathan again eyed down the rocky bank toward the swirling river. Even if he reached Charlie, he would be useless. Exhausted. Freezing.

He turned and looked toward the car. *Twenty yards. That's it. Just twenty yards of flat ground.* Maybe he couldn't drag himself to Charlie, but he could reach Danny. He turned his body around and called out, "I'm coming to you. Hang in there."

Pulling with his right arm, Nathan aimed his body toward the wreckage and dragged his legs across the wet leaves. The pain flared but wasn't unexpected that time. He could do this. Reach forward. Grab a rock or dig frozen fingers deep into the mud. Pull. Slide. Repeat.

He felt a fingernail pull away from his numb hands, the pain from that worse than he expected, so strong that, for a moment, it made him forget his broken bones. But only for a moment.

Reach. Grab. Pull. Slide.

He inched his way around the back of the car and looked through the shattered back window. He caught his first glimpse of the back of Danny's head resting where the driver's door met the ground. "I can see you. Almost there."

Reach. Grab. Pull. Slide.

Danny sniffled, choking back tears. "I'll be okay. Have to be. But I ain't heard from Charlie in a while. Can you see him?"

"Barely."

Reach. Grab. Pull. Slide.

"How long has Hank been gone?" Danny's voice was weaker, his breath more labored.

"I don't know. I passed out. Thirty minutes? An hour?"

Reach. Grab. Pull. Slide.

"He's the slowest of all of us. Matt would have been there and back by now. We've all passed him doing laps at practice. Maybe he can't find anyone. Maybe no one is coming. I don't wanna die out here."

"Stop it. No one's dying. They're coming."

Reach. Grab. Pull. Slide.

His foot snagged on a rock. The pain flooded his brain, and he couldn't choke his scream down again.

"Nathan? You okay? Talk to me!"

The world swam in front of Nathan's eyes as he fought to stay conscious. Gray faded to black, and he squeezed his eyes shut.

Ignore the pain. Just focus.

He reopened his eyes, and trees drifted back into view as his vision cleared. Rising up on his good arm, he spat blood from his mouth. In his anguish, he had bitten his tongue. "I'm okay."

Lying still to build his strength back, Nathan heard a splash from the river then a gagging cough and water being spit up.

He called in the direction of the sound, "Charlie? You there? Keep your head up, damn it."

The gagging subsided, replaced by an uneven breathing pattern. The sound chilled him more than the wind and rain, but he couldn't help Charlie from here.

He turned his focus back to getting around the roof of the car to the front windshield. "Coming, Danny."

Reach. Grab. Pull. Slide.

"I ain't going anywhere. Wish I could." The voice was barely a whisper.

Reach. Grab. Pull. Slide.

He reached the front windshield and stared down into the car. Except that direction wasn't down. With the car resting on the driver's door, he was looking sideways. Danny's eyes were wild with fear. Scratches and cuts crisscrossed his face and framed a broken nose dripping blood. His hands gripped the steering wheel so tightly his knuckles were white. The darkness and crumpled metal below the steering wheel hid his crushed legs from view.

Reach. Grab. Pull. Slide.

Nathan dragged his body even with the front window. One more time, and he could reach his friend.

Reach. Grab. Pull. Slide.

His head touched the hood of the car. He lay down face-first on the ground, his chest heaving to suck in air, blood dripping from his mouth. He reached through the shattered windshield and wrapped his hand around Danny's hand, feeling the fingers loosen their grip on the steering wheel. "I'm here."

"Thank God." The rain pelted them as they huddled for shelter in the wreckage. A sputtering cough came from the darkness of the river and then settled back to a raspy breathing, rougher than earlier.

Far in the distance toward town, the volunteer fire department shattered everyone's sleep with its piercing siren, calling for firefighters to respond. Lights would be turning on in bedrooms, boots pulled on, trucks started.

"Hear that, Danny? Hank made it. The cavalry is coming."

Danny coughed weakly and gasped for air. "Not sure if I can hold on much longer."

"Yes. You can. You have to. Just focus."

"Not sure I should." Danny swallowed, his throat clicking with dryness. "I damn near killed you all. If I had, I couldn't live with that. Couldn't live one day. I wouldn't deserve to live."

Nathan stared nervously at the swirling river, wondering if he had heard Charlie lately, but the approaching sirens were too loud. Police cars. Ambulances. The blasting of a fire truck air horn.

"Stop it," said Nathan. "Don't talk like that. We're all okay. Just one of those stories Coach says we will sit around and tell one day, right?"

"Some story." Danny sputtered, choked, and spat blood out. "I'm sorry. Sorry for everything."

"No need to be. We were all there."

"Yeah, but—"

"Stop it."

The sirens grew louder, approaching far below them, then faded away.

Danny's breathing accelerated, and panic flared in his voice. "He's going away. Not coming for us."

"No, Danny, around the industrial park. They have to go

around to get to the fire road. They're coming." Nathan pulled his soaked coat close, trying to warm his chilled body. His teeth chattered, and his legs and arm throbbed. He could feel every beat of his heart as blood gushed from the gash in his forehead. His swollen tongue clogged his mouth, making it difficult to spit out the blood.

The sirens regained volume as they approached the fire road, then they shut off. Silence descended.

"Nathan? Why did they stop?"

"Don't need sirens on the fire road, Danny. No cars. Nothing but deer. They're close. Hang in there. Couple of miles, max." Hard, slow miles through the rutted logging road, but Nathan felt no need to distract his friend with that detail.

The river rushed over the rocks. The wind rattled the trees. Charlie coughed again from the river. Minutes ticked by.

"Danny, see that?"

Danny moaned, licked his lips, and replied in a thick voice, "See what?"

"Lights. Flashing against the leaves over there. They're close."

Danny's eyes drifted shut, and he moaned. In the river, Charlie gagged and coughed.

Nathan squeezed his friend's hand. "Danny. Stay with me. You hear me?"

Danny nodded but didn't open his eyes. He mumbled, "Still here."

The red lights pulsed brighter. Minutes away. Danny's breath rasped in and out.

Charlie sputtered in the water, choking. A gagging breath. Something heavy slipped under the surface of the river. Then only the sound of rushing water.

PART II

FRIDAY

PRESENT DAY

6

"Come on, Little Man. Your mom's making pancakes."

The sounds of scrambling came from inside the room as the boy searched through clothes—probably strewn across the floor—for the right outfit. Nathan fondly remembered the little boy who didn't care if he had worn his lucky shirt five days in a row.

"Almost ready, Dad. Just a minute."

"Better hustle. You'll be late for school. And you'll make me late for work."

"I know. I know." Still a few months shy of thirteen, Jacob had already perfected the exasperated teenage growl. The sweet kid who thought his dad was a superhero was long gone.

Rather than provoking an argument, Nathan turned his attention to the tiny hall bathroom. Tucked between the master bedroom in the back of the house and the front bedroom Jacob occupied, the single bathroom was shared by everyone, which was a constant irritant for Donna.

When he and Donna had bought the small house, Jacob was taking his first tentative steps as a toddler. They didn't need savings, because the banks offered no-down-payment, low-interest mortgages. The monthly payment was not much higher than their old rent. They figured by the time their son was a teenager, they would've traded up for a bigger house. After all, houses always went up in value. Everyone knew that.

However, theirs didn't, and housing prices crashed. They owed more money than the house was worth and couldn't afford to sell it. Rather than dreaming of a bigger house and a bigger yard, they were figuring out how to live together as two adults, a teenager—a near-teenager—and only one bathroom.

Fog shrouded the mirror over the sink except for the streaks from the fingers of a small hand. A dripping washcloth hung over the edge of the shower-tub combination. Soap bubbles streaked the shower curtain shoved against the wall. A pair of pajama pants lay crumpled on the floor.

To avoid arguing with either Donna or his son, Nathan cleaned the small room. To allow the steam to escape and the spring air to circulate, he opened the bathroom window. He wiped the mirror and sink clean with an old hand towel and returned a hairbrush to a drawer. Turning his attention to the toilet, he cleaned dribble from the seat—*How can a boy throw a baseball across home plate but not have better aim in the bathroom?*—and closed the lid. In the shower, he scrubbed the curtain and pulled it open to air out. He closed the shampoo bottle and placed it on the shelf, along with a bar of soap found on the tub floor.

His cleaning efforts would avoid a fight, but Donna still wouldn't be satisfied. As soon as he and Jacob were out the door to work and school respectively, she would scrub the bathroom and take her morning soak in the tub—her time away from the mess and chaos of the boys, the big one she married and the little one who was growing up too fast.

Nathan picked up the wadded pajama bottoms and folded them as he noted the towel missing from the rack. As he neared his teenage years, Jacob had developed modesty around the house, one of the few welcomed changes of puberty, so he wrapped himself in a towel to take the few steps to his bedroom. Somewhere behind the closed door, a crumpled towel would mildew if not rescued.

Nathan rapped his knuckles on his son's door. "I have your PJs."

"Just leave them out there, Dad. I'll get them."

He draped the pajama bottoms over Jacob's bedroom doorknob. "Don't forget to hang up that towel. Don't let your mom find it on your bed again."

"Okay." Jacob made that exasperated sound of a teenager again.

Thinking of how exhausting the next few years would be, Nathan placed his hand on the door and listened to Jacob harrumphing around the room. He wanted to say more, but that could set off the teenage temper—better to pick another moment.

Nathan returned to the master bedroom and opened the closet door. Work pants and shirts hung neatly in one corner beside the jeans and flannel shirts he wore on weekends. The rest of the closet held Donna's clothes.

As with the small section of closet, he used only two drawers in the dresser, one for underwear and socks and another for his T-shirts and a couple pairs of shorts. The rest of the dresser was for Donna. He didn't resent it—well, not much—because women needed more space. At least, that is what he told himself.

He pulled the dark shirt over his black tee, buttoned it up, and tucked it into his pants. He brushed the lint off the white circle with his embroidered name. Though he could never tell the guys at work, he took pride in the way he looked. They ribbed him for how neat his uniform was, all the creases sharp and ironed. He would roll his eyes and blame Donna's meticulousness.

The uniform—neatly ironed by him and not her—fit his body well. Maybe he was not as cut as he'd been in his high school football days, but the physical labor at work and the effort of keeping up with a near-teen boy kept him in shape. Despite having passed the big three-oh birthday the past year, a milestone he kept trying to forget, he was mostly still trim and fit. Mostly.

Turning sideways to examine himself in the mirror, he patted the small bulge growing around his waist. To avoid the spread, he would cut down on the beers, pizzas, and burgers— a promise he made often and never achieved. Those uniform pants were getting a little tight around the waist.

Nathan closed the closet door and inspected the bedroom, a habit ingrained by years of marriage. His dirty clothes were in the hamper hidden in the closet. Both drawers that were his were closed. The wrinkles he had just created by sitting on the bed to get dressed were smoothed out.

Unlike Jacob's front bedroom, which was all preteen boy, the master bedroom reflected Donna's influence. Knickknacks highlighted the dresser. The two bedside tables were clear except for a lamp on each side, an alarm clock on Nathan's, and whatever trashy romance novel Donna was reading on hers. Not a speck of dust could be found. The queen-size bed had been made and covered with a brilliant flower-print bedspread, a purchase that made Donna quite proud—and made Nathan grimace, though never in front of her. The floral curtains flapped around the open windows, welcoming the warm spring air and scent of gentle morning rain. Despite the cloud-covered skies, the bedroom was bright and airy.

Sock-footed, Nathan walked through the den, a room as orderly as the master bedroom. His recliner, which Donna hated but allowed him to keep, sat in one corner. Her chair sat on the other side of a single table with a lamp. Both faced an old TV against the opposite wall. The room was too small for a couch, so Jacob would sprawl on the floor when he joined them.

The carpeted den yielded to the linoleum floor of the last room of the house. At one end sat the usual kitchen trappings —refrigerator, free-standing stove/oven, a sink, and cabinets. A small microwave took up part of the precious counter space. The kitchen lacked a dishwasher, something Donna reminded him of regularly, but they hadn't saved the money to buy one yet.

At the open end of the kitchen, a round table and three chairs, a yard-sale find discounted because of the missing chair, sat tucked into the small space. They ate breakfast and dinner there, but it also doubled as Jacob's desk. Evenings found his books spread across the table, his face scrunched while studying homework problems.

A door led from the kitchen to the driveway outside. A small closet held winter coats and Nathan's work boots. Each night, he took off his boots before entering the house, not daring to track dirt or grease inside. In the mornings, he would sit on the stoop outside and pull them on as he left.

Donna stood beside the stove with a cigarette pinched between two fingers, carefully blowing smoke out the open kitchen window. She had stopped smoking in high school as soon as she found herself pregnant. Over the years since, she had restarted several times, trying to hide it from Nathan, a lifelong nonsmoker. He could always smell it and chastised her to stop, reminding her that Jacob might emulate her—and besides, they didn't have the money to buy cigarettes.

She had last restarted several months earlier, just before Halloween, and his nagging efforts had failed to curtail the habit so far. As he entered the kitchen, she looked at the wall clock hung over the side door and emitted an impatient sigh. "Why does he take so long in the bathroom?"

Amusement crossed Nathan's face. "He's a twelve-year-old boy. Don't ask. Don't tell."

Donna waved the cigarette-free hand in protest. "You men are all alike."

"Don't blame me. Takes me two minutes to get dressed."

"You aren't trying to impress twelve-year-old girls."

Nathan groaned. "Oh, yeah. Them." He knew his son was beginning to fall for the siren song.

"Come on, Proud Papa Bear, don't kid me. I saw you grinning ear to ear while he talked to Missy and Cora at the baseball game last Saturday."

Nathan chuckled at the memory of the two girls leaning over the dugout and chatting with his son. The coach had yelled at him three times before getting his attention, proof of how distracting they were. "Can you believe those girls are only twelve? They looked so grown-up."

"Bad news. Cora is eleven."

"Holy cow. Eleven?"

Donna motioned toward the closed bedroom door. "You weren't the only one who noticed how grown-up she looked."

Nathan shook his head but smiled. "Remember when he caught that line drive and then turned to see if they were watching? I had to laugh at his swagger. He could not have been more obvious if he had winked at them. The boy was showing off."

Donna took another drag on the cigarette. "Hmm, I've seen that swagger somewhere before. Guess he inherited his subtleness from good old dad. Besides, you're just shocked he thinks about something other than baseball."

"Things were easier when all he cared about was baseball, baseball, baseball. That's just swinging and taking bases."

"Uh-huh. If I remember your buddies in high school, you talked about girls like baseball too. First base. Second base. Third base. Home run." Though Nathan's face reddened,

Donna didn't relent. "Have you had a talk with your son about girls? And being careful and all of that."

"For Pete's sake, he's twelve."

"Uh-huh. How old were you when you first kissed a girl?"

"Twelve. But it's not like I slept with her."

Donna shot Nathan a withering look. "All I'm saying is girls fall for baseball players as much as they do football players, so that is a conversation you need to have with your little man-child. And soon. Following in his dad's footsteps does not have to include getting his girlfriend pregnant before high school graduation."

"At least we got him."

She crossed her arms. "And neither one of us got to do all the things we planned to do."

He collapsed into one of the kitchen chairs. "Not like my friends did what they planned either. Charlie and Danny sure didn't." Memories of lying in that cold mud beside the river, waiting for help to arrive, drifted through his mind.

"Well, Hank did. Joined the Marines just like he always said he would. Did his tours and now works for a big security company down in Atlanta." She smothered her cigarette into a ceramic ashtray—a hurried school project from their not-artis-tically-inclined son—and clanked the frying pan on the stove.

Nathan knew well how successful his friend was because Donna constantly reminded him. Hank had walked away from the accident with only a few bruises and scratches and didn't spend weeks recovering in a hospital. He glided across the graduation stage without even a limp and left two days later for the Marines. Nathan had only progressed from crutches to a cane and hobbled across the stage for his diploma. Danny was sitting in a wheelchair in a jail cell, convicted of drunk driving and manslaughter, not to return to Millerton until his early twenties.

Donna flipped pancakes with a vengeance, the spatula

clanking against the pan. "Don't you want Jacob to go to college? To have opportunities?"

"You know I do. I think about it all the time."

She scooped pancakes onto a plate and slammed it in front of her husband. "So make sure he doesn't make the same mistakes we did."

"I'll talk to him. I promise." Nathan picked up a fork and poked at the food on his plate. "Hal called. He has an opening at the truck stop for someone to run emergency repairs on the weekends. Pays good. We could put all of that money into a college savings fund."

"You mean going out on the interstate and fixing trucks?"

"Yeah."

"It's dangerous. And you don't want to miss Jacob's Saturday games."

"No, I don't, but I could catch some games until I get dispatched out on calls. Besides…" Nathan attempted to stop himself from going too far, but Donna had heard him.

"Besides what?"

He set his fork down on the plate and sighed. "Just in case, you know, they ever shut down the plant, maybe Hal could take me on full-time. At least I would already be there and proving myself."

"Proving yourself? Hal already knows you can fix anything. That's why he called you rather than just hire one of the hundred guys hanging around the unemployment office. He ought to make you the manager, and then you can just quit that factory."

"He can't put me in charge because he ain't going to fire Paul. He managed the place for Hal's dad for years. Loyalty matters, but Paul is going to retire on Hal someday or drop dead of a heart attack, and that's my chance. If I'm there on the weekends, he gets to know me, and maybe I'm in line to be the manager when Paul quits. I can prove to him I can run the place, not just fix engines."

Donna shook her head. "Of course you can run it. You should own it."

"If I ever win the lottery, I'll just open my own place."

"If we win the lottery, it won't matter."

"A small lottery, then. Just a little seed money."

"If you get a little seed money, you're building me a master bathroom with its own hot-water heater. Tired of having only cold water after that boy's marathon showers." She turned back to the bowl of batter and whipped it again, waiting for their son to appear. "Besides, you better not be wasting money on lottery tickets."

The words slipped out of his mouth before he could stop them. "And how much money do you waste on those cancer sticks?"

She spun and glared at him. She defiantly picked up her pack of cigarettes, tapped one out, and lit it. She glanced at the clock over the door and yelled through the house, "Jacob, get a move on, boy!" No reply came from the closed bedroom, so she leaned against the counter and sipped her coffee. In a quieter voice, she asked, "Do you really think the plant will close soon?"

Nathan shrugged. "I'm the only one left in the maintenance department since they laid off Carl a few weeks ago. What kind of company can survive without fixing the equipment? Not like we have bought any new machines in years."

She stared into her coffee cup. "Poor Carl. Does he have kids?"

"Two. Both still in diapers."

"Jesus." She took a sip and settled the mug back onto the counter. "What's he going to do?"

"Last I talked to him, he had a lead with one of the fracking companies."

"I didn't know anyone was fracking around here."

"Out west somewhere. Texas? Oklahoma? Arkansas? I can't remember."

"Will they move?"

"No. He is going to leave the kids with Heather and go. Come back when he can. Or if anything opens up here."

"Fat chance of that."

"Yeah, well, fracking jobs come and go, so he can't move them around that much."

"Poor Heather, stuck in that trailer with those two kids all day." She turned and looked out toward the backyard. "Those fracking jobs pay well, right?"

Nathan looked up and studied her back as she stared out the window. "Why? You trying to get rid of me?"

"No." She paused and took another drag on her cigarette. "I was just thinking, you know, if you took one of those jobs, we could scrape together enough money, sell this house, and pay off the mortgage."

"And do what? We wouldn't have the money to make a down payment on another house. We would have to rent."

"Renting wouldn't be so bad. At least we wouldn't get upside down on another house. Besides, we could move somewhere else, somewhere there are more jobs." Since high school, Donna had always talked about moving to a big city, like Atlanta or Charlotte or Nashville, but neither one of them had ever lived anywhere but Millerton.

"We'll consider it if the plant closes. But for now, I have a job."

"Some job. You haven't had a raise in years, and they cut out all the overtime. You keep making less every year."

"Ronnie can't help it. Corporate told him not one penny of overtime."

"Ronnie." She sucked deep on a cigarette and exhaled it harshly. "He's the only reason you still work there."

He took his time to chew his food before answering, angling to avoid an argument so early in the day. Yes, he felt obligated to Charlie's father. The man had taken him in when Nathan's own dad had died and he had nowhere to go. Gave him a place to sleep. Put food on the table. Bought clothes as he grew. And after the accident, they grieved together, mourning the loss of a son and a best friend.

Donna sighed and extinguished her cigarette. She sat down in the kitchen chair opposite her husband and folded her hands on the table. "I get it, Nathan. I do. You're as loyal as an old dog. But we've got to be loyal to ourselves first."

Nathan leaned forward and cupped his hands over hers. "That's why I'm talking to Hal about getting extra hours out of the truck stop. Save that money for Jacob's college, and maybe we can get out from underneath this house too."

She nodded and hung her head before speaking quietly. "Well, I need to help with that." She pulled her hands free from his and waved at the pack on the counter. "And to pay for my own damn cigarettes. I'll get back on at McDonald's. I can get an assistant-manager job."

He collapsed his empty hands together. "You hated that job."

"I know. But it's more steady than temp work. The damn service promised me at least twenty hours a week, but they barely scrape together eight. Some weeks, nothing. McDonald's will be steady work, and we need the money. And we might need their insurance if you get laid off."

"It just doesn't seem right, you doing work you don't like. At least I'm doing something fun. And we're better off than most folks. Both cars are paid off. We have a house. Small and only one bathroom, but we have it."

"Both cars are paid off because I've had mine for ten years and yours is your dad's old truck. It's older than you, and it will break down beyond your repair skills one day, Superman. The bank owns the house. They just let us live in it as long as we make the payment every month." Donna crossed her arms and issued her edict. "I'm calling McDonald's today. Tell them I want to come back."

"They will want you to work weekends and nights. What about Jacob?"

"The plant ain't giving overtime, right? So you'll be here for Jacob while I'm working nights and weekends."

"But, Donna, we will never see each other."

Donna shrugged nonchalantly as Jacob walked into the room.

She busied herself making a breakfast plate for their son and placed it in front of him. "You have your homework?"

"Yep."

"Yes, what?" Nathan asked.

A puzzled look spread over the boy's face before realization hit. "Yes, ma'am."

She brushed her hand through Jacob's hair as she stood beside his chair. "And is it done?"

"Yep." With a hasty glance at his father, he added, "Yes, ma'am."

"All of it?"

Jacob stuffed pancakes into his mouth and mumbled, "Most of it."

Donna put on her stern mom face and studied him. "Most?"

"All but one math problem, I swear. I tried like three times, but it was super hard. I couldn't figure it out. Luke will help me between classes." Jacob reached for a strip of bacon and glanced sideways at his dad. "If I had a cell phone, I could have called him last night."

The cell phone had become a daily discussion. According to Jacob, every kid at his school—every kid on the planet—had a cell phone except him. Nathan found it strange that something no kid had when he was in school was now considered a necessity.

He put on his best serious-dad face—not as good as Donna's, but he tried. "You could have used that phone right there." He pointed to a holdover from his own childhood, a rotary phone mounted on the wall with a long cord to the handset. The thing should've been in a museum, not a home, but wireless phones were too expensive, and that one worked.

Donna grinned and kissed the top of Jacob's head. "He couldn't have done that. Because then they couldn't have talked about baseball and girls with us listening."

Jacob's face turned bright red. He dropped his eyes to his plate and shoveled more pancakes into his mouth. "I'll get it done before math class. I promise."

Nathan continued, "And did you hang up that towel?"

"Uh, no," Jacob shoved more bacon in his already full mouth, "sir."

"But you will, right?"

"Yes, sir."

"Don't forget, Little Man."

Donna finished cleaning the skillet in the sink. She leaned against the counter and sipped her coffee, watching her men at the breakfast table.

Nathan asked, "You aren't eating?"

"Yogurt and coffee. Breakfast of champions."

"Yuck," Nathan and Jacob said in unison. They turned to look at each other, pointed, and shouted together, "Jinx!"

Donna rolled her eyes at the two of them as they laughed. "Boys. Both of you."

Nathan grinned. "Always."

Jacob pushed away from the table, placed his empty plate on the counter, and raced back across the small house. "Gotta brush my teeth."

Nathan called after him, "You just sat down. How are you done already?"

"How are you so slow, old man?" Jacob yelled as he disappeared into the bathroom. "Don't make me late."

"Make *you* late? And don't forget that towel." He turned back to Donna. "Brush his teeth? Without being told? You are right. That kid is girl crazy."

She grimaced and shook her head. "Which is why you will have that conversation with him this morning, right?"

Nathan groaned. "This morning? What if I did it tonight?"

"Can't. He's sleeping over at Luke's tonight, and then they are going together to the baseball game tomorrow."

"Again? He stays over there all the time. They could stay here tonight. Be cool if they did. We could toss the baseball around."

"Cool, huh? And how many thirty-one-year-olds did you want to hang out with when you were twelve?"

"Hey, I'm the cool dad."

"Sorry, Mr. Cool Dad, but Luke has the latest, greatest Xbox game, shooting space aliens or monsters or something. Your coolness factor can't compete with that."

"Ouch." Nathan grinned as he stood and walked to the hall closet. He retrieved his jacket—dark blue with an embroidered name, just like the shirt—and work boots. He shouted toward the back of the house, "Jacob! Hurry. You'll be late."

His son emerged from his room with his book bag slung over his shoulder.

Nathan asked, "The towel hung up?"

Jacob stopped with an "oops" look on his face, raced back across the den into his room, grabbed the towel, hung it up roughly in the bathroom, and trotted out the door. They caught the unmistakable scent of Nathan's cologne, liberally applied, wafting through the air behind him and exchanged glances as Donna shook her head in amusement.

"You're right. I got to talk to him about girls." Nathan wrinkled his nose. "About not overpowering them with aftershave."

"Great. Tips on how to impress girls from his old man." She rolled her eyes but laughed.

He leaned over and kissed her cheek. "I'll talk to him on the ride to school. Lose even more cool-dad points."

She teased back. "You're assuming you have any cool-dad points left."

"Ouch. That's low." He smiled as he walked outside, sat down on the stoop with his cup of coffee, and pulled his boots onto his feet.

7

Mitch Thomas, Nathan's father, had purchased the 1983 Ford F-150 pickup truck shortly after his return to Millerton from the Navy. Other than the semi he bought after being laid off from the plant, the pickup was the only vehicle he'd ever owned.

Rust patches marred the faded two-tone walnut-brown paint. The vinyl seat cushion, cracked from years of sunshine, crinkled under their weight and stuck to their bodies on humid days. The knob on the end of the gear shift was polished smooth from years of handling. Sometimes, it came off in the driver's hands midshift.

But the old truck represented numerous childhood memories for Nathan—rides to and from school, sports practice, or errands; father-and-son conversations, sometimes inane chatter about nothing, laughing and telling fart jokes, swapping sports stories or tall tales.

And sometimes they had serious discussions. The importance of grades. The disappointment of losing a game. And, of course, the most mysterious subject in the world to a teenage boy: girls.

The first girl to confound Nathan was Marissa Whittum. Seventh-grade fall dance loomed. Nathan sat in the passenger seat, chewing his lip, wanting to ask for help but embarrassed to do so.

Mitch shifted gears, the numbers on the knob already fading. He was taking a longer-than-normal route home, giving extra needed time for his son. "What's on your mind?"

He struggled to explain the effect Marissa Whittum had on him. Only stupid stuff fell out of his mouth every time he tried to talk to her. She sat in front of him in class, turning to ask him questions and mesmerizing him with her eyes. She flipped her hair over her ear as he breathed in the scent of her shampoo. Her mere presence aroused him and made it impossible to stand up at the end of class. He had to gather his supplies slowly as everyone left the room before he dared to rise to his feet then position his books so no one could see how much she drove him crazy.

He stammered, "How do you ask a girl to a dance?"

Mitch respected the gravity of the situation to the young boy and didn't smile but nodded in sympathy, a weighty look on his face. "Scary, isn't it? But it's the same way you deal with anything that scares you. You hit it straight on. You just ask her."

"But how do you know if she will say yes? I mean, what if she laughs? Or says no? The guys will all laugh at me."

Mitch turned to his son with a look of warmth and comfort. "How many of your buddies have a date for the dance?"

"Hank."

"Just Hank?"

"Yeah, he's not scared of nothing."

Mitch passed on grammar correction and stayed focused on the issue at hand. "Anyone else?"

"Nope."

"Then they can't laugh because they haven't even been brave enough to ask a girl. It's easy to avoid failing if you never try, but then you can't succeed either. So just call her. Ask. Whatever her answer, I've got your back. Right, Sport?"

The wall phone in the kitchen—the same one that hung on their wall today—had taunted him, daring him to pick it up and dial her number. Mitch busied himself making dinner, leaving Nathan to stretch the long cord into the privacy of the den.

He dialed the phone with shaking fingers, heard the first ring, raced back into the kitchen, and slammed the phone down on the hook. He stood, head against the wall, breathed deeply, and dialed again. As the phone rang, he prayed—harder than he had in ages—that his pubescent voice wouldn't betray him with a squeak. He lowered his voice, tried to hide the quaking, and asked Marissa to the dance.

She said yes.

In his excitement, he started a celebratory jig, hung up the phone, and whooped in revelry, only to realize that he had forgotten to plan any details. He called back and apologized—nothing like getting the first apology done before even having a first date.

The night of the dance, Mitch drove to her house in that old pickup, Nathan quaking with nerves, and coached his son on how to behave. He escorted her down the sidewalk and helped her into the truck. They rode together in the front seat, Mitch quietly shifting gears and trying his best to be unobtrusive.

They danced. They chatted. They sat on the bleachers between songs. She kissed him—his first kiss, a kiss that fueled his late-night fantasies, already running wild based on ill-informed locker-room tales from older, supposedly more experienced boys.

Rumbling to school in the truck the next Monday, Nathan

felt more confident in asking, "Where do I take her for a second date?"

Mitch pondered the question seriously and answered with authority. "A movie, but let her pick it. Something she wants to see. And no matter what she picks, agree."

That Saturday afternoon, Mitch dropped them off in front of the theater with a promise to return and pick them up in two hours. He claimed to have shopping to do though Nathan had rarely seen him shop for anything other than groceries or hardware. But when the movie ended, Mitch was sitting in the pickup truck in the parking lot. On the ride home, Marissa held Nathan's hand.

When they dropped her off in front of her house, Mitch elbowed Nathan and whispered in his ear, "Walk her to the door."

She kissed him under the glowing porch light. Nathan glanced nervously at his father but was surprised to see he was studying something across the street, not looking at them at all.

At lunch on Friday, Marissa caught Nathan going into the cafeteria and pulled him aside. Thinking only of another kiss, he was stunned when she announced she wanted to break up. Another boy had asked her out. Hank.

Two weeks and two dates was a long romance in the seventh grade, and the breakup crushed him. After school, he crawled into the truck and broke into tears as soon as he shut the door. He bawled like a baby all the way home. Mitch said little as he kept an arm wrapped around his son, helping him through his first heartbreak.

As promised, his dad had his back through it all. Nathan could never forget sitting in the truck, the warmth of his father's embrace, feeling safe despite the heartache. He didn't even object when Mitch gently touched the black eye from the fistfight with Hank—the first but not the last the two friends would have over a girl.

One evening several months later, when they pulled in the driveway, Mitch shut off the engine and turned to his son. He explained about having been laid off from the plant, but Nathan wasn't to worry, for he was going to drive a semi and deliver freight. He would be gone for days at a time and have to leave Nathan behind, but Ronnie had already agreed that he could sleep there whenever his dad was on the road. In the cocoon of the pickup, that sounded like an adventure, just sleepovers at his best friend's house a few doors down.

Several years later, on a crisp fall night, a highway patrolman knocked on Ronnie's door and asked for Nathan. He sat, hat in hand, and delivered the life-altering news of Mitch's death.

Late that night, Nathan slipped out the bedroom window once everyone else had fallen asleep. Tears flowed as he walked down the street to his own house, which sat empty and dark. He climbed inside the truck, parked out front, and stretched out on the bench seat, comforted by the smell of his father's aftershave and sweat. Through his sobs, he felt the arm wrapped around his shoulder, assuring him he wasn't alone in the world, comfort enough to drift off to sleep.

A gentle rapping of knuckles on the glass woke him as the sun peeked over the horizon. He sat up, wiped his tear-stained eyes, and opened the door so Ronnie could slide onto the bench seat. They talked for hours as dawn turned to day. How alone Ronnie had felt when his wife had succumbed to cancer. How scary dealing with social services would be. How badly Nathan did not want to leave Millerton for some orphanage or foster home.

The sun was hanging in the middle of the sky before Ronnie cranked the truck, drove it back to his own house, and parked it in the driveway. He handed Nathan the keys, looked him in the eye, and said he could park his truck there for as long as he needed.

His truck. No longer his dad's truck. His.

His friends sat waiting for him on the covered porch: Charlie, Danny, Hank. Ronnie made lunch for them as they huddled with their grieving friend.

Even all these years later, when the world confounded him, he sat in the pickup truck and asked for fatherly advice—how to treat his wife; how to raise his son; how to keep this blasted truck running; how to make his paycheck cover all their bills; how to stay loyal to Ronnie for taking him in when he had nowhere to turn.

The answers would come to him as if Mitch were sitting right there, arm draped over a little boy's shoulders, teaching him lessons between days of long absences delivering freight around the country—teaching him how to be a man.

Not just a truck. A sacred father-son space.

NATHAN SILENTLY PRAYED for his dad's strength as he opened the driver's door, pushed aside his son's overstuffed book bag, and settled onto the bench seat of the pickup truck. A sneeze threatened to explode as the crushing scent of aftershave emanating from his son tickled his sinuses. With a twist of the crank in the door, he rolled down the window and pretended to enjoy the spring breeze despite the drizzling rain.

The key went into the ignition, a silent prayer was uttered, and the truck sputtered and choked but sprang to life, never a certainty despite Nathan's vigilance in maintaining the engine.

He licked his lips as he peeked out of the corner of his eye at Jacob. The boy was staring obliviously out the window, just as Nathan had years before, trying to avoid awkward conversations. His dad never seemed nervous starting these discussions. He sure seemed calm and in control, but maybe that had all been an illusion.

Come on, Dad, give me the strength to talk to him as clearly as you talked to me. But uh, Dad, could you let me be a little more effective? After all, Jacob exists because I got Donna pregnant in high school.

Nathan took a sip of his coffee, balanced the cup on his knees, and shifted gears. He cleared his throat and asked, "Jacob, can we talk a minute?"

The boy looked up warily. "About what? I'm not in trouble, am I?"

"No, of course not." Nathan paused, studying his son. "Unless there's something you've done I should know about."

Jacob vigorously shook his head, a little too strong of a denial, but then wasn't the time to get distracted.

Nathan focused on his task. "I want to talk about girls."

"Ah, Dad." Jacob's face turned beet red as he jerked his head back toward the window. His left hand twisted the book-bag strap into knots.

"I saw you talking to Missy and Cora last Saturday. They're cute."

"Dad! You're being stalker gross."

"No, I don't mean to me. I meant… you know what I meant." Flustered, Nathan gripped the steering wheel until his fingers turned white. He breathed deeply and tried again. "I want, you know, well, girls will like you, and you will like them, and that's cool and everything, and well, I want…"

Award-winning dad conversation. Donna was right. I have zero cool-dad points.

"Look, I want you to be careful and, you know…"

"Dad. We've had this talk, remember? I do. Besides, I learned all about rubbers and stuff in school."

Shocked, Nathan pivoted and stared at the back of his son's head. "You did? Have you, uh, you know, done anything?"

"God, no! I kissed Missy one day, which was weird and all, and she told everyone, which was weirder, but that's it."

Nathan struggled between wanting to laugh at his son's stricken face and wanting to gasp because his son had kissed a girl. "You kissed Missy?"

"Yeah." Jacob shrank down in his seat and crossed his arms. "I don't wanna talk about this."

Nathan sucked in a lungful of air, held it, and slowly exhaled. He willed his fingers to loosen on the steering wheel and flexed them. "Look, Jacob, a little secret, okay? It's as weird for me to talk about this as it is for you. I know. I get it. But sometimes, the weird things… they're also the important things. So as hard and weird as it is, we gotta do it anyway. Deal?"

Jacob looked at his dad for a moment, studying his face. Ever so slightly, he nodded agreement.

"Good." Nathan breathed deeply. "Look, I made a lot of mistakes with girls. Somehow, I ended up getting it right with your mother because she's awesome, you know?"

Jacob nodded.

"But even there, well, we should have waited longer."

"For sex, you mean. Because you had me."

"Yeah, for sex. Because we had you earlier than we should have. Don't get me wrong, Champ. Having you is the greatest thing ever. I mean it. But we would have been able to give you so much more if we had waited a few years. Maybe we both would have gone to college and had jobs with more money. And then we could have given you all of the cool things like the latest Xbox games."

"Xbox is okay, but baseball is cooler."

"Yeah, baseball is cooler." Not to mention a safer topic, but he guided the conversation back. "What I want for you is to go to college and have all the choices I didn't have. I won't tell you that sex is dirty or any of that because that's a lie. And I won't lie to you. Ever."

Jacob's eyes were wide open, his mouth slack, his face still red. But he wasn't staring out the window.

"So I promise to be straight with you. Answer any question you ever have. And you talk to me about anything on your mind. Does that make any sense?"

"Yeah."

"And I'm okay dealing with the weirdness of talking about anything. And I want you to be able to tell me anything. Is that cool?"

Jacob nodded. "Cool."

They drove in silence for a few moments, the tires hissing on the wet pavement. "So you kissed Missy?"

"Ah, Dad." But Jacob didn't look out the window. He held his father's gaze as the blush blossomed across his cheeks.

Wait for him. Don't push too hard, or he won't say it.

Jacob looked down at his hands. "It was cool but weird too."

"Weird how?"

"I don't really like her like that. I mean, I wanted to kiss a girl but not kiss *her*, you know? Cora is so much cooler, but Missy just pushes and does stuff. So it was cool to kiss, but it was weird too."

"Yeah, I get that."

Jacob looked shocked. "You do?"

"Yeah, I do. When I first started dating your mom, one girl, Emma, kept trying to get me to…" He glanced over at Jacob as he mentally edited the details of the story. "To kiss her. But I didn't really like her like that."

"Really?"

"Yeah, really. Once upon a time, girls chased me, too, you know."

"No way!" The shock in Jacob's voice was genuine.

No cool-dad points. Zip. Zero.

Jacob rode for a few seconds in silence before speaking. "So, what did you do?"

"I told Emma no. I was with your mother, and no way was I going to do anything with Emma."

Okay, that wasn't accurate. He hadn't said no so much as waited too long to say yes, but this didn't seem like a good time to split hairs.

"What did she do?"

"Got mad at me. Then she dated one of my friends."

"Lucky friend."

Except they didn't really date because the relationship didn't last more than a romp in bed. *Hank took one for the team that time, didn't he?* But he couldn't say that out loud. "It didn't last. Emma was not right for him either. And I won because I got your mother."

Jacob chewed on his lower lip, mulling over the conversation. "When Missy tried to kiss me, I started to say no. But the guys, they would make so much fun if they knew I wouldn't do it."

Ah, locker rooms. Where lies and bravado are easy because the girls who knew the truth weren't allowed inside. "I get it. I do. Here's the thing, though, Champ. Don't do something because of what the guys think. And don't do something because of what some girl wants. You have to do what you think is right."

They rode in silence for a few moments, Jacob twisting the book-bag strap and chewing his lip. His face brightened, a decision made, and he piped up, "Okay. I will not let Missy kiss me again."

"And Cora?"

"She can kiss me," Jacob replied, grinning. He turned toward Nathan, his face a look of innocence. "But nothing else, I promise."

"I am okay with that. But that other stuff—you can talk to me about that too." Though Jacob groaned, Nathan didn't relent. "Any questions for me, Little Man?"

Jacob thought for a minute. "You coming to my game tomorrow?"

Nathan laughed, relieved to be back in safe-conversation territory. "Wouldn't miss it for the world. Heard you are headed to the high school for their practice after school."

Jacob's face brightened. "Yeah, they are so cool. I even hit against Carlos Estrella."

The high school star pitcher—tall and lanky, he had a deceptive throwing style that challenged high school batters. Nathan was very impressed his son had an at bat against an older, more skilled player of that caliber. "You took pitches from Carlos?"

"He's unreal. And he has a wicked curve."

"Had you chasing it, huh?"

"All over the place."

"How did you hit?"

Jacob shrugged. "I barely touched it. A few foul balls. A bunch of whiffs."

"No shame in foul balls. Keeps the pitcher working."

"I got one sweet line drive off of it."

"You did?"

"Yep. Right to the shortstop. He had the ball to the first baseman before I was halfway down the line, but Carlos was still steamed I hit off him."

"What did he do?"

"Threw the fastest ball I've ever seen." Jacob paused and shook his head. "Or didn't see, you know? Just heard the damn thing hit the catcher's mitt. I think I pissed him off, getting that hit."

"Language."

Jacob shrugged. "Sorry. Made him mad."

Nathan smiled and decided not to point out the other curse word. "Made him mad, maybe, but earned respect too. Remember, your old man was in football for a reason. I never could hit a baseball like you can. Proud of you for connecting on Carlos."

"Yeah, I loved it," Jacob said, beaming with pride. "But I was careful. You know, not celebrating. Coach says never make them mad, even when you beat them."

He thought back to his own taunting of Ricky Ward after his last football game. "Good advice. Coach is smart."

Jacob shrugged. "Yeah, after that fastball, Carlos talked with me for a while after practice and let me sit in the dugout with them."

"What else did you get to do?"

"Mostly, they had us shagging foul balls for them, but they let Luke and me do a few fielding drills."

"How did that go?"

"Hurt like hell. They throw fast." Jacob proudly held up his bruised left hand. "See?"

Nathan ignored the language that time. "Ouch. Luke's hand look like that?"

Jacob shook his head. "Nah. He's got that fancy new fielder's glove. Plus, he has those inner gloves."

Nathan picked up the glove lying in the seat between them. The padding in the glove was worn thin from use. "This glove has about had it. Let's get you a new one and an inner glove just like Luke's."

Jacob glanced sideways at his father. "It's okay. I'll make this one work."

Nathan returned the glance. "You don't want a new glove?"

"It's okay. They're expensive. Luke's was a hundred and fifty dollars. Plus another fifty for the inner glove."

Nathan whistled. "Wow." He pulled the truck into the turn lane for the school and crept toward the drop-off point.

"Yeah, his Uncle Hank gave it to him for Christmas. As few balls as Luke catches, he will never wear it out."

Nathan chuckled. "Talking smack about your pal."

Jacob threw his shoulders up in an exaggerated shrug. "It ain't smack if it's real. I run circles around him on the field, and he knows it."

As they glided to a stop at the entrance of the school, Jacob unbuckled his seatbelt, gathered his backpack and baseball glove, opened the truck's passenger door, and stepped out onto the sidewalk. He turned to his father and said, "Coach says all the time, 'It ain't the glove. It's the hand.' I don't need no new glove, Dad."

"You don't need *a* new glove," Nathan corrected.

"That's what I said." After the door slammed shut, Jacob disappeared into the mass of students, but the aroma of after-shave stayed.

8

L ying on his back underneath the conveyor system he was disassembling, Nathan saw only a worn pair of Red Wing work boots and the legs of blue work pants, but the distinctive voice calling his name told him Ronnie had walked up.

With a kick of his feet, he rolled the shop creeper from under the machine and looked up from his supine position into the glare of the overhead factory lights. Ronnie's white short-sleeve shirt, stained from ink pens, machine grease, and coffee contrasted against his black arms and face. The top button of his tieless collar gaped open. A collection of pens gathered in the shirt pocket, ready to add notes to the neatly organized reports in the bulging notebook he carried.

When visitors from the corporate office came, his shirts were clean and pressed. A tightly knotted tie hung from his neck. Slacks replaced the work pants. A sport coat indicated the visitor was an executive.

The break room buzzed with a perpetual debate. Did he dress up to impress the bosses? Or did he dress down on other days to ingratiate himself with the worker bees? But Nathan never wondered. Ronnie was a wrench-turner at heart and was more comfortable in the working-man's uniform.

"I have bad news, Nathan."

Nathan sat up on the wheeled creeper and planted his work boots on the shop floor. Tension tightened his muscles, and his pulse accelerated as he wiped grease from his hands. He wondered if today was the day his job was being eliminated. "How bad?"

"The parts for the boiler weren't in this morning's shipments. Seems they got held up at customs."

Nathan exhaled slowly, but relief was quickly replaced with a stomach-churning guilt. Every layoff notice Ronnie delivered ripped a piece of his heart from him, graying his already salt-and-pepper hair. In his mind, he failed every employee who lost their job through no fault of their own. His job was to protect them by running the factory as profitably as possible.

Along the same vein, Nathan took great pride in keeping the aging equipment running. A broken-down machine meant someone was sent home early, their pay shrunk even though they had done nothing wrong.

"Customs? I thought they made those parts in Alabama."

"Not anymore. Nothing is made in the good old USA anymore. Cheaper crappy Chinese parts now, so the idea must have made some accountant giddy." Ronnie fiddled with the stacks of reports in his hands. "You thought I was over here to lay you off?"

Caught, Nathan could only shrug. "It's Friday."

Ronnie smiled sheepishly and shook his head. "They don't do layoffs on Fridays anymore. Some stuffed shirt in HR came up with this brilliant strategy that it was bad for morale to do layoffs on Friday."

"They think the problem with morale is *when* they tell people they're unemployed?"

"They aren't worried about the feelings of the people they fired, just the ones left. Something about 'people will talk about it all weekend,' so you do reductions earlier in the week so you can manage the chatter."

Nathan shook his head in disgust. "I guess I should have gone to college so I could understand crap like that."

"I think college just teaches how to spew garbage with a straight face." Ronnie shrugged. "Anyway, the good news is the parts cleared customs and are on a truck to the FedEx depot now, but they won't get delivered until tomorrow morning— around eight, nine at the absolute latest."

The bad news wasn't the delay but that the parts were arriving on a Saturday. With corporate visitors coming Monday morning, Nathan knew the answer before asking, "So you want me to fix it first thing Monday or come in over the weekend?"

The echo of clacking machinery from the distant end of the building muffled Ronnie's quiet reply. "Sorry, but the vultures are here Monday morning. Can't have anything down while they are in the building. Hate to ask, but I need you tomorrow."

Of course that was the answer. No surprise. And he would work simply because Ronnie asked. The question was how to balance his desire to be with his son. "Jacob's ballgame starts at two. If I get here at seven and shut everything down, I can get the old parts torn down by nine. Take an hour or so to install the new parts. Give me another hour to power up and run tests. I should be done by eleven and still make Jacob's game."

Relief spread over Ronnie's face. He bled for every employee, past or present, but the bond with Nathan was special, more family than business. "I'll have the door open by seven and fresh coffee brewed. Hell, I might even stop at Abe's and get some of Martha's homemade biscuits. Help you get started and then head to the office so I can keep an eye out for the packages to come through the gate. As soon as they get here, I'll hustle the parts out to you."

"Fred can't watch for them?" At sixty-seven years of age, Fred wasn't much of a physical threat as a security guard, but he could sign for packages on weekends.

Ronnie looked down at his boots, studying one speck of grease among the many. "Fred's gone. The sons of bitches cut the security budget."

"Jesus. Poor Fred. How they gonna keep people from stealing stuff on the weekend? At least he could call the police if he saw anyone who wasn't supposed to be here just walking in."

"The geniuses think a padlock and chain on the gate will do it. They said there's nothing of value to steal."

Nathan rolled his eyes. "The copper thieves will love that."

Copper in electrical wires could be easily stripped and sold to recyclers who melted it down and manufactured new wire, making it a prime target for anyone trying to make enough money to buy illegal pain pills. Some people risked electrocution to steal copper wire from live street lights, so jumping a fence and ripping out wires from disconnected machinery was easy in comparison.

"You try convincing the damn bean counters. The copper doesn't show up as a line item, so they can't figure out it's inside the machines. These are the same geniuses who look at people as costs." Ronnie waved his hand toward the people working hard on the assembly line at the other side of the cavernous building. He took a deep breath and shook his head, an attempt to keep his frustration in check. "You need an extra hand getting the work done tomorrow?"

"How about Carl? He could use a few dollars."

Ronnie loosed a mirthless chuckle. "And get in trouble with both the accountants and the soulless wonders in HR? They would tell me how I cost us money because I restarted some stupid unemployment benefit clock. I wish I could, Nathan, I really do. But I meant me. I'm afraid you're stuck with me as your helper."

"Because they pay you a salary, so you working on a Saturday doesn't cost them a penny?"

"See? You don't need college to be executive material. With that logic, all you have to do is lose your heart, sell your soul, and you, too, can make the big bucks."

"No, thanks. I prefer working for a living." Nathan grinned at the old joke. "I'll take your help, but don't slow me down, old man."

The return smile was genuine, the ease of banter. "Don't even go there, son. I've forgotten more about boiler repairs than you will ever know."

"That's what I'm worried about—everything you've forgotten about real work since you became management," Nathan shot back. "You and Dad probably put this old thing in, didn't you, Ronnie?"

"Yep. That's why it lasted so long."

"Funny. I was going to say that's why it's falling apart."

Both men laughed. After honing his skills in the Navy, Ronnie had installed and repaired more manufacturing equipment than Nathan had ever seen—including, ironically, being sent by the company to install equipment in China and unwittingly helping to move so many jobs overseas. In turn, he taught Nathan everything he knew.

"We'll put you to the test tomorrow and see how much you remember," Nathan said.

"Deal. Just don't slow me down, youngster."

Nathan stood and scanned the building, planning the rest of his day out loud. "I got parts to harvest off these old conveyors anyway. The machines on Line Five aren't going to last much longer. And I can attack that old press to see what I can salvage off of it. We'll need those parts sooner or later." He gestured at the pile of what they called "carcasses" in one corner of the plant—old machines that had been decommissioned as layoffs reduced the plant employee count. Those machines coughed up parts needed to keep the remaining production lines running. Nathan tried hard to buy supplies only when absolutely necessary.

The smile on Ronnie's face faded. "Sorry, Nathan, but no overtime. The bean counters are all over me about that."

"But how am I supposed to fix that machine tomorrow without overtime?" Nathan's voice trailed off. He knew how. The only way to stay below forty hours this late in the week was obvious. "That's not fair."

Ronnie did his best to paint a stern face, but the hurt in his eyes betrayed him. He was powerless to fight the corporate office. He wiped at a coffee stain on his shirt. "Accountants suck, but you don't want to appear on one of their damned lists, particularly with the suits here Monday. You know as well as I do that the only thing that happens when they show up is there are less of us around."

Nathan nodded. He did understand how that worked. "Same idiots as last time?"

"New idiots." Ronnie glanced around to make sure no one was listening.

No risk in that—people in a dying factory knew to avoid management as much as possible. No one wanted to be remembered when it came time to draw up the next layoff list.

"The people coming Monday are from Ireland or something."

"Ireland?"

"Yeah. The venture-capital moneybags who bought the company a couple of years ago have this big plan to do some sort of merger so the company will be headquartered in

Ireland. Something about taxes—I don't know. Anyway, since they closed the McKinnon plant, they need us for a while."

"I thought that work went to China or something."

"Vietnam. Can you believe they think China is too expensive? Go figure that one out. But no, they closed McKinnon because of some EPA regulations. They were going to have to replace the scrubbers and retool the waste-water plant. It was cheaper just to close it down and move the work."

"So, what does that have to do with us?"

"Only that they are busy with moving that plant and now the latest corporate merger. That makes us small fish. And small fish don't get fried."

"Well, not until they are hungry enough."

"Survival is about today. Not tomorrow."

Nathan leaned against the machinery and crossed his arms. "I don't get it. You said that this plant is profitable."

"It is. Just not as much money as the suits want. Profitable ain't profitable enough anymore."

"Too bad we can't buy it ourselves."

Ronnie studied the floor before speaking quietly. "We mapped out a plan once."

"We?"

"Bob Torrington, Chad Rivers, and me." Bob was a long-time salesman who came in and out of the plant at least once a week and had been working there almost as long as Ronnie. Chad was the plant controller, a smart accountant who understood the need to invest to make money.

"So, what happened?"

"Fifty million reasons not to."

"I don't get it."

"Chad ran the numbers. Figured out what it would take to buy this place off the suits. And invest in needed repairs. And get the sales channels going. Fifty million dollars."

Nathan whistled low. "Wow."

"The weird part is that's really cheap and much less than what it used to be worth. But if you have a spare fifty million, we would probably make you a partner."

He chuckled and tapped the pocket holding his wallet. "I'm a little short."

A sly grin crossed Ronnie's face. "Aren't we all, son? In the meantime, we just keep working for the man as long as he will have us."

Nathan picked up a rag and wiped grease off his hands as he looked over his half-done project. "Okay, I'll clean this up and clock out. See you in the morning."

Ronnie nodded, turned, and walked toward the lights. After a few steps, he hesitated and studied his clipboard. He turned back around. "Why are you still here?"

Nathan spread his hands wide. "It takes a few minutes to pack up."

"No, I mean why are you still working here?"

"I'm not leaving you, Ronnie."

"Well, you better. And soon. There are still companies who hire thirty-one-year-olds who know how to fix things."

"I ain't quitting on you."

"This company is quitting *you*. Not today. Not tomorrow. But maybe next month or next year. Certainly not much longer."

"And go where? No one around here is hiring."

"Which is why you've got to leave. The town's quitting you too, and you know it."

"I can't sell the house. And even if I could, I'm upside down on it. Besides, I've never been anywhere else."

Ronnie studied his hands before speaking. "That's the same crap your dad and I used to say to each other over beers on Friday nights. Cooking burgers on the grill, watching you and Charlie toss a football. Nora making baked beans in the kitchen and getting the potato salad out of the refrigerator. We couldn't even imagine another way of living. Another place. I wonder, sometimes, what if we had moved? Would city doctors have caught Nora's cancer in time? Would Charlie still be alive, married with kids? Would Mitch have been able to avoid driving that damned truck?" He looked up at Nathan, his eyes glistening. "Just promise me you'll think about it. Take Donna and Jacob and go somewhere that boy of yours can have a future."

"If I leave, how will you keep this place running? Fix everything yourself?"

Ronnie shrugged. "Bring Carl back. And I can work a wrench while I wait for them to pull the plug on this place."

"Yeah, but with me here, maybe we can keep this place running longer. And keep you in a job."

"Son, don't worry about my job. Worry about yours."

"Don't work that way."

"Yeah, it does. You owe it to Donna and Jacob, not me. That's the way it works." Ronnie crossed his arms. "If your dad had lived and Charlie had lived, would you still be here in Millerton?"

"Probably. Hank and Danny wanted the Marines. Charlie wanted to teach and write books. But me? I like it here. Always have."

Ronnie uncrossed his arms and hung his head. "I like it here, too, but a simple question. Where do you want Jacob in twenty years? Here in Millerton or out there somewhere?"

"Wherever he wants to be."

With a nod, Ronnie replied, "Then what you gotta do is make sure all his options are open. And being here when they close this place isn't going to do it. So now I'm about to do what your dad would have done—kick you hard in the seat of your pants and tell you to go find something other than this plant. You hear me, boy?"

"But—"

"No back talk. Do you hear me?"

"Yes," Nathan said. "Yes, sir."

"Good. Now pack those tools up, clock out, go home to that wife of yours, and start figuring out another job in another town."

MIST ROSE from the puddles as Nathan walked out of the factory and across the expansive parking lot. The clouds were breaking up after the morning rains, and the bright sunshine was warming the humid air.

Sweating by the time he reached his pickup truck, he unlocked the door and cranked the driver's window open. He tossed his jacket on the hot vinyl seat before unbuttoning his shirt. It joined the jacket as he savored the sun beating down on his now-exposed black T-shirt.

An afternoon off work. Jacob was in school then heading over to Luke's house for the night, which meant they would have the house to themselves. He couldn't remember the last time he and Donna had had some alone time.

He knew other men ogled younger, skinnier girls, but he had never strayed or wanted to. Donna was a good partner and a great mother to Jacob. And he thought he loved her—was fairly sure. The old high school days of getting her out of her cheerleading outfit—as she eagerly removed his football jersey —might have been long behind them, but maybe leaving work early on a Friday and surprising Donna would be good for them.

Trying to stay ahead of bills and raising a son was so time-consuming that they had settled into a routine: breakfast as they scrambled to get ready, separation for the workday, dinner in the kitchen, chores, sleep, repeat. Donna had commented many times that they never ate out except for pizza or burgers, the primary diet of a near teenager. On a special night, they splurged at the town's Mexican restaurant out by the highway, as exotic as it got in Millerton.

During the weekends, they shepherded Jacob to sporting events and activities with friends. Evenings were helping him with his homework and making sure he actually did it. Despite all the time demands, Nathan carved out opportunities for a little father-and-son pitching of a baseball, dribbling a basketball, or tossing a football. By the time Jacob was asleep in his bed each night, Nathan was exhausted from hours of parenting piled on top of hours of hard physical work. He and Donna had little time or energy for intimacy.

Having the day free would be a blessing. He could surprise Donna with some couple time—maybe even some playtime in bed. They sure had not had much of that lately, and he couldn't remember the last time they had done anything during the daylight hours. And since Jacob was spending the night with Luke, he might even take her to that Mexican restaurant—just the two of them.

He planned the afternoon and decided to start the surprise off on a good foot: flowers, maybe some of those fancy chocolates, even some of those fruity wine coolers she liked and he detested. They tasted like the nasty punch the school used to serve at dances—and he and his buddies always tried to spike.

Nathan reached into his back pocket and fished out his wallet. A few small bills lay tucked inside. He had a credit card, but that was reserved strictly for emergencies. He had taken nearly a year to pay off the deductible when Jacob had fallen off his bike at the age of eight.

So forget the wine coolers, which meant he could avoid driving out to the stores by the interstate since Abe's Market no longer carried beer and wine. Abe had not sold a single bottle since he'd walked into the store the morning after the accident and found the envelope of cash for the illicit beer. But he could still stop there for flowers. And maybe some chocolate.

Donna would love it.

9

Nathan guided his pickup truck through the open gate of the factory, an empty guard shack serving as a lone sentry against trespassers, and turned onto Millerton Industrial Park Road. At the entrance of the industrial park, a battered traffic light swayed in the breeze from the overhead wires, its yellow caution flashing. To his left was a faded wooden sign marking the entrance to the Millerton Municipal Park. The two-lane Hilltop Road traversed to his right, leading to the next rural county as well as the paper company's fire roads and the Point.

Straight across the intersection, the road changed to the aptly named Broad Street, the main road through the center of town and the primary access to the interstate. During Millerton's heyday, traffic had filled the two lanes in each direction though only a few vehicles traveled the road's length any longer, semitrucks hauling their wares to and from the factory and locals running errands.

A semi sat parked in the underutilized left-turn lane, its hazards blinking. The driver, no doubt, was inside Abe's Market grabbing a snack, a soft drink, or lottery tickets. Or if

Abe was lucky, all of the above. The truck stop by the interstate offered better parking for the big rigs, but Abe's Market sold fresh biscuits handmade by Martha, a popular breakfast delicacy much tastier than fast-food fare.

Nathan drove into the store's parking lot, past the gas pumps, and parked beside a row of other pickup trucks. The lines marking parking spaces were faded and difficult to see in the cracked asphalt, but order reigned anyway. As he stepped from the truck, he spotted a flash of green trapped in the weeds growing beside the crumbling curb. What appeared to be a dollar bill was buffeted by the wind from a passing truck. Nathan leaned down to pick it up, smoothed the wet bill, and discovered a twenty, more money than he had in his wallet. He glanced around to see if anyone was looking for it, but no one was in sight.

As always happened at moments like that, Nathan heard his father's voice echo in his head with lessons of honesty and integrity. He had been dead for half of Nathan's life, but the voice was as loud as if he stood in front of him. Pocketing found money was not an option without a reasonable effort to find its owner, so he held it between his fingers as he crossed the parking lot and pushed open the glass door.

Fluorescent lights hung from the ceiling, interspersed with ceiling fans slowly turning to move the warm, humid air. To the left, grocery staples including cereals and canned goods lined four rows of tall metal shelves. Baskets overflowed with fresh vegetables and fruits delivered by the farmers each morning when Abe opened the doors at six a.m. During the winter months, vegetables, fruits, jellies, jams, and preserves canned on local farms replaced the fresh produce.

Beyond the shelves at the far end of the store, a group of elderly men huddled in a booth, sipping coffee and swapping tall tales. A handmade sign adorned their table: Reserved for the Liar's Club. Not that the sign was necessary, because the same men occupied the same space every day.

Beside the tables at the back of the store, glass-fronted cases displayed a small selection of meats for sale. Martha would slice the meats for take-home, but she also served fresh biscuits in the morning and created deli sandwiches and home-made potato salad for lunch. In the winter, she might have a pot of chili or beef stew cooking.

Beside the deli counter, shelving displayed fresh flowers gathered from her own gardens at their house behind the store. She called it the "just because" section, saying men should buy flowers for their wives periodically "just because." Abe called it the "I screwed up" section, but never when Martha might overhear him.

To Nathan's right, behind a counter overflowing with racks of candy bars, Abe ran the cash register, a folded newspaper laid down on his stool while he helped a paying customer. The truck driver from the rig in the street handed over cash for a pair of biscuits and a lottery ticket, another person hoping for a magical win to take him away from the drudgery of work. With the sale complete, he exited the store and ambled back across the pavement to the idling truck.

Abe picked up his newspaper and settled onto his stool. "Morning, Nathan. Did Ronnie give you a lunch break today?"

"Nope. I have the afternoon off because I have to work tomorrow. No-overtime rule and all that."

"Try owning your own place. You never get overtime, no matter how many hours you work." Abe shrugged as he positioned his reading glasses on his nose. "You see this article about your old nemesis, Ricky Ward?"

"What did he do?"

"Got arrested again, pulled over for DWI, and they found a bunch of pills on him. Stolen prescriptions again. Is that the third or fourth time? What a waste of talent."

"Poor guy."

Abe looked over the top of his glasses. "His choice to have the pills."

"Yeah, sure, but you have to feel for him. Great college-football career. Left school early for the draft. And tears his ACL in a stupid pick-up basketball game before signing a contract. No money. No future. Some doctor gets him hooked on pain medicine. It's like he was the luckiest guy on the planet with all that talent, and then suddenly he's the unluckiest."

Abe harrumphed and snapped his newspaper. "You didn't feel sorry for him the last time you saw him—lying on top of him in the mud after walloping him."

"That was different. He was trying to beat me then." Nathan grinned and held up the twenty-dollar bill. "Found this out front. Must have been out there in this morning's rain."

"Must be your lucky day."

"Don't want my luck coming from someone else's misfortune. Anybody been asking about it?" He motioned toward the old men at the table.

"Not heard a word. If you asked them, one of them might 'remember' it, but I wouldn't trust it. The four of them have been at that table since seven and haven't spent twenty dollars yet."

Nathan looked around the store, hoping to see someone frantically looking for lost money, but no one else was in the aisles. "I don't want to take someone's money."

"Take? I didn't see you knock some old lady down and steal her purse." Abe shrugged. "You feel guilty about it, then put it in the offering plate on Sunday. I think you should just buy Donna or Jacob something and be done with it."

Nathan grinned as he pointed at the cash register. "Then you end up with it with absolutely no guilt."

Abe spread his hands in mock protest. "Hey. It's just business."

Nathan laughed. "I was here to buy Donna some of Martha's flowers, so I guess it's your lucky day."

"Uh-oh. What did you do?"

Nathan shook his head. "Nothing. I swear. Since I was off work early anyway and had to work tomorrow, thought I would show up with some flowers in hand." Holding up the found money, he continued, "And since I have a little spending money, maybe some of those chocolates she likes."

"Good plan. Martha will be glad to pick out a good bunch." Abe popped open the newspaper to read the latest Carolina Panthers' news as Nathan went to the back of the store.

Buying flowers was such a trap. If he spent too much, she would think he was asking forgiveness—too little, and she would think he didn't care, which meant he *would* ask forgiveness. If he didn't buy them at all, she would claim he took her for granted, so he would ask forgiveness. Nathan had learned long before that the three magic words in a marriage weren't "I love you" but "I am sorry," even if he had no clue what he was apologizing for.

Martha beamed as he explained what he needed. "You men are such clueless creatures. Donna deserves flowers, but stop looking at those roses. Expensive flowers mean you're guilty, and she'll wonder what you did wrong. Get her roses on her birthday, anniversary, Mother's Day, but not the rest of the year unless you get them all the time."

She motioned toward bundles of flowers still sparkling from the morning rains. "Now, these wildflowers are the perfect 'I was thinking of you' message. Simple, sweet, and beautiful. Let me make her a special bouquet real quick."

As Martha assembled the blooms, Nathan walked down the aisle to the display of chocolates left over from Valentine's Day and Easter. He picked up one box and whistled low at the price tag.

Martha slipped up beside him with the flowers and shook her head. "Nope, wrong. Fancy chocolates are like roses. Guilty before the charges are even read. Donna loves these little Dove chocolates. Get her a small bag of those."

Nathan placed his purchases on the counter in front of Abe, who folded his newspaper, slid his reading glasses on top of his head, and grinned at the pile. "Chocolate and flowers, a lethal combination. You sure you aren't in trouble?" He took the found twenty from Nathan's hand. "Or maybe you're just trying to continue your lucky streak once you get home to that beautiful wife."

As Nathan's face reddened, Martha's voice floated from the back of the store. "You stop it, Abe, or you better show up with flowers in hand if you want dinner tonight."

Abe winked as he returned Nathan's change of a dollar and a few coins.

Nathan looked at the money. "If today is my lucky day, maybe I should just buy one of those lottery tickets."

"Sure. You never know. One of the scratch-off ones?"

"Nah, I mean the big one."

"There's two big ones. The Powerball drawing is Saturday, but someone out in California won it Wednesday, so it's only a forty-million jackpot."

"Only forty million? A man couldn't put food on the table with that pocket change."

"Wise guy." Abe grinned. "I meant the Mega Million is the one you want. Jackpot is one hundred fifty-four million. You win that in tonight's drawing, and I will never see you again, now will I?"

"Only if you visit white sandy beaches on a tropical island." Nathan shrugged and handed back the cash.

Abe printed the ticket. "You never know. That could be the winner right there."

"Sure. Why not? It's found money."

"Good luck with the missus," Abe called as he shuffled open his newspaper.

Walking across the parking lot, Nathan glanced around and noted with relief none of his friends saw him carrying the flowers or chocolates. He felt as self-conscious as he did holding Donna's purse in a store and didn't want their ribbing. After opening the door of his truck, he placed the chocolates on the seat, with the flowers resting on top so they would not be damaged. He slipped the lottery ticket into the pocket of his jacket as he climbed into the truck.

10

A dozen small houses sat snugly on the short street—standard salt-box floor plans with two bedrooms, one bathroom, a kitchen, and a den—built decades earlier by the plant owners as housing for workers and their families. As distant, cold corporations replaced the paternalistic mill owners, they retreated from owning the homes and sold them to their employees.

Nathan's neighbors prided themselves in maintaining their homes. Toys cluttered the small yards, but summer flowers bloomed amid mowed grass. Homeowners tackled minor repairs on the weekends. Those with special skills pitched in to help their neighbors with advanced projects.

With his diverse mechanical talents, Nathan spent many a Saturday afternoon helping a neighbor patch a leaking roof, dig up a broken waterline, or replace a shattered windowpane. No one expected money to change hands for these tasks, certainly not Nathan, but he readily accepted cold beer and grilled burgers in payment. Or a return of a favor when he needed an extra hand keeping his own home standing.

With school still in session, quiet reigned over the neighborhood as Nathan dodged cars parked at the curbs in front of the houses, inching his way down the narrow path. Each driveway was big enough for only one car, so those families with two cars parked the second car on the street. Without a word ever discussed, the neighbors had long agreed that no one should park in front of another's house. Only two families owned a third car, both because of older teenagers still living at home, indicated by the worn grass in the front yard.

A shiny black Dodge Charger with tinted windows was breaking those unspoken neighborhood rules and occupying the curb in front of Nathan's house. He knew the car didn't belong to any of his neighbors, not just because it was new and expensive but because of the out-of-state license plates. It must have belonged to a visitor to the neighborhood, but Nathan couldn't figure out who they were visiting.

The driveway next door sat empty. Seventeen-year-old Josh often skipped school and hung out with his buddies, smoking pot, blasting music, and playing video games. But his beat-up old Honda Accord was not in their front yard, so he might have been in school that day. And his mom and stepdad were at work. Besides, none of Josh's friends could afford a new car.

Across the street, Betty's Buick was parked in the drive while Maury's Chevy pickup sat on the street. Long retired, they rarely moved their cars except for a weekly grocery excursion and church services on Sunday mornings. Maury waved at Nathan as he pushed his noisy, smoke-spewing lawnmower across their lawn. If the Charger-owning visitor was theirs, Maury would have been moving it as soon as he spied Nathan coming down the road.

On the other side of the house, Chad's truck occupied the driveway. Unemployed for months and collecting a disability check, he rarely left the house. The old Camaro parked at the curb belonged to a blond, chain-smoking woman, the girlfriend of the month. Perhaps a third person was visiting around midday and Chad thought Nathan would be at work—a reasonable assumption.

Donna's car occupied the drive, so he parked in the only open space he saw, the curb in front of Josh's house. He vowed to keep an eye open for the boy if he came home early from school—a distinct possibility on a sunny spring Friday. He hoped that by then, the owner of the Charger would appear and Nathan could claim his rightful parking spot.

He draped his work shirt and jacket over his arm and gathered the candy and flowers. The possibility of afternoon sex eradicated any frustration of dealing with a visiting car blocking his way. Chad wouldn't be the only man in the neighborhood getting laid on a Friday afternoon if the presents Nathan carried worked as hoped.

He sat on the stoop and removed his boots before entering the kitchen. He hung his jacket neatly in the closet and draped his shirt across a kitchen chair, mentally reminding himself to haul it to the hamper before Donna griped about dirty clothes strewn about the house.

Thanks to the loud sputtering of Maury's lawn mower floating through the open window, he couldn't hear Donna anywhere in the house. The den was vacant, and both bedroom doors and the bathroom door were closed. With a glance out the back window, he confirmed Donna was not on her knees toiling in her precious flower bed. She must have been enjoying a late-morning shower after cleaning Jacob's whirlwind of the morning.

Pleased to have time to set up his surprise, he retrieved a large glass from the cabinet, filled it with water, and arranged the flowers before placing them in the center of the kitchen table. He propped the candy bag in front of the flowers and stepped back to admire his handiwork.

He glanced around and realized she still hadn't heard him in the house. With visions of her naked in the shower, he decided to strip off his own dirty, greasy clothes and surprise her by slipping under the streaming water with her. An hour or so later, covered in the sweat of sex, they could climb into the shower again.

The thought aroused him as he picked up the dirty shirt from the back of the chair—*don't give her something to complain about*, he thought—and crossed the den just as Maury shut off his mower across the street to accept the glass of lemonade Betty was delivering. Through the living room window, Nathan saw the two of them chattering in their yard and looking across the street, likely speculating whether the factory had laid off Nathan since he was home so early.

Without the background roar of the mower, he heard a woman's moaning coming from the bedroom and froze just outside the door, his hand resting on the knob. No mistaking the noises emanating from behind the door, sounds he expected—had expected—to make within the hour himself, the rhythmic cries of passionate lovemaking. His heart pounded in his chest, a drumbeat denying what his brain knew.

Donna?

But then the sound of a man grunting hammered his ears. Giggles floated through the closed door. And the creaking of the bed.

My bed. Our bed.

Sweat beaded on his forehead as he squeezed his eyes shut.

The Dodge Charger. Parked where I park.

He leaned his head against the door. A tear slipped down his cheek and clung to his jawline before plummeting to the floor.

Walk away. Right now. Go get drunk.

But he couldn't. His feet wouldn't move. Couldn't move. He remained stuck to the door, listening to the ecstasy on the other side. He hadn't been so hurt, so crushed, since the night his father died. The ache spread through his body as he quietly sobbed.

Donna called out, and Nathan's head snapped up. His jaw clenched, teeth grinding against each other. She had yelled out a name.

No. Can't be. Not him.

Out-of-state license plates. Georgia. An easy drive into the mountains of Western North Carolina.

He wouldn't.

A state that printed the county name on the plates. DeKalb county. Atlanta.

No friend would.

A Marine Corps sticker on that tinted window.

She wouldn't. Not with him.

Someone in law enforcement would drive that. Or someone who wanted to look like they were in law enforcement. Like someone with a high-end security job.

No!

An ex-Marine. Who worked in security. From Atlanta.

Hank.

Son of a bitch.

He leaned his head against the door frame, willing the accusation out of his mind. Arguing against it.

Couldn't be. Hank would never break the one inviolate rule of the Fearsome Foursome—never, ever, ever interfere with a buddy's girlfriend. That rule certainly included wives.

But that rule only existed because of Hank and his womanizing ways, starting with Marissa Whittum in the seventh grade.

But that was then. Friends grew up and respected each other.

But are we really still friends?

Hank came to town two or three times a year to visit Matt, Colette, and their son, Luke. After Hank and Matt's mother had died several years before, he had no other relatives in town.

During those increasingly rare visits, the three remaining members of the Fearsome Foursome would gather in Sammy's Pub to raise a toast to Charlie's memory, but those nights had grown shorter—halting conversations, mainly old stories of pranks. Without the bond of football, they had little in common. And with Hank in Atlanta, they didn't even share Millerton.

Even if the bonds had waned, Hank still would not cross this line. He wouldn't do that.

But someone was in there. Whoever was with Donna, the sounds were unmistakable. *Open the door and confirm it. Or walk away and let it eat you forever.*

Nathan took a deep breath, steadied the shake in his arms, turned the knob, and pushed the door open slowly.

THE COVERS of the bed lay twisted in a pile on the floor, the interlocked couple exposed and so enthralled with each other they didn't notice their intruder. Donna stretched on her back, eyes closed, moaning in pleasure. Her legs wrapped around the man, ankles hooked on his thighs, pulling him deeper inside her. Her fingernails dug into the small of his back. A series of semicircular nail marks peppered his skin.

The man's hands cradled her back and lifted her to him while he suckled her breasts. He pushed her back onto the bed, arched his back, and thrust deep inside her, rewarded with a squeal of delight from her. His hairy buttocks clenched as he propelled himself forward.

Nathan stood paralyzed in shock, his work shirt squeezed in his fist. Outside the door, despite the sounds, the tryst had been only imagined. But seeing them together shattered all illusion.

Turn and run? Yell and scream? Grab the naked man and pull him off her?

Donna screeched in delight, and her eyes fluttered opened as she arched her back and rose upward to receive the man more deeply. Her eyes locked with Nathan's and widened in shock. The man, oblivious to the interruption, continued to thrust as Donna tried to push him off. He only stopped when she stammered a question.

"Wh-wh-what are you doing home so early?"

The man froze, his back muscles tense, and he turned his head slowly toward the door. All doubt left Nathan's mind. Hank Saunders. Fellow high school football teammate. Life-long friend. Stealer of girlfriends.

Add stealer of wives. And traitor.

As Hank slid out of her, reached to the floor, and pulled the sheet over Donna's naked body, she protested, "You aren't supposed to be home."

Anger exploded through Nathan's body, a splattering of red crossing his field of vision. His chest tightened, and his hands shook. He felt the pounding of his pulse along the sides of his head. "I'm not supposed to be home? All you care about is I'm not supposed to be home. Here's one for you—you aren't supposed to be fucking another man." Spittle sprayed from his lips as fury rose with his voice.

Donna trembled and clutched the sheet to her chin. "I'm sorry. I'm so sorry."

"What if Jacob came home and caught you in bed?"

Tears flowed down her face. "I would have heard him come in."

Nathan flung his shirt in the air. As it floated to the floor, he threw his hands onto the top of his head and pulled his hair.

His head throbbed as his body quivered. He shrieked in anger, a primal scream of rage.

The neighbors could probably hear every word through the open windows, but he couldn't bring himself to lower the volume. "You didn't hear *me* come in. Why would you have heard him? And even if you heard him come in, how would you have explained his best friend's uncle walking out of our bedroom?"

Donna's voice dropped low, almost to a whisper. "He wouldn't have caught us."

"But I sure caught you, whore."

Hank stood from the bed, his erection accusingly pointing at Nathan, and held out his hands in front of him. "Easy, Nate, just calm down. Don't call her names like that."

Explosions ripped through Nathan's chest, blinding him with rage as he stepped toward his former friend. "Calm down? Who the hell are you to tell me to calm down? I ought to rip your cheating dick off and shove it down your throat."

Donna sat up in bed, the sheet dropping and exposing her breasts. Rage filled her face. "Nathan! Stop it!"

He pivoted back toward Donna. "Me? You're pissed that I'm mad? Are you kidding me? You're the whore in bed with another man!"

Hank stepped closer, his open hands still outstretched, and spoke in a quiet, authoritative voice, the voice of a Marine trying to command a situation. "Nate, I already warned you. Donna doesn't deserve to be called that."

"Fuck off, Hank."

"Nate." Hank reached forward and touched his forearm.

If Nathan had thought about Hank's military training, he would have never swung. In a fair fight, the bigger, stronger man would win. But Hank's weakness had always been his speed, a weakness exploited daily by his younger brother in their high school days. He never saw Nathan ball his hand into a fist and reacted too late to avoid the incoming punch.

Nathan's swing slammed into Hank's nose. Blood spewed as the crack echoed in the bedroom. His hands flew to his face as he stumbled backward and fell over the corner of the mattress. Trying to break his fall, he stretched his arm out and collided with the lamp on the nightstand, toppling it to the ground. The ceramic base shattered on the floor, scattering shards throughout the room.

Donna screamed and jumped out of bed. She bent over Hank, crying and touching his face.

Watching her tenderness, Nathan's anger ebbed slightly as a crushing ache of loss swelled within him. He leaned his back against the wall in shock as Hank staggered to his feet.

Donna sank onto the bed, sobbing and glancing back and forth. "I'm sorry."

"Donna..." Nathan started but stopped as she waved her hand in dismissal. He hung his head.

"You broke my nose, you son of a bitch." Hank grabbed Nathan by the throat with his left hand and pinned him against the wall. He balled his right hand into a fist and cocked back as he prepared to swing.

Donna jumped in the middle of the two men and pushed Hank in the chest. "Stop it."

Hank stumbled backward, stepping on the broken ceramic with his bare feet. He howled in pain and pushed Donna onto the bed. "Stay out of it." Anger flared across his face as he turned back toward Nathan and charged.

Nathan hadn't been on a football field in over a decade, but the sight of his wife being pushed caused instinct to kick in. He viewed Hank as a receiver breaking for the end zone and dropped his head to drive his lowered shoulder into his rib cage.

But Donna had bounced back off the bed to put herself

between them again, catching Nathan's shoulder in her chest. With an "oof" of escaping air from her lungs, she fell backward, collapsed into a heap on the floor, and groaned.

Horror coursed through Nathan as he saw his wife crumpled on the floor. Like all couples, they had had fights over the years—some yelling, some tense moments—but he had never, not a single time, hit her, grabbed her, or harmed her. Even the thought of doing so—or of any man hitting a woman—sickened him.

Shocked and horrified, he dropped to one knee. "Donna. Are you all right?"

With gentle hands, he helped her sit up and draped the sheet over her naked body. Tears flowed down her face as her body shook. He reached to stroke her face.

From behind him, he heard a metallic sound—an action being pulled back on a pistol, a bullet sliding into a chamber.

Still on his knees, he rotated slowly and found a 9mm pistol pointing between his eyes. Hank stood naked, gripping the pistol. His voice remained soft and firm, yet anger rumbled in the background. "Get out, Nathan."

Nathan gritted his teeth. "It's my house. *You* get out."

The gun held steady. "Look at her."

Donna looked up through red eyes, tears rolling down her face. Her arms were wrapped around her chest as she fought to catch her breath.

"Now look at me."

Hank stood in front of him, hands gripping the pistol. His nose was misshapen, blood flowing freely and dripping from his chin. His face was swelling around his eyes.

"If we call the cops, they will take one look at the two of us and not care about anything else. They will just slap the cuffs on you and drag you to jail. Do yourself a favor, and get out of here."

The fight had oozed out of Nathan. His voice came out defeated and quiet. "You were screwing my wife."

"We were making love to each other, not screwing. And not for the first time." Hank waved the pistol toward the bedroom door. "Get out of here. Go find somewhere to stay the night. We'll deal with this later. I need to take care of Donna right now."

Nathan rose to his feet, careful to keep his hands open and out. The pistol followed his movements, Hank's hands steady and sure. With a glance at his crying wife, he backed toward the door, stepping over the broken lamp and his crumpled work shirt, and slipped into the den. Hank lowered the gun and scurried around the bed to Donna. He dropped to his knee and kissed her head, his eyes still warily watching Nathan.

The tenderness Hank showed Donna hurt Nathan more than anything else. That simple scene revealed a deeper, longer relationship than a single afternoon of adultery.

As he crossed the den to leave, he glanced out the window. Maury and Betty were standing arm in arm, horrified looks on their faces as they stared back across the street.

Nathan opened the closet, picked up his work boots, and walked out the door.

THE AFTERNOON SUN BLAZED, the wet ground steaming from the morning rains. Boots in hand, he stumbled down the driveway, past his wife's car, and toward his own truck. He leaned against the hot frame and stared at that black Charger as angry questions bounced through his head.

How many times? How many times have they been together? How often has that black Charger been parked in front of my house?

They weren't sneaking off to some cheap motel. They were meeting in his house, in front of the neighborhood, which meant the neighbors had seen it. All of them would have seen it. They saw everything. Nothing happened without the whole neighborhood knowing.

Do all the neighbors know about the affair? Do they whisper behind my back?

He wiped his hand across his eyes, clearing tears, and looked around. Maury and Betty had retreated to their porch, where they stood watching. The looks in their eyes said it all. They knew. He and Maury had changed the oil in their cars together only a month before. Maury had talked about Jacob and baseball, not about Donna and affairs, but he must have known.

A curtain fluttered in the house beside Maury's. Shelly was peering out her window, tracking the secrets of the neighborhood, just as she always did. He had helped Shelly fix a broken screen door just the last weekend. Yet she saw everything through those curtains, so she knew. Of course she knew.

Chad and his girlfriend-of-the-month were standing on his front porch, smoking cigarettes, sipping beers, and watching Nathan.

How often have they heard Hank and Donna's lovemaking through the open window?

Even Josh—that pot-smoking, hooky-playing Josh next door. *Bet he knew what was going on, too, despite his weed-addled brain.* He skipped school enough and hung out. Of course he knew what happened during the day. Donna wouldn't mention how often he was at home during the day if he didn't mention how often Donna had company—a deal to keep each other's secrets.

So the whole neighborhood knew. How could they not?

Only Nathan was clueless.

He froze as a horrible thought entered his mind. *Does Jacob know? Has Jacob ever come home and found Hank still there?* Maybe they tossed a baseball back and forth while Nathan was working. Maybe Hank helped him with his homework at the kitchen table or made him an after-school snack.

He glanced back over at Chad sitting on his porch, who raised a beer. Nathan didn't know if that was a wave of hello or an offer to drink a few beers and commiserate over ex-wives, but he nodded in return as though they were having an everyday moment. He needed a beer, but he couldn't stay in this neighborhood, not knowing Hank was inside his house with his wife. He leaned against the hot metal of his truck and fished his cell phone out of his pocket. Through blurred eyes, he scanned his contacts and tapped one.

The phone rang twice before a cheerful voice boomed, "Hey, Nathan."

"Danny. You free?"

"Are you kidding? What else would I be doing?" He paused. "Aren't you at work?"

"Can you meet me at Sammy's Pub?"

"After work?"

"Now."

"Now? What's wrong? Did Ronnie lay you off?"

"Worse. Much worse. I'll tell you there, not over the phone. I need a friend. A real friend. Can you get there?"

Danny's jovial tone disappeared. He didn't need to know why. "I'll be there in twenty minutes."

Nathan hung up the phone and stuffed it into his pocket. He shuffled his feet and spun slowly around, surveying his neighbors as they watched him back. None of them came over or offered condolences or even an explanation. They just watched.

He reached for the door handle, paused, and looked back at the house. He was leaving with just the clothes on his back. He didn't have fresh clothes for the next day. And the work shirt and jacket he'd worn that morning were inside too. If he didn't go get them, he would show up tomorrow at the plant out of uniform for the first time since high school.

But the next day was Saturday. Ronnie wouldn't care because no one else would be there. And, after work, he could arrange to get his stuff because this wasn't his home anymore —just a house. Danny would let him sleep on the couch that night. He had done it before. And Danny would let him stay as long as he needed until he could find an apartment or a trailer to rent.

Not that he could afford rent *and* a mortgage, so Donna would have to find work if she wanted to keep the house.

Regardless, the marriage was over. He couldn't live there. He couldn't go back to Donna even if she wanted him back. He couldn't even go back for his clothes right then—not with all the neighbors watching, not with all of them knowing.

He would find a time to come get what he needed. Later. The next day maybe or the next week.

Right then, he needed to get drunk.

11

In what had once been a bustling center during Millerton's heyday, half the buildings of the three-block-long downtown area sat vacant. The second- and third-floor apartments and rooms for let, from an age when people lived above the stores, sat vacant except for a handful of attorneys' offices and a bookkeeping service.

The ground-floor retailers, already victimized by the declining economy as the town's manufacturing base shifted overseas, couldn't survive the opening of a Walmart out by the interstate. A consignment store had opened in one of the spaces, selling rows of hand-me-down clothes, banged-up furniture, and discarded toys for sale at prices even the big discounter couldn't match. A hardware store struggled to stay afloat, selling single nuts and bolts so you didn't have to buy a whole box when you needed just a few.

The city hall, with the attached police station and volunteer fire department, anchored one end of downtown. Three blocks away, on the other end, Sammy's Pub, the most prosperous and longest-running business in the center of town, occupied a squat single-story building beside an expansive asphalt parking lot.

The original Sammy, a lumberjack who'd realized he could make a better and easier living running a bar than harvesting trees, opened the business long before even the city hall. The generic moniker became a proper name when a carved wooden sign was tacked above the door. His grandson, Sammy III, was running the business now though generational doubt loomed about the future. Sammy IV talked of moving to a bigger city when he graduated from high school.

In addition to liquor and cold beers, always domestic and never microbrews, Sammy had a small kitchen serving burgers, sandwiches, wings, and various snacks. The lunch rush for the day, such as it was, had dwindled to four men sitting around one of the front tables overlooking Main Street—lawyers in no hurry to head back to their offices, if they even made it back at all on a Friday afternoon. Iced-tea glasses were drained, and sandwich plates sat empty except for crumbs and a few straggler French fries soaking in pools of ketchup.

Behind the cluster of tables at the entrance, a large wooden bar jutted out into the center of the room. Two men perched on barstools at opposite ends of the bar, sipping their beers and arguing sports. Two TVs hung on the wall above the liquor bottles. With limited choices early in the day, one showed a poker tournament, and the other featured two anchors discussing sports news. Ricky Ward's mugshots from the day before were being featured.

The back wall held a rack of pool cues while two pool tables occupied most of the floor space. Dartboards hung on the wall beside the doors to the bathrooms. The walls were pockmarked with holes from errant shots, highlighting the treachery of bathroom trips on some nights. Photos of Sammy, his father, and his grandfather with various patrons or on fishing or hunting trips occupied most of the back wall, which hid the kitchen.

Later in the evening, the pool tables would be busy, but no one played that early on a weekday. For the moment, Nathan sat alone at the last table along the side wall. In the shadows, he gripped a mug and stared at a half pitcher of beer in front of him.

He looked up as the heavy wooden front door opened, allowing the dark bar to be invaded by sunlight. Danny rolled his wheelchair through the door and greeted Sammy—the third—who leaned against the cooler behind the bar with his tattooed arms crossed. With the slightest tilt of his head, the bartender pointed out Nathan without moving his arms.

Danny squinted through the shadows at the back of the bar until recognition crossed his face. The wooden floor creaked as he rolled his wheelchair down the aisle. He grabbed a chair, moved it out of his way, and rolled his chair up to the table. He poured himself a beer into the waiting glass and stared at his friend.

They sat in the dim light, sipping their beers, occasionally eyeing each other but neither speaking. Danny was patient—he could wait as long as Nathan needed. They had played the opposite roles countless times as Danny struggled with guilt from the accident and the frustration of his own physical infirmities.

With a toss of his glass, Nathan finished his beer, slammed the mug down on the table, and poured another. Sammy glanced back at them but remained leaning against the bar.

Danny took another swig and broke the silence. "I need a clue here. What's wrong?"

Nathan opened his mouth to answer, but no words came out—too hard to say something out loud and make the nightmare a reality. Maybe if he didn't say it, it wouldn't have been true.

"Jacob? Did he hurt himself? Get into a fight at school? Get a B in something you and I failed? Get cut from a sports team?"

A good and rational first guess. Nathan worried more about his son than anything in the world. He wanted him to be successful, to have better chances, but those were easy things to discuss. He held his hands in front of himself, twirling the wedding band on his finger as he shook his head. Strike one.

"Work? Is the factory closing? Did you get laid off? Is something wrong with Ronnie?"

The ring continued to circle around his finger, but he couldn't bring himself to look up at his friend. He dismally shook his head. Strike two.

"That only leaves Donna."

He pulled the ring off his finger and balanced it on the table. A flick of his finger sent it noisily spinning across the table.

Danny sighed and took a big swallow of beer. "So, what happened?"

Nathan cleared his throat. He hadn't spoken since ordering the pitcher and didn't trust his voice. He leaned forward, not wanting the words to travel across the quiet bar, and croaked, "I caught her in bed with a man."

Shock spread across Danny's face as he uttered a simple "Oh." He gulped the remaining beer in his glass and poured a refill. He was hesitant, choosing his words carefully. "Caught her? Or suspect something?"

Nathan wrapped his hand around the ring and balled his fist. The words flooded out of his mouth. "Walked in on them doing the horizontal bop in the house. In my own bed. Naked as the day they were born. Saw everything, so no, there is no doubt."

Danny cursed as he held his mug in midair, ripples rolling

on the surface of the beer as his hand shook. "Do you know him?"

Weirdly, Nathan dreaded this more than Donna's infidelity. Danny would be put in the middle, between friends, the second he revealed who. He would have to choose sides and might just elect to take the other. Breathing deeply to calm his nerves, Nathan muttered, "Hank Saunders."

Danny sat back in his chair, his eyes wide and the color draining from his face as he cursed again. He sat in shock before picking the mug up and draining the liquid down his throat. He settled the glass back on the table and let loose a small burp as he wiped his mouth with his shirtsleeve. "Did you beat his ass?"

"Broke his nose."

A nod of satisfaction. "Good. He deserved it."

Relief spread through Nathan's body as he realized his friend was going to pick his side—a bitter victory, but he needed the support.

Danny studied the empty glass in front of him. "Is it a one-time thing?"

"Sounded like they've been doing it for months."

Danny picked up the pitcher and drained it into the two glasses. "We're going to need another pitcher." He twisted in his chair and signaled for Sammy. "And I'm ordering nachos. We need some food."

"So I won't get too wasted?"

"Don't worry, my friend, I plan to get drunk with you. We'll get a ride back to my place. I'm just gonna need food too."

"Good idea." Nathan leaned back in his chair. "Believe it or not, I gotta work tomorrow."

"Ronnie's giving you overtime?"

"No. That's the kicker. That's why I went home early, because they're too cheap to pay overtime. Otherwise, I still wouldn't have had a clue about the affair." Nathan slumped deep in the chair and muttered, "In my own bed. They didn't even have the decency to get a cheap motel room. Now I know why she was always putting on clean sheets."

"Something to be thankful for."

Danny ordered a full plate of Nachos Deluxe—Sammy's most popular menu item, with cheese, chili, beans, sour cream, guacamole, and other toppings poured over a large stack of tortilla chips. A coronary delight. And a fresh pitcher of beer to wash it down. Sammy looked at them quizzically but shrugged his shoulders. Business was business, and whatever was driving them to drink so early on a Friday was not his concern.

They sat in silence, no words needed. Sipped cold beer. Breathed. Waited. Nothing more to be done. That's what friends did. Sat with each other.

The nachos were delivered, along with clean plates, fresh cold glasses, and more beer. They ate. They drank. And Nathan finally told Danny every detail of his day.

ONLY SCATTERED remnants of the devoured nachos remained on the plate when the front door opened again and light flooded the dark bar. Two uniformed police officers entered, their radios squawking in the relative quietness. All eyes in the bar followed them as they scanned the room, locked eyes with Nathan and Danny, and walked straight to the back table, purpose in their steps.

The older of the two approached the table while the second stood a few feet back, watching them.

"Nathan Thomas?" the older officer asked.

Nathan gulped. He hadn't spoken to a police officer since a traffic ticket six years before. "Yes."

"You probably don't remember, but I'm Brett Carrington. Played JV at Millerton High when you guys beat Roosevelt." Not waiting for acknowledgment, he continued, "The Fearsome Foursome. What a great game. I will never forget that last play. The hit you laid on Ricky Ward was awesome."

Startled, Nathan blinked before replying, "We won't forget it either."

The officer looked at Danny's wheelchair and nodded. "No, I guess you won't. Danny Morgan, right?"

Danny locked eyes with the officer and nodded. "You were a running back?"

"Yes, exactly. You do remember. Not that many people do because I followed in Matt Saunders's footsteps. I kept thinking he was going to college to play some real ball, but he went and got Colette pregnant. How dumb."

Nathan looked down at the beer mug in his hands and twisted the glass. "Lot of that going around back then."

Danny interjected, "Look, Brett, Officer Carrington, thanks for stopping by, but Nathan and I have some things we were discussing."

Brett turned to his partner. "Why don't you head up front and get a Coke or some water or something? And ask Sammy to get me a water."

Frustration crossed the younger officer's face. "But I should back you up."

"You will... from up there."

With an exasperated sigh, the other officer turned, walked to the front of the bar, and leaned against the front door.

Brett turned back to the table. "Sorry, this isn't a social call. Mind if I sit?"

Nathan and Danny exchanged glances before Nathan waved a hand at a vacant chair.

Brett settled in, his equipment belt clanking. "My partner is young. He thinks it's all about car chases and arrests. I was the same way when I started." He took a sip of water from the glass Sammy set in front of him. "You guys probably don't know, but I went to work for the Atlanta PD after graduating from community college. A good learning experience, but all they cared about was stats. How many tickets you wrote. How many arrests you made. When I got a chance to come back to Millerton, I took it. We still make arrests—and we should—but it's more about solving problems."

Nathan shook his head. His boozed brain couldn't figure out what the cop wanted. "So?"

"I need to ask you some questions about what happened at your house today."

Nathan's eyes dropped. "Figured that's why you're here. Donna called the cops?"

"No, sir. Your wife was pretty upset we showed up and wanted us to go away, but once we got there, we had to find out what happened."

"Maybe I shouldn't talk to you."

"Totally your right not to. It's all right here in the Miranda warning." Brett pulled a card out of his pocket, read it word for word, and laid it on the table.

Nathan picked up the card and studied it through bleary eyes. "So what happens if I refuse?"

"I arrest you and take you to the station. You sit in a jail cell while you arrange an attorney and bail."

"Arrest me?"

"If you don't talk to me, the only stories I have are from your neighbors, your wife, and Hank Saunders." Brett leaned forward. "Your choice. We can do this all official and go outside or down to the station. Or we can just talk here."

"And I talk, you don't arrest me?"

"Can't promise that because it depends on what you say."

Nathan laid the card down and slid it across the table. "Then let's talk."

"In front of your friend?"

Nathan looked at Danny. "I have nothing to hide. He's my best friend. He knows everything about me."

"Fair enough." Brett studied his face. "Looks like you're pretty drunk. You okay to talk?"

"Sure." However, the word came out "shhhhure."

Brett hesitated but took a deep breath and plunged ahead. "So you want to tell me what happened today?"

"I caught my wife in bed with another man. We yelled at each other. I left. End of story."

Brett nodded but kept his unblinking eyes on Nathan. "Come on, I think the story is a bit longer, don't you?"

Nathan played with the glass on the table. "I hit Hank, but only after he grabbed me." He hung his head and studied the water rings on the table. "Maybe not exactly grabbed."

Brett studied him. "The marks on your neck. Hank do that or your wife?"

His head popped up. "Hank. Donna never touched me. I swear."

"Okay. Hank grabbed you, and you hit him?"

"Not quite." He lowered his eyes to his hands and told the story, responding to questions as the officer flushed out details.

With the tale done, Brett scribbled notes on a pad before looking up. "So no weapons?"

"Just Hank's pistol."

Brett's eyebrows shot up. "Pistol?"

"Yeah. He pointed it at me and told me to get out."

"You were still fighting?"

Nathan shook his head. "No, the fight had stopped."

"Interesting. Your stories match up pretty close except Hank left out the pistol." Brett bit his lip, thinking through what he had heard. "So the stuff between you and Hank. You find him in bed with your wife. He stands up, the two of you exchange words, and he touches you. You hit him. He grabs you. The two of you fight some. The fight ends. He pulls a pistol and tells you to get out. That cover it?"

"Yeah."

"This is why I like just talking through things. You figure out what's real." Brett sighed. "So here's the deal. I have to swing back to them and ask some follow-up questions, but it sounds like Hank could press assault charges against you. Like you said, you hit him first. But you could probably press charges too. Not so much for grabbing you since that was already in the fight, but for the pistol coming out after. Since the fight was over, he can't really claim he felt in danger at that point. A judge might rule for him, might rule for you, might rule for both of you, or might throw it all out as mutual combatants. Or maybe neither of you presses charges. That's up to you two."

Brett locked his stare and continued, "But let me be clear. You hitting him first and hitting him as hard as you did—that's wrong. Pure and simple. You understand me?"

"Yes."

"I'll write it all up and let you look at it when you're sober and sign it."

"And you don't arrest me for assault?"

"Not unless Hank presses charges. If he does, then I have to. And if you press charges for pulling the gun, then I arrest him."

"I won't if he won't."

"Usually the way it works." Brett twirled the pen in his fingers. "But there's more, and it's not as easy."

"What?"

Brett sighed. "How did Donna's ribs get cracked?"

Nathan sat up in horror. "They're cracked? Is she okay?"

"She's at the hospital getting checked out, but she's going to hurt for a while."

"Oh God."

"So did you do that or did Hank?"

Nathan whispered, "Me."

"You just hit her in anger?"

Nathan's eyes flashed. "No, I swear. It was an accident. He was coming at me, and I was going to tackle him. Donna stepped between us to stop the fight. I never meant to hurt her."

Brett leaned back, his eyes squinting, and studied Nathan's face. "Okay, I'll write up your story just like that."

"Does Donna say different?"

The officer hesitated before replying, "No, she said exactly that. It's just, sometimes, a wife lies for her husband. I've seen it way too much."

"I'm not lying, I swear. And Hank could tell you."

"Well, that's the problem. He says it was deliberate."

Nathan crumpled back in his chair. "What?"

"Don't get worked up about that. Let me do my job. Now that I have your side of the story, I will circle back with them and ask some more questions. Like about that pistol they didn't mention."

Nathan meekly nodded. "Okay, I'll stay right here."

Brett grimaced. "Sorry. Not going to happen."

"What do you mean?"

"Listen to me, and don't do anything crazy. Remember my partner is watching."

"Why would I do anything?"

"Nathan, I have to arrest you."

Nathan's mouth dropped open. "But I thought you weren't going to arrest me for hitting Hank?"

"I'm not. That just goes in the report. The problem is Donna's injuries."

"She wants me in jail?"

"She doesn't even know. And she doesn't have a choice. It's the law. Period."

"Wait. She doesn't want me arrested?"

"No. That's not the way domestic-violence laws work. When there is a fight between husband and wife and there are injuries, we have to make an arrest. She doesn't have a choice. And I don't have a choice."

"Even if it was an accident?"

"Arrest and conviction are two totally different things. The judge will hear you out and listen to her and to Hank. And I will tell him what all three of you told me and what I saw. He'll look at your history, which is clean, and make a decision. If what you said holds up, you stand a good chance with the judge. But that's not for me to decide."

"So you have to arrest me?"

"Yes, I do."

Nathan looked at Danny, helpless. "I guess I am going to jail."

Danny said, "It's Friday. Will he be in all weekend? Can I bail him out?"

Carrington flipped his wrist over and checked his watch. "You're in luck. I can probably get him booked before the magistrate leaves. Since he's been cooperative, I'll do everything I can to make it happen. Bail will be set there, and then you can get him out if you want."

"You can't afford bail, Danny," Nathan objected.

"I'll get it. That's my problem."

Brett looked at Danny. "He can't go back to his house. Period. You bail him out, you keep him away."

"No worries, Officer, he was already going to stay at my place. That's why we're here. He was getting away from them. He won't go near them."

The officer nodded and stood up. "Okay, Nathan, can you come with me?"

"Please not the cuffs in here... please?"

"No need as long as you continue being good. We'll walk out to the car, and then I will have to search you and put them on. Just don't make me regret waiting."

Sammy stood behind the bar, arms crossed, and shook his head as they walked out into the sunlight.

12

Fingerprints. Mugshots. Wallet, change, keys, phone, and wedding band inventoried and sealed in an envelope. Belt and boots removed, a precaution against hanging by shoelaces, though Nathan couldn't understand how that could happen when the two holding cells faced the desks the officers used for reports.

Then, the waiting. A clock hung from the wall above the desks crammed into the workspace. The second hand crept along its face, inch by inch marking the achingly slow passage of time. Phones rang, and conversations chattered until, after an excruciating hour and a half, a grim-faced officer came for him and escorted him sock-footed up the stairs to face the magistrate.

He expected the trappings of a majestic courtroom with deep-mahogany walls. Rows of wooden benches for spectators, pews in the church of court. An ornate bar protecting the well. Two fashionable tables, one each for the prosecution and the defense, occupied by well-dressed lawyers. A dais for witness testimony and an even higher platform for a judge in a flowing black robe. A jury box to one side. That was the way it always looked on TV.

Instead, the magistrate, a loosened tie hanging from his dress shirt, sat behind a metal desk facing two plastic-topped folding tables for the defense and prosecution. A sparse number of spectators were scattered throughout the room, some standing and some seated on a mishmash of metal folding chairs and ancient office side chairs. The sheetrock walls had once been painted white but were covered with scuff marks and crooked pictures, photographs of the town throughout history. The room served multiple purposes and could be quickly rearranged for town-council meetings or public hearings or set up as a training room or conference room.

The magistrate picked up a file folder and asked Nathan to confirm his name and address and whether he understood what he was charged with. When Nathan attempted to explain what had happened, the magistrate waved his hand and asked a series of questions.

"Do you have an attorney?"

"No, sir."

"Can you afford an attorney?"

"No, sir."

"Do you understand that you will have to prove that you cannot afford an attorney by filling out an application and disclosing all of your holdings?"

"That shouldn't be a problem."

"Do you want this court to appoint an attorney for you?"

"Yes, sir."

The magistrate scanned the courtroom, pointed at one the lawyers sitting in the gallery, and motioned him to come forward. The lawyer didn't glance at Nathan but looked at a folder handed to him by the magistrate.

"This attorney will represent you only today and may or may not take your case. A permanent attorney will be assigned next week. Do you understand?"

"Yes, sir."

His lawyer for the minute looked up, announced that Nathan had no priors except for a speeding ticket, and asked for release on his own recognizance.

The magistrate shook his head and ordered bail. He stared at Nathan with a stern face. "Do not go to your wife's house. Do you hear me? I'll revoke your bail if you do."

"Yes, sir."

The lawyer laid the folder back on the magistrate's desk and turned to Nathan. "Don't talk anymore to the police until your attorney is assigned." He returned to his conversation with other lawyers, his back to Nathan.

A police officer escorted him back down the steps and into his jail cell. The clock had moved only seventeen minutes.

He settled into the cell, eyes on the clock, where the second hand made a sloth look fast. With his head bowed and eyes closed, he napped until a rapping on the cell door woke him. A glance at the clock showed two hours had passed since his return from the court appearance.

Standing in front of the door was an intimidating bruiser with a shaved head and scraggly goatee. His T-shirt was stretched across a bulging chest. The sleeves had been cut off, revealing massive, tattoo-covered arms. "I'm Zach."

When Nathan looked blank, no recognition on his face, the brute continued, "Triple-A Aaron's Bail Bonds. Danny Morgan hired me for you."

"Where's Aaron?"

"Who's Aaron?"

"Of Triple-A Aaron's Bail Bonds."

"Oh, I just picked that name to be first in the phone book."

Zach dismissed the conversation with a wave of his hand. "Is your wedding ring here?"

Startled, Nathan could only point at the sea of desks. "They have it."

"Your friend said you don't need it anymore, so you'll give it to me as part of your fee."

"Part?"

"He's arranged a payday loan secured by your truck."

"I don't know if I want to give up my ring."

"You got anything else of value?"

Nathan hesitated. "No."

"Then sit here all weekend if you want. Or give me the ring."

"Do I get it back?"

The hulk shrugged, his massive shoulders touching his ears. "Between you and the pawn shop. I'm just going to hock it for cash. You can buy it back from them if you want it."

Nathan hesitated and looked at the clock, and the minute hand ticked one spot. "Take the ring."

"Deal. Rules are simple. Show up for court anytime they tell you. Don't be one minute late. You fail to show, the cops and I'll hunt you down. And you better pray they find you before I do. Got it?"

Nathan had no other choice. He nodded agreement and watched Zach sign paperwork with the officers. A form was passed through the cell wall to him, and he signed and returned the paper and the pen.

He settled back onto the metal bench and watched another hour creep by on the clock. Through the glass of the front door, the daylight disappeared, and the black of night fell before his cell door was opened. His personal effects were returned, minus the ring. He walked out the door, stringless boots on his feet, and climbed into Danny's waiting van.

As he strung the shoelaces back through his boots, he asked, "How did you survive?"

Danny looked at him quizzically. "Survive what?"

"Jail. I was bored out of my mind, and I only had to sit there for a few hours. I can't imagine doing months of that."

"That was the Hilton compared to a real jail." Danny cranked the engine of his van. "The truth is it wasn't easy. Day in and day out, monotony. I had days I wasn't sure I wanted to survive it."

Nathan clicked his seat belt on, a habit never broken since that horrible night long before. "I'm not sure I could make it. I always thought the worst part was the other inmates, but I couldn't believe how slow time moved."

"Trust me, the other inmates are the worst part." Danny guided the van away from the curb. "Good news is I don't think you'll ever find out what jail is like. I talked to Brett again. He checked in with Hank and Donna, and they admitted to the pistol. Even better, Donna was insistent you weren't trying to hit her."

"Is she okay?"

"Seems to be. Matt's with them in the emergency room and is going to drive them home."

"They're still at the hospital? It's been hours."

"When is an emergency room ever fast?"

"Let's go."

Danny stomped on the brakes and pulled the van over to the side of the road. He threw the vehicle into park and turned in his seat to face Nathan. "Are you nuts? What part of keeping your nose clean did you miss? Didn't the judge tell you to stay away from her?"

"He said not to go to her house."

"Judges don't have a sense of humor. You know what he meant."

"I just want to see how she is for myself. I feel terrible that she's hurt."

Danny drummed his fingers on the steering wheel as he watched the passing traffic. "So how about this? We park in the lot but don't get out of the van. Just watch them walk out, get in Matt's car, and leave. You promise not to try and talk to them."

"Deal."

THE MOSTLY EMPTY parking lot of Millerton Community Hospital on a Friday evening reflected the facility's primary purpose, performing elective surgeries for people who wanted to avoid traveling to a larger hospital. The parking lot, crowded with cars during the week, emptied out for the weekends. Only the small emergency room—more equipped as a large urgent-care center—would be busy as the night wore on. Traffic accidents, drug overdoses, and domestic violence contributed to a steady flow of patients. Those cases started slowly in the early evening and increased with the later hours.

Danny maneuvered his van through the nearly empty parking lot. Nathan spied the vacant helipad and shivered, memories of the car accident years earlier flashing through his mind. The ambulances had transported them here. The doctors stabilized them and loaded them onto the MAMA helicopters—Mountain Area Medical Airlift—for the flight to the Mission Trauma Center down in Asheville. That flight was the only time Nathan had ever flown, and he didn't remember it because he had been barely conscious.

Matt's car was parked in the second row of the lot, just beyond the handicapped spaces. Danny slipped the van two rows over, close enough to watch but far enough away to avoid conflict. They settled back for a long wait in the dark parking lot, eyes focused on the sliding glass doors to the hospital's main entrance.

Smokers, many of them nurses, sat on the benches under the covered portico, puffing away, unhindered by the large Smoke Free Campus signs posted on the columns. A few people wandered around with cell phones stuck to their ears, hands waving as they talked. An ambulance sat parked by the curb.

Every time the glass doors swished open, they sat up to see who appeared before settling back down, disappointed again. After a dozen false alerts, Matt appeared with car keys in hand. Walking a few steps behind him, Donna leaned on Hank's side. With his arm wrapped around her waist, he guided and supported her. Her own arms wrapped lightly around her midsection, hugging herself as she walked gingerly, wincing with each breath.

A metal splint secured with strips of white tape covered Hank's face. Packing stuffed his nostrils, and his raccoon eyes were a deep purple.

Nathan's body tensed as he examined them, surprised at the amount of damage he had done. "Jesus, they look terrible." Without thought, he reached for the door handle.

Danny's hand grabbed his arm. "Stop. You promised to stay in the van."

He hesitated, torn between wanting to comfort his wife and the desire to avoid further conflict. Reluctantly, his grip loosened, and he lowered his hand to his lap. His eyes glistened with tears as he settled back in the seat and watched them walk toward Matt's car.

Matt strolled ahead of them and pressed the button on his key fob. The hazard lights of his car blinked in acknowledgment as the sound of the unlocking doors carried across the empty lot. The flash momentarily blinded the van's occupants, accustomed to the dim light from the overhead poles.

Matt stopped midstride, his eyes locked on the van, and recognition spread on his face. He turned his head toward Hank and pointed them out.

"We've been spotted. Time to go." Danny reached to turn the dangling keys in the ignition.

Nathan's outstretched hand stopped him. "Too late. They've already seen us, and we have to drive right past them to get out of here. We might as well find out what they have to say." The words came out relaxed, but his body tensed as the trio walked toward them.

Hank stepped up to the passenger side of the van and signaled with a crank of his hand to roll down the window. Nathan complied, and the bigger man leaned in. "What are you doing here?"

"I just wanted to see how Donna was doing."

"Pretty rough, thanks to you. Cracked ribs taped up and some potent pain meds are kicking in. I need to get her home so she can rest." Hank patted her hand hooked around his elbow.

"Donna, I'm really sorry. I never meant to hurt you."

Tears flowed down her face as sobs overcame her. Nathan opened the door to comfort her, but Hank shoved it closed again. He kept his grip on the door as he turned to his brother and asked him to get her settled in his car. With Matt's support, she ambled back toward their car.

Once she was settled, Hank turned his attention back to Nathan. "Thought you would be sitting in jail all weekend."

"Bail."

"You need to stop stalking Donna, or we'll call the cops."

"I wasn't stalking. I just wanted to make sure she was okay. If Matt hadn't seen us, you would never have known we were here."

"She'll be fine if you leave her alone. Don't go near her again, do you understand?" Hank's hand drifted up to his face and rubbed the metal plate. "You won't get the drop on me next time. Don't even think about going near the house because I'll be keeping an eye out, so stay away."

"Don't worry. I'm sleeping at Danny's until things calm down."

Hank leaned against the side-view mirror. "You aren't hearing me. I mean don't go near her ever again. You'll be served with divorce papers next week."

Nathan's chest tightened, and his breath caught. He knew the marriage was over the second he'd found them earlier in the day, but hearing the word aloud was painful. "I understand. We'll get to all that, but we have to talk to figure it out."

Running his hand though his hair, Hank glanced back over at Donna in the back of Matt's car. He refocused his blue eyes sternly on Nathan and spoke quietly, keeping his voice from carrying across the parking lot. "She isn't divorcing you because of today. This isn't some rash decision. We met with an attorney two weeks ago. The divorce papers are already drawn up and ready to be served. Donna was just trying to find a way to tell you as gently as she could."

Numbness crept down Nathan's body. His tongue felt thick and bloated, strangling his ability to speak. "Two weeks ago?"

"We've been talking about it for a while. You need to understand this was coming even if you hadn't walked in on us today. But now that you know, no reason to delay any more."

Nathan tried to swallow, but his mouth had gone dry. "How long have you two…?"

"It's been months, Nate, since before Halloween. She stopped by Matty's to pick up Jake after school. She had some temp job, and Colette had agreed to watch the boys. I just happened to be there, nothing planned, but we started chatting. Catching up on old times. Neither one of us meant anything else, but we talked until she was almost late getting home before you did. But that rekindled things."

"Rekindled?"

Hank glanced back toward the car. Donna was settled in the backseat, the door open to capture the night air. Matt was leaning against the fender, twirling his car keys, watching them, and waiting to insert himself if needed.

"Yeah, rekindled. We were always good friends in high school. You know that. If you two hadn't been dating, she and I probably would have. Then the accident happened, and she announced she was pregnant. You married her, and I took off for the Marines. But when we saw each other last fall, all those warm feelings came back. We started talking a lot on the phone, just as friends at first, but it became more. I would catch up with her when I was in town and have lunch. One thing led to another."

"You seduced my wife."

Hank shook his head, those piercing eyes never leaving Nathan's face. "The seduction was very mutual."

"No way would she do that to me."

"Think about it, Nate. You didn't know we ran into each other. Or that we talked on the phone. Or that we had lunch when I was in town. If she wasn't planning anything, if she had nothing to hide, why didn't she tell you? But she never said a word, did she?"

Nathan swallowed hard. "No."

"Why is that? Would you have thought anything weird was going on if she mentioned that she saw me and caught up? Of course not. Two old friends having lunch? You probably told her about the last time we had beers down at Sammy's. She didn't tell you because she knew it meant more to her. She knew from the moment she saw me that she had feelings for me, or she would have told you. The first phone call after we ran into each other? She called me. So no, I didn't seduce your wife. In a lot of ways, she seduced me."

The numbness was complete. Nathan couldn't think of

anything to say as they stared at each other. With a final warning to stay away, Hank turned and walked back across the parking lot. He slid through the open car door and wrapped his arm around Donna's shoulders as he closed the door, extinguishing the interior light. Matt cranked the engine and drove away, the taillights fading with distance.

13

D anny drove his battered van into the trailer park, a resigned Nathan riding beside him in the passenger seat, and parked in the dirt spot in front of his dark home.

Overgrown brush crawled up the sides of the old trailer, partially hiding the faded paint. Gaps in the skirting exposed the cinder-block supports. A wooden ramp stretched up to the small front porch, a plastic chair its only furnishing.

He spun the driver's seat around, transferred himself to the waiting wheelchair, and operated the lift to move himself to the ground. "You coming?"

Nathan nodded glumly and climbed out as Danny wheeled up the ramp, opened the front door of his trailer, and flipped on the overhead den light.

He rolled through the small den, grabbed the remote control, and turned the television on just as the late-evening news from Asheville was starting. A serious-faced anchor provided updates on the latest arrest and downfall of Ricky Ward.

Nathan shuffled in, closed the door, and collapsed on the couch. Danny wheeled into the trailer's kitchen area and filled two glasses with water. "You sure you don't want a beer instead?"

"I have to work tomorrow." Shocked that he hadn't automatically removed his boots as though he was at home, Nathan untied and slid them off his feet and tucked them beside the couch. He had no home to go to and no clean clothes to change into. Even his truck was still parked at Sammy's Pub. "After everything you've done for me, I hate to ask, but I need a ride in the morning. I can't lose my job too."

"I'll get you to work, but you deserve a good rip-roaring drunk tonight. We both do."

"I wish I could. I want it more than about anything except for the nasty hangover I would have tomorrow if I did it. Fixing a boiler is bad enough sober."

"Grasshopper has learned over the years," Danny said in a fake and weak TV-Asian accent.

Nathan leaned back into the couch and propped his feet up on the arm. "Facing Ronnie with a hangover would be the worst. It's already going to be miserable when he hears what happened today."

Danny handed over a glass of water and wheeled into position at the end of the couch, his usual TV-watching spot. On the screen, a young guy with microphone in hand breathlessly reported from some darkened street with crime-scene tape around a now empty house.

Nathan waved his hands at the television. "Why do they report 'Live! From the Scene!' of something that happened hours ago. Why not just do it from the comfort of the studio?"

"Because they couldn't show off that they can be live, I guess."

They watched the next few stories in quiet before Nathan spoke up again. "I learned one thing today. Jail sucks."

"I think that's the point."

"I wish I had had more of the nachos and beer than that

stale sandwich they gave me. No mayonnaise or mustard and dry as a desert. I couldn't swallow it."

"From my personal experience, they only serve nachos and beer on Saturday nights."

A faint smile crossed Nathan's lips, the first in hours. "I'll make a point of being arrested on Saturdays from now on."

He sipped water and watched as the serious-looking middle-aged white guy and the coanchor young enough to be his daughter laughed at some silly joke. "Thanks again for arranging the bail."

"That bondsman was scary and as big as a house. And he had some serious ink all over his arms. I don't want him knocking on my door."

The words were no sooner out of Danny's mouth than a loud banging interrupted them. They exchanged worried looks as he rolled his chair over to the front door and turned the knob.

The reflection from the porch light glistened off a police officer's badge, sparking a flashback to the highway patrolman who'd knocked so many years earlier to tell a young Nathan that his father had died. He braced himself for bad news as Brett Carrington removed his hat and stepped inside the trailer.

"Mr. Thomas, did the judge not tell you to stay away from your wife?"

Nathan was shocked by the officer's formal approach. "He said not to go home. I didn't."

"But you went to the hospital to confront her?"

"No. Not at all. I mean, yeah, I went to the hospital, but only to see how she was. I never meant her to see me." Nathan cocked his head. "Is that what she said? That I confronted her?"

"She was sleeping off the pain medication when I took the report. I spoke to Hank Saunders."

Nathan buried his face in his hands, fighting to keep his frustration under control. "I went just to see if she was okay but only spoke to them because they approached us."

"They approached you?"

Danny spoke up. "That's right. We were sitting in my van in the parking lot away from the entrance. We never got out of the van and never approached them."

Brett extracted a small paper pad from the breast pocket of his shirt, read something, and scribbled a note.

"I wish you hadn't done that. I'm trying hard to work with you, but that was a big mistake."

"I'm sorry. I didn't mean for her to see me."

Brett sighed and pulled out a sheaf of papers. "Fair enough. The magistrate wasn't too happy with the late call, but he signed off on a restraining order. You aren't to approach your wife or your son until further notice. Don't go to their house or to his school or anywhere else they are. If you see them somewhere, you have to stay at least a hundred feet away. You also are not allowed to contact either of them in any way." He looked up and focused stern eyes on Nathan. "Let me be clear. If you violate the order, you will be arrested immediately. And trust me, the magistrate isn't coming in over the weekend to hold another bail hearing, so you will sit there all weekend long. Is that clear?"

"My son? Why can't I talk to my son?"

"If you have any questions or complaints about the order, you need to schedule a hearing in front of the magistrate and take it up with him. Until then, no, you may not speak to or approach your son. If you do, you will be arrested. Any more questions?"

Nathan stared down at his feet, willing his anger to stay in check. The realization that Donna could keep Jacob away from him was just sinking in. And in a divorce, the woman always got custody. Or, at least, Nathan thought that's the way it worked, then she would use it to keep them separated forever. He couldn't let that happen.

"No, sir. No more questions."

Brett put his hand on the doorknob but paused and turned before opening the door. "Nathan, do yourself a favor. Be smart about this."

"HANK's with her right now. The two of them together."

Danny had locked the door after escorting the officer out and then retrieved beers from the refrigerator. The water was no longer enough.

"Stop it," Danny said. "You're torturing yourself."

"He's lying in my bed with her right now, and Jacob is wondering what's going on."

"Jacob is at Luke's house, remember? He knows nothing about what happened today, so he isn't wondering anything."

The TV continued to ramble in the background, something about why the stock market was down for the day. Nathan grabbed the remote and lowered the volume to a mere whisper. "This is all about custody, isn't it? She'll want custody of Jacob."

"That's a question for a divorce attorney."

"I can't afford a regular attorney. How do I pay for a divorce attorney?" Nathan wrung his hands together, squeezing his knuckles until they popped. His fingers faded white from a lack of blood. "I should have just walked out when I caught them in bed. All I was thinking was I saw my marriage disappear before my eyes. I wasn't even thinking about custody. Now, with the whole domestic violence thing and restraining order... man, I'm so stupid."

Danny took a long swallow on his beer. "One day at a time, okay? See how things go next week. Donna knows it's better for

Jacob if his life stays somewhat stable. Besides, he's almost a teenager. He'll insist on seeing you, and the courts will listen to that." He looked at the can in his hand. "Probably. Hopefully."

Nathan cleared his throat. "But what she wants matters a lot, right? I mean, don't the courts usually side with the woman in these things?"

"Like I'm an expert?" Danny thought about it a moment but shook his head. "Do I think she will get custody? Sure. But I don't see her trying to keep Jacob away from you. That doesn't make sense."

"But how do we know that isn't what she's thinking?"

"We don't."

Nathan crumpled the can and retrieved another beer from the refrigerator. He settled back into the couch. "That restraining order. It's on me and not you."

"So?"

"Can you call Donna tomorrow and see what her plan is?"

"You think she would tell me?"

"She would if you ask it right."

"And how do you propose that?"

He traced a water droplet rolling down the side of the can. "Ask if you can stop by and pick up my clothes. That's a reasonable request, right?" When Danny nodded, he continued, "Then you can just say you feel stuck in the middle. Trying to help me with a place to live, but also trying not to pick sides. See what she says."

"Hank will be there."

"That's fine. Maybe even better. He's always been cocky, so maybe he just tells you their plan."

They locked eyes, Nathan studying Danny for any sign of resistance. Finally, Danny nodded slightly. "I'll do it if you promise to stay away."

"I have to work anyway, right? We can meet at Sammy's for lunch, and you can tell me everything. Deal?"

Danny nodded and turned his attention back to the TV. White balls with black numbers filled the screen—the lottery drawing. Some lucky SOB somewhere was getting rich. He rolled his wheelchair over to the kitchen, slid open a drawer, and pulled out a lottery ticket with five sets of numbers.

As the third number flashed on the screen, he dropped the ticket and cursed under his breath.

"Guessing you aren't buying a new house, huh?" Nathan said.

"I wasn't close. Guess it isn't my lucky day."

"Want to hear the stupidest thing?"

"What?"

"I bought one of those today."

"You? Really? Thought you considered lottery tickets a waste of money."

"I do. You know I think it's all rigged. But I found some money in Abe's parking lot and thought today was my lucky day."

"No offense, but I think this has been the unluckiest day of your life."

"Tell me about it."

"So?"

"So what?"

"Did your ticket win?"

Nathan shook his head. "I have no idea. Stuck the ticket in my jacket pocket. Left it at the house when I stormed out of there."

"Unluckiest day ever."

PART III

SATURDAY

14

Nathan opened his eyes but quickly squeezed them shut again. The bright rising sun streaming through the trailer's front window hammered his brain.

He lay still, willing the pain to eke out of his body. With a great deal of reluctance, he pried his eyes open. The morning brilliance forced him to blink several times before he could focus.

Several empty cans cluttered the small dining table. The reek of stale beer hung in the air. He remembered having drunk only three or four the night before, so Danny must have emptied the rest. At least, he hoped that was true though he may have just blanked the rest out. His body certainly felt worse than a few beers.

His skin itched against the wool blanket draped over his body. After tossing aside the blanket, he dropped his feet to the floor with a thud, sat up, and stretched. His back creaked and popped in protest of a night on the lumpy couch. The room swayed as his head pounded from a hangover.

Clad only in his boxers, he stumbled to the sole bathroom in the trailer. He leaned a hand against the wall to steady himself, his head still fuzzy from the lack of sleep and late beers, and pissed away the night before.

Sleep had been scarce, as he'd woken up every half hour or so, wondering how badly he had screwed up his life. What little time had been spent in slumber was punctuated with vivid dreams.

Before the previous day, his run-ins with the police seemed minor. His adult history included a lone speeding ticket, a surprise that his rickety old truck could even beat the posted limits.

As a teenager, he and his friends had been caught rolling a teacher's yard with toilet paper. The officer had called their parents—or in Nathan's case, Ronnie since his dad was in Phoenix delivering a load with his semi. The next morning, he and Charlie, joined by the others involved, cleaned the toilet paper out of the trees under Ronnie's stern supervision. Two days later, when his father came home from the road, he was grounded for a week. Coach Burleson made them all run extra laps for the next two weeks. Plus, the teacher kept calling on them in class. The coordinated punishment was effective. Nathan and Charlie swore off ever toilet-papering a yard again.

The worst, of course, was the accident. Nathan had hobbled into a courtroom on his crutches to face a citation for underage drinking. The judge glared at him, lectured sternly, and sentenced him to community service. After the leg casts were removed, he spent six Saturdays leading up to high school graduation picking up trash under the supervision of a deputy. The others in his work crew shared their own tales of being caught driving drunk, losing their licenses, and jail time in addition to the trash detail.

But as tough as facing that judge was, the real punishment was everything else. The emptiness of his room as the bed along the other wall sat vacant in accusation. The awkward silence around Ronnie as he mourned his son's death. The absence of Danny from school as he sat in jail, awaiting his own trial—and then his time in jail after his conviction. The gnawing fear the state would swoop in, remove him from Ronnie's care, and assign him to a foster home. And his own painful weeks in the hospital followed by outpatient physical therapy. Picking up trash was more a relief than a punishment, getting away from the other repercussions for a few hours.

But this was a whole different level of trouble. Never before had he worn handcuffs, sat in a jail cell, or had to worry about bail. Shame washed over him, a paralyzing ache of regret, at the mere thought of standing in front of a judge and being accused of shoving his wife and slugging one of his childhood best friends. He collapsed on the couch and held his head in his hands.

His worst fear was whether Jacob knew. He wondered if they had told him.

Probably not yet. Either Matt or Colette would drive him and Luke to the ballgame. Donna would probably wait until after, leaving him to enjoy the innocence of the game.

The thought of the game sent Nathan's thoughts racing.

How was Donna going to explain my absence to Jacob? Or, worse, how could she hide her injuries? Jacob would see her pain and wonder what kind of monster he had for a father. They would be forced to tell the story.

And, of course, he would hear *their* version of the story before his dad's. She would conveniently skip over Hank in the bedroom. Her explanation would make it sound like Nathan's fault.

Unless he wanted his son to hate him forever, he had to tell Jacob before she did, to control the story, and to ensure he understood that Nathan had never meant to harm his mother. And he had to explain that no matter how wrong he had been to react violently, he had been pushed by her horrible betrayal.

Damn the restraining order. Nathan needed to explain things. He promised himself to be fair, to highlight his own mistakes. He just wanted to frame the story so that Jacob could be prepared when his mom's turn came.

Danny's closed bedroom door confirmed he was still sleeping off the drinks. A few minutes was all Nathan needed to make a quick, quiet phone call.

He pulled himself up from the ragged couch and lifted his pants from the back of the kitchen chair to retrieve his cell phone. The pockets were empty, and no frantic searching changed that. Slipping the dirty pants over his boxers, he surveyed the room until he spied a pile of personal effects on the kitchen counter. His wallet and keys and a collection of coins waited for him, but no cell phone.

He scanned the kitchen counter and cluttered dining table, shifting beer cans. The top of the TV held the old remote. The blanket was tossed on the floor. He slipped his hands between the couch cushions. Dropping to his knees, he searched underneath the couch—a few coins and some dust bunnies, but no phone.

Balancing himself on the edge of the couch, he surveyed the small room. He was positive he had remembered to take his phone when he was released from jail. It came out of the same envelope as everything else, except for his wedding ring, which he'd hocked for bail.

Memories flashed in his mind. Last night. Sipping a beer and studying his phone. Scanning for a text or a call. Thinking Jacob might call to say good night. *Like he would withstand embarrassing himself in front of Luke to call home.* The look from Danny, telling him not to call. His sheepish grin in reply. Laying the phone on the table with his keys and change and wallet. Danny had sat right there and watched him do it.

Damn it. Danny had watched. And when he drifted to sleep under the weight of beer, Danny had swiped the phone and hidden it to prevent a desperate call in the middle of the night —or in the morning.

To prevent exactly what he was trying to do.

Someday, he might thank Danny, but not then. That morning, he ached to talk to his son. With no land line in the trailer, the only other phone was Danny's cell. With a glance at the bedroom door, Nathan resigned himself to not calling—at least, not right then. *Maybe later. From work. When Danny won't know.*

He picked up his T-shirt and slipped it over his head. He sat on the couch and pulled on socks and boots before clumping around the small kitchen, purposely making noise. He needed Danny to drive him to work. And he wasn't going to let him hide his phone without some punishment in return.

Within a few minutes, the bedroom door squeaked open, and Danny wheeled into the den, his hair mussed and clothes wrinkled. "Morning."

"Phone," Nathan demanded.

"Someone woke up a little grouchy this morning."

"I want my phone back."

"So you can call Donna?"

"No."

"Ah, so you can call Jacob." When Nathan didn't deny it, Danny rolled into the kitchen and scooped grounds into the coffee maker. "Calling your son is an even worse idea than calling your wife. What time is it?"

"I don't know. The only clock I have is on my phone. If I had it, I could see the time."

Danny ignored the dig and continued, "Six a.m. Do you think Jacob is awake at six a.m.?"

Nathan dropped onto the couch and sighed. Jacob was smart in school, a talented athlete, and a good kid, but he was also a late sleeper. That boy was impossible to pry out of bed on weekend mornings. "I have to try. Please."

"If you call right now, you know as well as I do that Matt or Colette will answer the phone and not Jacob. You won't get to talk to your kid. But they will tell your wife that you called. You think you can smooth it over with her after the rest of this mess? Do you want to spend the rest of the weekend in jail for violating the restraining order?"

Nathan rubbed the back of his neck and stared at the ceiling. "So I'm just supposed to give up?"

"No, of course not." Danny rinsed two coffee mugs as the pot gurgled out the dark liquid. "I have a plan, but you need to listen first. And then I need you not to screw everything up, but let's start with listening."

"A plan?" Nathan bit his lip. Danny wouldn't return his phone until he was confident no call would be made. He could always sneak a call later, but listening was his only choice now.

"Not really a plan," Danny said, "but a step. After I drop you off at work, I'm going to call Donna and arrange to go get your clothes."

"That's it? You get my clothes? And that was my plan for you anyway."

Danny poured two cups of coffee. He balanced one on his chair as he wheeled to Nathan and handed over the cup. "And here I thought you were too drunk to remember. While I'm getting your clothes, I can talk to her. Find out where her head is. Maybe even without Hank standing there."

"I'm still waiting for the new part."

"Very simple. I'm going to tell her the truth."

Dumbfounded, Nathan sat the coffee cup on the table. "I'm not following."

"I'm going to tell her you are worried about Jacob and his need for stability. You're willing to work with her to make the divorce go smoothly because all you care about is how your son handles it."

Nathan sat still, eyes blinking. "What's that going to do?"

"I've known Donna as long as you have. What she's doing with Hank, going behind your back, that's wrong. Here's the thing—deep down, she knows it. She's just not that type of person."

"So, what, you think she would break it off?"

A wan smile crossed Danny's face. "No, I think she really cares for Hank. Maybe even really loves him. But I also think she cares for you."

Nathan's face scrunched up. "Then I don't understand. What are you going to accomplish?"

"Now that everything is out in the open, my bet is she feels bad about hurting you. If it didn't bother her, she would have told you about Hank months ago."

"I wish she had."

"Exactly. So does she."

"So how is this a plan?"

"Simple. She feels bad about hurting you and doesn't want to hurt you any more. And she really doesn't want to hurt Jacob. She would protect that boy from anything. So when she figures out you can accept her being with Hank, she'll understand and want things to be the best for Jacob."

"Which means working with me on custody so that we both can see a lot of him?"

"Exactly."

Nathan scratched the side of his head. "But won't Hank object?"

"Why would he? He wants Donna. Jacob's just part of the package. In fact, he might even be cool with the kid being around less. I've never thought of Hank as a paternal kind of guy."

Nathan laid his head back on the couch and stared at the ceiling. "You think she really will back off this whole domestic violence thing?"

"Why wouldn't she? Jacob needs you in his life."

"And I need him."

"Exactly." Taking a deep breath, Danny counseled, "You need each other, and Donna knows that. She loves Jacob too, and you know it. So go to work, get that boiler fixed, and I'll do my best to plant those seeds in her head."

Nathan sat in silence. He could barely think of life without Donna, but he couldn't imagine life at all without Jacob.

Danny reached out and patted Nathan's knee. "I'm only asking for a few hours. When you get off work, meet me at Sammy's for lunch. I will tell you how it went, and then you can decide what to do next. But whatever you do, stay off that phone until then. Do I have your word?"

Nathan dropped his face into his hands. Minutes ticked by without a sound in the trailer. Danny sat and waited until he muttered through his fingers, "Deal. I won't call Donna or Jacob until I get your report. I'll be a good boy."

Danny leaned back in his chair. "Good. Now, here's your phone." Danny pulled the phone from his pocket and held it in the air. "You get this only on your promise you do nothing and we meet after you work. Agreed?"

"I promise," Nathan mumbled.

Danny tossed him his cell phone. "Look, Nathan, Donna might be mad at you, but she loves that boy. I think she will do anything for that kid, including making sure he gets to spend time with his dad. But even if I fail this morning, what could change in a few hours? We can still work out another plan."

Nathan nodded, resigned. "For Jacob. For a few hours. No promises after that."

"Fair enough. For Jacob." Danny wheeled into the small kitchen. "And now we have a couple of minutes to kill before we go retrieve your truck, so you get some of my world-famous omelets."

Nathan looked incredulous. "World-famous? In what world? I've eaten your cooking before, remember?"

Danny smiled. "In my own little world, my friend. The only world that matters."

The truth was that Danny's omelets were awesome. As kids, they'd all thought it funny that the brusque football player was so comfortable in the kitchen, but Martha had taught him well. And breakfast food was his specialty.

Nathan's stomach growled as he watched his friend chop onions, peppers, and mushrooms and sauté them in a cast-iron skillet along with some diced ham. After moving the cooked fillings to a plate, Danny cracked and whisked three eggs before pouring them into the hot pan. As they cooked, he grated cheese and added the vegetables and ham before folding the eggs over them. He delivered the steaming omelet to the kitchen table before starting a second omelet for himself.

Nathan poured a cup of fresh coffee, settled into the chair, and cut a first bite. The rich flavors melted across his tongue.

When Danny rolled over to join him at the table with his own breakfast, Nathan had already eaten half his omelet. He mumbled through a mouthful of food, "Not bad."

Danny chuckled. "Best omelet ever, and you know it."

Nathan scooped another mouthful of eggs and savored the flavor. "You really should have your own breakfast place. The restaurant would be packed every day."

Danny dropped his fork on his plate with a clatter. "Don't start."

Nathan opened his eyes wide in mock protest of his innocence. "Oh, have I said that before?"

Danny picked his fork back up and jabbed at his friend. "You and my mother conspiring against me. The thanks I get for letting you sleep on my couch."

"After sleeping on that couch, I should sue you for bodily injury."

"Sue me. Go ahead. You could get all my worldly possessions, and that might buy you a cup of coffee. And that, my friend, is why I can't afford to open my own breakfast place. No money. No credit. No business."

Nathan scooped in another bite of the omelet, closing his eyes as he savored the taste. "Take over the deli side of the business from your mom and add a full breakfast menu to go with her biscuits. We can scrounge an old grill from somewhere, and I can get it working. You got room to add some more tables. It won't take a fortune."

"My dad would get a kick out of that, me cooking breakfast rather than fixing cars like I was supposed to. Without the garage open, that old store barely breaks even, and you know it."

Nathan twirled the fork in his hand, thoughts racing through his mind. Second only to the Marines, the four friends had often talked of working on cars in Abe's garage. However, by then, they imagined the store would belong to Danny and Colette. But Danny never wanted to discuss car repairs after being confined to his wheelchair.

"So we reopen the garage," Nathan said. "I fix cars. God knows no one around here can afford to buy new ones. You run the restaurant and the store. And you know the store would be more profitable if you added beer back to the coolers. People wouldn't have to drive out to the interstate stores then."

After gathering the empty plates from the table, Danny balanced them in his lap and wheeled to the kitchen sink. "My dad would never go for beer back in the cooler."

"Oh yeah? If you offered to come back to the store, he would probably agree to anything."

Danny scrubbed the dishes and stacked them in the drying rack without speaking. He didn't utter his next words until he picked his van keys up and spun back around. "Ready to go? Got to get you to work."

They settled into the van and drove silently toward Sammy's Pub and Nathan's truck.

Nathan watched his friend drive before speaking. "Would you at least think about it?"

Danny's thumbs thumped against the steering wheel. "I *am* thinking about it."

Nathan cocked his head. "Really?"

"That night, the wreck—it's haunted me ever since. Being in jail wasn't the worst. Even this damn chair isn't the worst. I deserved both of those. Some nights, sitting in that god-awful trailer, I thought about just ending it."

"Danny—"

"No, wait. Let me say it. Do you know why I didn't?"

Nathan sat twisting his fingers. "Why?"

"You kept coming by. Taking me out to Sammy's. Or for a sandwich. Or a pizza. Or just to sit on that couch and watch a football game with me. You don't know how much that means to me."

"Danny, I'm your friend. That's what friends do."

"But that's why I'm thinking about it. I know I need to get out of that trailer and get a job rather than live off a disability check. I've just never felt worthy of it after what I did."

When Nathan started to protest, Danny waved him off. "I know we talked about it in high school. When I got back from the Marines, I would take over the store from my folks, and we would fix cars together. But then, after that night, I thought you wouldn't want to be with me every day. And then when I thought maybe you would, I figured you would never leave Ronnie high and dry. Donna would freak about the lack of a steady paycheck. And you wouldn't do anything she didn't agree with." He pursed his lips as his fingers drummed on the wheel. "But if you two aren't together, if the factory closed, you might actually do this."

Nathan turned and looked out the passenger window.

Danny was right. Being on his own, he could take the risk that some weeks wouldn't bring in much money. And Ronnie would be proud if he struck out on his own with a real business plan. "Go into business with my best friend? Yeah, I would definitely do that."

Danny pulled the van into the pub's empty parking lot and stopped beside the pickup truck, sitting alone in the far corner. He shifted into park and wiped his eyes with his shirt sleeves. "Let's get you through the next few days and then talk some more about it."

"Deal."

"But remember your promise for today?"

Nathan's hand rested on the door handle. "Yes, I promise. I won't call. I'll go to work and then meet you back here for lunch."

"Good," Danny replied. "Are you going to tell Ronnie?"

"I have to." He climbed out the door and stood in the parking lot. "He'll hear soon enough about it anyway, and he would be madder if I didn't tell him first."

Danny nodded and handed him a thermos.

"What's that?"

"Coffee. I figure it's just you and Ronnie at the plant, and I wouldn't want to drink the coffee either one of you makes."

Nathan smiled and took the thermos. "Thanks. For everything."

"See you at noon. I'll bring the best news I can."

"And I'm serious about the garage. If I'm going to change, maybe it's time to change everything."

"I'm serious too." Danny shifted the van into gear and drove away.

15

N athan navigated his pickup past his usual spot on the far side of the empty factory parking lot and took the space beside the only other car, Ronnie Mills's old Buick, the same car he'd had when Nathan was in high school. True to his word, Ronnie would never ask anyone to show up on a weekend unless he did himself.

After turning the engine off, Nathan pulled his cell phone from his pocket and flipped it over and over in his hand. He couldn't remember the last time he'd gone so long without hearing Jacob's voice. He wanted to know how the sleepover at Luke's went. *Did they play Xbox all night? What was he thinking about today's baseball game?* The answers weren't that important, but the conversation would be everything.

Even a simple phone call to say, "I love you." Like that wouldn't arouse suspicion in a twelve-year-old.

"Yeah, sure, Dad, thanks. Why did you call to tell me that?"

If he had broken down and bought Jacob that cell phone, he probably wouldn't have been able to resist the urge. But knowing he would have to get through Matt or Colette stopped him. Even if they allowed him to talk to Jacob, a questionable outcome at best, the repercussions would be too great.

He stepped out into the cool morning air, shivering in his T-shirt against the breeze. He reached for his jacket before remembering he had left it at his house the day before. After a last glance at his phone—still no calls—he pocketed it and swiped his employee card through the electronic lock on the door. The lock popped, and he stepped into the darkened plant, the lone light shining from Ronnie's office at the front of the building.

After punching his time card at the nearby clock, he walked across the cavernous floor to the boiler room, picking his way through the shadows. Using the keys hanging from his belt to unlock the door, he turned on the overhead lights and stared at the hulking structures. The operating panels were dark, an indication that Ronnie had powered them down when he'd arrived earlier.

Nathan gathered his tools and disassembled parts, stacking them neatly on the floor. As his mind concentrated on the task, he soon forgot his troubles and settled into the rhythm of work. Physical labor had always been that way for him. Moving. Working. Tinkering. All better than replaying troubles in his mind.

He didn't hear Ronnie approach until he spoke.

"Good morning, Nathan."

Turning in his crouched position, Nathan spied the Red Wing boots and blue work pants of the plant manager. "Morning. Got coffee in the thermos there if you want some."

"Donna didn't trust my coffee, huh? I don't blame her."

Nathan hesitated, not ready yet to explain all that had gone wrong since he had last seen Ronnie the previous day.

Before he could work up his nerve to start that conversation, Ronnie filled a cup with coffee and continued, "I'm listening for the FedEx truck. Even have a fork parked at the loading dock, ready to go. As soon as it gets here, I'll bring you the parts."

The need to confess seemed to have passed, so Nathan just muttered, "Great."

Ronnie sipped the coffee, murmuring his approval. "So how was the afternoon off? Was Donna surprised? She okay with you being here this morning, or is she mad at me?"

Telling a boss was bad, but telling Ronnie was so much worse. Disappointing someone who'd raised him was a different level. "Very surprised. Had no clue I was coming. If she had known, she would've made sure Hank Saunders wasn't in my bed."

Ronnie jolted at the words, spilling coffee from his full cup. He brushed the spreading stain on his shirt. "Jesus, really? Hank Saunders?"

Nathan told him the whole story—the fight, the police, being arrested.

"You spent the night in jail? Why didn't you call me for the bail money?"

"Danny bailed me out."

"Yeah, guess he would know how that works." Ronnie clucked. "Do you need a place to stay?"

"Slept on Danny's couch."

Ronnie sipped his coffee. "Your old room is available if you need it. We need to put clean sheets on the bed. More comfortable than Danny's couch, and you would have a closet for your clothes. Especially if, well, if it will be longer than a few days."

Nathan twirled the wrench in his hand. "It will be until I can find a new place to live or she moves out of the house. The marriage is over. I wish it wasn't, but it sounded like the thing with Hank is more than we can fix."

"I'm so sorry, Nathan. You don't deserve that. So, what's the next step?"

"Danny's going over this morning to get my clothes and

stuff and find out the temperature. She already lined up a divorce attorney, but there's not much to fight over. My truck, her car, the house, and the crap in the house."

"And Jacob."

Nathan winced. "I will fight her to the end of the world over Jacob. I mean, your son, you'd do anything, right?"

Before Ronnie glanced away, his eyes watered. He sniffed and swallowed before nodding. "How's Jacob handling it?"

"I don't think they have told him yet. I can't talk to him because they got a restraining order."

"Ouch." Ronnie slurped coffee, looking at Nathan over the cup. "Listen, son. Just leave it be now. Do nothing else. He deserved to get hit, but anything else makes you the bad guy. Do you hear me?"

"Yes, sir."

"I mean it."

"Yes, sir. I understand, sir." It felt like all those lectures in high school. Ronnie hadn't just given Nathan a bed and food. He had treated him as firmly and fairly as he had his own son. Being an orphan didn't give him any special favors in Ronnie's eyes.

"Good. That's settled." Ronnie pushed off from the machinery. "Need anything else? You have a lawyer? How can I help?"

"Nothing yet. I'll know more after talking to Danny at lunch."

"Smart to let Danny do that. Don't you try. Be cool for a few days. If he doesn't get through to her, I'll try."

Nathan breathed deeply, steadying his voice before replying, "Thanks, Ronnie. I mean it. Not sure I could have handled you being mad at me."

"You showed more restraint than I would have. Not sure how I would have reacted if someone had touched Nora."

Ronnie shrugged with a wry smile and started to walk away. He hesitated and turned back. "Look, Danny's being a good friend. I know I'm harsh on him. It's hard for me to look at him."

"I understand, but he regrets that night. He would give anything to change what he did. You should give him a chance."

"Someday. I just can't yet," Ronnie nodded and looked at the ground. "It's good he's letting you crash there, but his couch will get old. Remember the offer of your old room for as long as you need it."

"I will. Maybe after tonight. I need to hear how things went with Donna."

"Fair. The offer is open anytime." Ronnie watched as Nathan busied himself breaking down the equipment. After a few moments, he turned and walked back across the dark plant floor to his office.

NATHAN SETTLED in to the repair work, his hands deftly handling tools. As promised, Ronnie brought the parts to him after they were delivered, and he offered to help, but Nathan declined and enjoyed the solitude of work. The machine slowly came back to life under the care of his talented hands.

Wiring, gears, pulleys—he had always had a natural talent with anything mechanical. Growing up, he grasped the most complex repairs with only basic instructions from his mentors. The work always brought a sense of calm to him, shifting the rest of his mind into neutral while he concentrated on the complexity of the equipment. Time slipped easily through the morning before he heard Ronnie's work boots echoing in their approach through the empty factory.

"How's it coming?"

"Good." Nathan's voice was muffled from behind the boiler, tools clanking as he continued to work.

"Need a hand, or got it under control?" Ronnie asked.

Nathan appeared in the shadows, wiping his hands on a soiled cloth. "Just about wrapped up with all the connections and getting ready to run tests. All the new parts were good, so the repair has been straightforward. Unless I missed something, I should be done before eleven."

"Good news. Thanks."

"No worries. And I'll get in early Monday to make sure all is humming before the suits get here."

"I appreciate it." Ronnie paused for a few seconds, glancing around the room. He stood and watched as the younger man finished checking the installation.

Nathan knew his boss wanted to say something more, but he could never rush the conversation. He returned to his work until he heard Ronnie clearing his throat to speak.

"Part of me hoped you wouldn't show this morning."

The sentence shocked Nathan, and he fumbled the wrench in his hand. It clanged to the floor, the echo reverberating off the walls. He stooped to pick it up and asked, "Why would you hope that?"

"I hoped you were the lucky one."

Puzzled, Nathan said, "Help me out. What are you talking about?"

"You haven't heard the news?"

"No clue."

"Someone won the lottery."

Nathan laughed. "Someone's always winning the lottery, but it sure ain't been me."

"Maybe, but I never heard of someone from Millerton winning the big one."

Nathan's mouth gaped open. "Really? From here? The whole jackpot?"

"Yeah. According to the news, Abe sold the winning ticket, not even one of those corporate stores over at the interstate exit. Probably not some trucker or tourist if it came from Abe's. It's got to be a local."

Nathan's hand drifted toward the pocket of his jacket but found only his T-shirt. If only he had the winning ticket, he could afford the best lawyers in the world.

Don't be a fool. The odds are crazy.

Out loud, he said, "I would be okay if a trucker with five kids at home who needs the money won."

"Yeah, fair enough," Ronnie said. "But it would be better if some local person won it. Anyone around here deserves it."

Thinking of Hank, Nathan said, "Not quite anyone. But, yeah, I hope someone nice won it. And someone local would be cool. How much was it?"

"The TV was saying one hundred fifty-four million dollars. Can you imagine?"

"Yeah, but then there are the taxes, and it's less for a lump sum and all."

"I can't feel sorry for somebody who has only fifty to sixty million after paying the taxes."

Nathan laughed again. "Okay. You got me. I could scrape by on that. I would like to win a hundred bucks on one of those scratch-off cards just once."

"I already checked my tickets. One of them won seven dollars. Might buy me a beer or two at Sammy's."

"Better than nothing."

Ronnie stood in thought for a minute. "Doesn't Abe get a big check from the state for selling the winner?"

"Yeah, I think he does. He deserves it."

Nathan started powering up sections of the boiler system as Ronnie joined him, testing the repairs. They worked side by side in a comfortable silence. Once they were both satisfied everything looked good, they brought the system up. They sat back and listened to the hum, the well-tuned machinery purring along.

After Nathan packed up his tools and closed up his toolboxes, he turned back to Ronnie. "You're more worried than normal about this meeting Monday. I can tell."

The older man sat silently, contemplating his hands, before speaking, "Look, I trust you to keep this quiet. Word gets out, and people panic. They haven't told me anything, but…"

"But what?"

"Chad and I submitted next year's budget."

"And?"

"Nothing. No questions. No revisions. No *try agains*. Nothing."

"That's different?"

"Very. Last year, we did twelve versions of the budget. Chad got so frustrated he told that weasel Wesley Gotham in accounting to just tell us what the numbers should be. It's this crazy game you play every year where you are trying to guess what they want you to say, but they want to pretend you get to make your own budget."

"And now… nothing?"

"Absolutely nothing."

"And the weasel?"

"Hasn't visited in months. None of the bean counters. They did some big financial analysis about three months ago, and I haven't seen a single accountant since then. But lots of HR people have been here. The only thing you want to see less of than accountants—HR people. At least accountants don't pretend to care. Those HR suits won't look me in the eye, so you know it's bad. And they keep huddling in our conference room with the door closed, on calls with corporate."

Nathan sighed. "I'm sorry, Ronnie."

"Yeah, me too. I keep hoping I'm wrong."

"You aren't. We have all known the plant closing was just a matter of time."

"Yeah. Me too. I hope it will be longer. Some good people in here don't deserve to be out of work."

They studied each other before Nathan spoke, "We'll be okay. Somehow."

"*You* will be. You're good. You can fix anything. Some people here, though, they don't know how to do anything else. And I'm scared no one will give them a chance to learn anything else. Especially the older ones. That's the part that sucks."

"And you?"

The older man shrugged. "Who knows? Go fishing, I guess. Try not to get sick before Medicare kicks in. Best plan I've got."

Nathan wanted to say something would come along, but they both would know it was a lie. And he respected Ronnie too much to lie to him.

Ronnie shrugged and continued, "Whenever they announce it, I will work for a few months, no matter what. They have to shut the place down, and that takes work. You and I will probably turn the lights out together. They need you to fix everything, and they need me because I know everything that's broken. And they would rather have me here fixing it than out there telling the EPA where to look for the crap that would get them in trouble. That's my big value. I know things they wish I didn't."

Ronnie paused again as he contemplated the younger man. "If something else comes up for you, take it. For Jacob. Just know you will have quite a few months, so don't take something bad. Maybe you will end up making more money. Or open your own business."

Nathan could only chuckle as the vision of the half-baked plan he and Danny had discussed flashed through his mind.

Not even half-baked—just an idea. "My own business... right. No way I could afford to start a business. And no bank would loan me anything."

"I've got some savings. I could help." Ronnie pursed his lips. "Well, something good will happen. You deserve it."

They stood in the silent darkness of the plant, lost in their memories of working in the vast structure. So many years of their lives were tied up in these machines. Thinking of the building sitting vacant was just too depressing, just another abandoned shell in an area filled with obsolete buildings, fading For Sale signs decorating the unkempt lots.

Ronnie sighed, staring off into the shadows of the idle plant. "Well, when you finish up, don't punch out. Just leave your time card with me. I will punch you out so you get a full forty."

"Thank you. It means a lot. I appreciate it."

Ronnie shook his head. "We should be paying you over-time, but at least I can make sure you get a full week."

"No complaints here."

Ronnie slapped him on the back. "I know. Thanks." He walked away, the echo from his work boots disappearing in the distance.

16

W ith the boiler repairs complete and paperwork and timecard dropped on Ronnie's desk, Nathan walked out of the factory into the warm midday sunshine, much as he had the day before. Rather than the lot being half full of other cars, only their two vehicles occupied spaces. And his thoughts were focused on divorce and the separation of lives, not flowers and candy.

He settled into the truck and rolled the windows down, letting the spring breeze chase the heat from the cab as he contemplated how much his world had shifted in the last day.

A glance at his phone showed no calls or texts, not even an indication from Danny whether the conversation with Donna had gone well or poorly—or if it had even happened at all.

But worse was the lack of a message from his son. He hadn't left a voice mail sharing a funny story from the sleepover with Luke or even asking if he was coming to the game.

Nathan slid his fingers across the glass screen, reminding himself that Jacob not calling this morning was hardly surprising. He ached to call his son but knew he shouldn't. He could hold out a little longer, at least another hour or two to hear Danny's report before trying to call.

The clock on the screen showed 11:15, too early to head to Sammy's Pub for lunch and wait for Danny's arrival. If he hung out at the bar, he would be tempted to have a beer, which would lead to another beer and another, not that a few patrons wouldn't already be bellied up to the bar. He couldn't think of anytime he hadn't seen at least one lonely soul nursing a drink at the bar.

But beer wouldn't help him think. And whatever results Danny shared, Nathan would need to process it. Analyze it. Plan a strategy.

For now, he could only plan how to kill an hour of time. Going back to Danny's trailer and sitting alone with Saturday-morning TV chatter rattling in the background had no appeal.

Driving around with no destination in mind was even less attractive, not to mention a waste of gas money, a luxury he didn't have especially with a looming divorce. They lived paycheck to paycheck, any savings they ever built up raided to pay an unexpected medical bill or buy clothes for the ever-growing boy.

Life would be great if he won that lottery and he never had to worry about paying a doctor or dentist again. They'd be able to eat in restaurants anytime they wanted, able to buy clothes for Jacob without shopping at the Goodwill or consignment stores.

But he couldn't even find that out because his ticket was jammed in his coat pocket in a home he wasn't allowed to enter. Just another thing he would have to wait for—Danny bringing his clothes.

Maybe Abe knew who'd bought the winning ticket. Maybe he would break out in a huge grin at the sight of Nathan walking through the door, applauding his luck as Martha hugged him and cried tears of joy.

Or at least Abe might tell him about a lucky neighbor or even truck driver.

One way to find out. Swinging by the market didn't break his restraining order or his promise to Danny.

His decision made, Nathan stopped strumming his fingers on the steering wheel and turned the ignition.

HE HADN'T SEEN Abe's Market that busy in years. Cars were scattered about the lot, parked at angles and blocking the ancient gasoline pumps, not that it mattered because no one was fueling. People he had never seen wandered through the glass doors.

He eased his truck around the bumpers of parked vehicles until he located the only vacant spot, the same beside-the-road space as he'd been in the day before. He exited the truck and couldn't help but glance at the ground, hoping to repeat yesterday's find, but no wad of cash rewarded his search. He spied only discarded cigarette butts among the overgrown weeds.

After navigating around the cars parked helter-skelter, he entered the store and nodded toward Abe. The older man's newspaper remained folded on the counter, not even opened for the morning yet. A line seven people deep stood in front of the register. None held groceries or snacks in their hands, just cash, as Abe busily rang up sales and printed lottery tickets.

Martha greeted him with a wave from the back of the store. She stood behind the counter of the deli, wiping the counters down with a rag. Unlike the crush of business up front, only the same four old men sat around the table sipping their coffee. With Abe unavailable for a quick chat, Nathan cut through the aisles and greeted Martha.

"Need me to make you a sandwich, Nathan?"

"No, thanks. I'm having lunch over at Sammy's in a bit."

"Honey, my sandwiches taste better, and you know it. And my sweet tea is much healthier for you than Sammy's beers," Martha teased with a grin.

"Yes, ma'am, they are, but I promised Danny I would meet him there."

Martha's smile faltered at the mention of her son, but she quickly recovered. "Make sure he doesn't get started too early on the beer. And let him know I would be glad to feed you boys here anytime."

"I will. I promise. Doesn't matter about the beer because I'm only drinking iced tea. I'm headed to the park for Jacob's game this afternoon."

The plan slipped from his mouth before he even realized he had been thinking it. Because of the restraining order, he knew he couldn't sit with the rest of the parents and cheer the team, but he could watch the game from the Point. He figured that was far enough away to meet the conditions of the restraining order but still close enough to see his son. Of course, he would be far enough way that no one would smell beer on his breath either, but he still would stick with tea.

"Best of luck to Jacob today." Martha's smile broadened, and her eyes twinkled. "Such a nice young man and getting strong. Not sure if Donna told you, but he carried crates of flowers from my house last week."

This from the same boy who couldn't remember to pick up his clothes off the floor. "She didn't tell me. Glad he helped."

"We were chatting while she was getting groceries. I said I needed to restock the flower racks. Jacob just piped up and said he would help me carry them. Neither one of us had to ask him. His dad sure is teaching him right, just like his dad taught him." Her face beamed with pride. "You know I always saw your dad in you. And now I see you in Jacob, so it's just like your dad is still around."

Nathan flushed. "Thank you. I try to raise him right."

"You're doing a great job."

Pride swelled inside him, but so did the ache of not having seen or talked to his son since the morning before. He diverted the conversation back to what he wanted to know. "I heard you sold the winning lottery ticket. Is that true?"

Martha rolled her eyes and waved her hand in dismissal. "Yes, we sold the big winner. At first, we didn't know if it was true or not, but then the TV station from down in Asheville called and said they had confirmation. They did a live report this morning from right here in the store about it. Cameras and lights and that pretty young reporter interviewing Abe. You should have seen him strutting around like he had something to do with picking those numbers himself." She gestured at the crowd waiting at the register. "The weird thing is that these people are buying lottery tickets, and most of them aren't even from here. They think if we sold it once, we have to sell another winner. Doesn't matter we have been selling them for a decade and never had a winner paying more than a hundred bucks."

"If lightning strikes twice, you'll really be popular." After they both laughed, Nathan asked the question he'd come to pose. "Do you know who bought it?"

"No. We didn't even know we had sold it at all, and we have no way of knowing which ticket it was. Maybe Raleigh could tell us what time it was sold, but even then, it would be a guess, especially since we don't have cameras to even go back and see who was here when. Guess we will find out just like everyone else." She glanced toward the front of the store and shook her head. "But then you know my silly husband will be swearing he knew the ticket was the winner when he printed it."

"At least it means someone local won it, right?"

"I would think so, just because mostly locals buy from us, but not necessarily. A couple of truckers and some salesmen peddling their wares over at the plants stopped before getting back on the road. Could have been one of them, I guess. At breakfast this morning, he listed off everyone he remembered buying tickets." Martha's eyes widened. "Hey, he said you bought one. Maybe you won."

"Wouldn't that be awesome?" Nathan laughed, implying he knew he hadn't won rather than admitting that he hadn't checked, because then he would have to explain why he didn't have the ticket. He was there to get information, not to tell his story, so he shifted the conversation again. "Ronnie says one of his won seven bucks. That was his big winner."

"Good for Ronnie." Martha reached out and grasped Nathan's arm. "I wish you had won it. That would be great for Donna and Jacob. That kid could go anywhere to college, then. He so deserves it."

"Maybe he'll get a baseball scholarship."

"I wish you had gotten to go to college. Your dad would have been so proud to see that." She busied herself behind the counter, cleaning in case anyone came back to order lunch, not that the lottery seekers in the front of the store looked as though they were going to spend cash on anything of value. "You seemed to have so much bad luck. Losing your mom. Then your dad. That wreck. Even Donna getting pregnant, though that boy sure is a blessing."

Nathan pressed his lips together. "I had better luck than some. Better than Charlie. And Danny."

Martha flinched at the second mention of her son.

"Besides, college was always a long shot. And once we found out Donna was pregnant…"

She reached out and patted his hand. "All Danny thought about was the Marines. I figured he and Hank would do that, but I always hoped you and Charlie would do something different. Both of you got good grades."

He smiled at the memory. "Shoot, Martha, we got good

grades because neither one of us dared take anything lower than a B home to Ronnie."

"Like a certain C in eleventh-grade history?" Martha's eyes twinkled at the memory.

"Oh, yes. I split two cords of firewood for that C. Ronnie just handed me the axe and pointed."

"And grounded you until the next report card, if I remember right. That sure cut into your dating life."

"I was so mad at him then. I couldn't believe he did that right after my dad died because I figured that was an excuse for everything."

"You don't know this, but Ronnie and I talked about that a lot."

"Really?"

"Oh, yes. He was so scared he was being too harsh. He felt so bad, knowing how alone and scared you were after losing your dad. He wanted to just hold you and tell you he understood the C. But he also knew your life wouldn't get easier as an orphan. He thought the state would take you and put you in a foster home if they had even the slightest reason to. He didn't want you to hate him, but he didn't want you to play victim either."

"I hated him for about ten minutes, but then I forgot it all as I swung that axe." Nathan stared out the window, lost in memories as he mumbled, "He always seemed to understand."

"Understand what?"

He shook his head as the memories flooded back into his mind. "I was mad at the world. Everything seemed so unfair. And Ronnie was determined not to let me wallow in pity."

"Losing your dad was unfair. No kid deserves to be an orphan."

"No, but Ronnie taught me bad luck happens. What you do about it? That's what matters." A faint smile crossed his face. "Do you know what he said when I told him Donna was pregnant?"

"What?"

"I was ranting about how unfair it all was. How could she be pregnant and ruin all my plans? Typical thinking-only-of-me bull." He shook his head at the shame of the memory. "He came up into my face and asked me if I got her pregnant. I gulped and said yes. His nose was almost touching mine when he asked what I planned to do about it. That's what he always asked when I complained about something being unfair. So what? Now what are you going to do about it?"

"And look at you now. Beautiful Donna and an awesome kid in Jacob. Couldn't be better, huh?"

Nathan looked down at the floor, studying the cracks in the linoleum—anything to avoid mentioning Donna. "He's the best."

Martha cocked her head, a look of puzzlement crossing her face. He felt her gaze on him and didn't want to look her in the eyes.

She asked, "How did the flowers and candy go over yesterday? And you getting home early? Was she thrilled?"

"Her reaction was, uh, unbelievable. Like nothing I've ever seen." Desperate to change the subject—and feeling guilty for lying by not telling her everything—he asked, "You get a check for selling the winning ticket, don't you?"

She hesitated with a look that said she didn't want to leave her questions alone, but she relented. "Yeah, we do. Bigwigs from Raleigh are driving over next week to take pictures and give us the check. I think they direct deposit the actual money. The presentation is just one of those big fake cardboard checks and smiles. Abe will be so happy in front of the cameras."

"That's terrific. You going to retire on it?"

"Oh, honey, I wish. It's good money, more money than we make off this place in a year, and we are thankful, but it's not like we can close up the store." Martha gestured at Abe, who was busy running the cash register and holding court with new customers who had never heard his old stories. "Besides, I think Abe enjoys hanging out in here and talking too much. If he retired, he would have to find a store just like this so he could feel at home."

She turned back to Nathan and smiled. "It gives me a place to do my flowers and stuff too. Same thing I would do if retired—gardening and finding somewhere to peddle my blooms." A wistful look slid over her face. "We sure don't want to retire down to Florida or something even if we could afford it. God's waiting room—sitting around and waiting to die. This is home."

"Running the store doesn't sound too bad, then."

Martha laughed in her good-natured way. "Maybe we are retired and just don't know it. We sure don't run this place to get rich."

They watched Abe take money and print out lottery tickets. Every time the door opened for someone to exit, another person came in and joined the line. "They really think you will sell a second winner?"

Her head nodded slowly in wonder. "Sadly, yes. Everyone wants to get rich quick. I just hope someone nice won it. Take care of others. Do nice things. Like you would. And you would treat Donna like a queen." Martha turned to look at Nathan and was shocked to see tears welling up in his eyes. "Oh, honey, what is it? Something wrong with Donna? Jacob?"

Nathan tilted his head back and sucked in a deep breath. He couldn't hide the truth from her anymore. "You won't believe me, Martha."

Martha guided him back to an empty booth in the corner, well away from the four gabbing men. "I will always believe you, Nathan. Now what's wrong?"

"It's a long story," Nathan replied and told her everything about the day before.

———

MARTHA'S warm hands wrapped around his, holding them as he slumped in the seat, exhausted from telling the tale. Her eyes brimmed with tears throughout his story, and one ran down her right cheek. "So, what are you going to do?"

"You sound just like Ronnie. 'Life screwed you, so, what are you going to do about it?' I can hear him now." He smiled weakly and shrugged. "I guess the first thing is to find somewhere to stay. Danny's offered his couch, and Ronnie said I could move back into my old room."

He turned and looked out the store window. Another car was turning in from the main road to join the crowd of fortune seekers. "I want to be with Jacob as much as possible, so I'll work as many hours as I can so I can get a decent place. Hal offered me weekend work with the truck stop, and that will help."

Martha tsked and shook her head. "If you work all those hours, how are you going to spend time with Jacob?"

"That's what Donna asked yesterday morning when I told her about the offer, but what else can I do? Ronnie can't give me overtime or a raise."

"Come open this garage like I been begging you to for years."

Nathan chuckled, a hollow sound since nothing felt funny at the moment. "It's like y'all are conspiring on me. Donna said the same thing yesterday morning. Danny and I talked about it this morning. Even Ronnie said I should take another job if I found something."

"So do it."

"I don't have that kind of money to open a business."

"What would you need money for? You have your own tools. And Abe's got his old tools sitting in there, gathering dust. Open the place up."

He looked down at his hands, noticing again the absence of the wedding band. "It's not like my old truck and the cars Abe used to work on. Modern cars have all these computers on board, and you need fancy diagnostic equipment."

"With the check we are getting from the state, we can help you update whatever you need and make sure everything is ready."

"I can't let you do that."

"Nathan, honey, you could pay us over time. We would figure the details out."

He shook his head firmly. "I couldn't borrow money from you. Besides, I would have to buy the business from you, and I really can't afford that."

"Get off your proud horse and listen. That garage is just an empty, worthless building to us right now, so anything you pay us is more money than we are already making off it." She gripped his hand in her own and stared into his eyes. "We work out a deal where you fix cars and pay us some rent or something. We put that rent toward you owning the building someday. It's a win-win."

Nathan's head swirled as he stuttered, "Not sure Abe would go for it."

She laughed, a musical echo off the walls. "Oh, honey, are you kidding? You think I talked to you about it without Abe knowing? He's wanted you to do it for years. Just a few weeks ago, he brought it up again when you fixed the freezer for him. It reminded him of how good you are at repairing things. He always said you were a natural mechanic when you hung out in the garage during high school."

Nathan barely remembered the freezer repair. He had walked in to pay for some gas, and Abe was hurrying to empty it of ice cream that was melting. He was trying to pack it in an already-full freezer, scared he would lose hundreds in inventory. Nathan grabbed his tools out of his truck and had it running in thirty minutes. It kept running until some spare parts arrived a few days later, parts that Nathan also installed.

"That was nothing," Nathan said. "Repairing it was easy."

"To you, yes. That's what you do. Fix things. You do it all the time. Randy Fletcher brags you fixed his tractor last fall for harvest. And he says it runs better than the Deere guys have ever had it running. Norma Caldwell can't stop talking about how you helped her when her car broke down up on Spring Street. Not only got it running but better than it had in years. I've heard dozens of stories like that."

"But helping a neighbor is different from asking people to pay me to fix stuff."

"You think they didn't pay you? Randy's wife sent you canned vegetables to last all winter. She could have sold them down at the farmer's market for a few hundred dollars. Norma cuts Jacob's hair for free. Abe funded Jacob's Little League uniforms. Every one of them still thinks they got a bargain. They gladly paid you." Martha's eyes twinkled as a smile spread across her face. "Besides, you fixing their cars without ripping them off—that would help people. People around here can't afford new cars every time they turn around, and they sure can't afford to pay the crazy repair prices of those dealerships."

Nathan sat back in the booth and stared at the ceiling fan slowing turning over his head. He couldn't understand why everyone else thought he could run a business but he didn't believe it. To daydream was one thing. To talk in generalities with Ronnie or plan with Danny was a little unsettling. But to have such a specific conversation with someone who could make it happen was petrifying.

He lowered his gaze to her waiting face. "We would have to work out something fair. I don't want to take advantage."

"No, I know you don't. And wouldn't. That's why we want you to do it." She relaxed as if she had just won a contest. "Besides, my bet is if you ran that garage, I could convince my wayward son to run the store itself. He sits around in that awful trailer and feels sorry for himself. If you were here every day, he might just figure out he could run the store despite that chair."

Nathan averted his gaze toward the front of the store, not wanting to break Danny's confidence by sharing how open he might be to the idea. "If Danny was running the store, what would Abe do?"

Martha's laughter rang like little bells, full of mirth. She pointed at the Liar's Table, the old men sitting around gabbing, with cups of coffee in their hands. "Probably try to outdo all them with their fancy tales… until I tired of him underfoot and kicked him out to the garage with you. You know how happy he would be changing oil again?"

His mind raced. "I want to. I really do. But I have to think about it. A lot."

"I wouldn't expect anything else. Come back next week. After all of this craziness has died down"—Martha waved her arm at the crowd buying lottery tickets—"and you and Donna have figured out your way forward."

Nathan spied the clock on the wall over the deli, startled to see it was after noon. Apologizing as he explained he needed to leave, he rose to his feet. "I'm late to meet Danny, but I promise to come talk more."

Martha surprised him by wrapping her arms around him and hugging. "Try to get him to come with you next time. Would be great to have you boys in the store again."

17

The door to Sammy's Pub swung closed behind Nathan. He stopped to let his eyes adjust from the bright sunshine to the murky shadows. The view that came into focus was a near replica of the day before.

Like a statue in a museum, Sammy occupied his usual space, arms crossed and back leaning against the mirrored display wall lined with liquor bottles behind the bar. He nodded a hello, the slightest tip of his head, as though Nathan had not been escorted out of the bar by a policeman the afternoon before.

Two men—the same two as the day before and perched on the same stools, as if they had never left—squinted against the light from opposite ends of the bar. They made blurry eye contact with a greeting nod and then returned their gaze to the golden liquid in the mugs in front of them. They showed no sign of remembering his perp walk the day before. Or they didn't care, too focused on whatever personal troubles kept them ensconced there.

A scattering of people sat at tables toward the front, eating their lunches. Four guys shot pool in the rear of the bar, a cash bet stacked beside a pitcher of beer and four mugs. The bright flash of light from the door caused them to look up and nod a hello. All were three or four years younger and vaguely familiar from high school days, but he struggled to come up with their names.

That was life in a small town. Everyone knew everyone, at least on a nodding basis, but Nathan was too mission focused to give them much thought.

He spotted Danny at a table midway down the wall, far away enough from the others so that they could talk. He settled into a chair across from his friend and eyed the cold pitcher of beer and two frosted mugs before declaring, "I'm just drinking iced tea."

Danny's eyes narrowed. "The only reason you would do that is if you planned to watch Jacob's game. But since you promised to avoid contact, you wouldn't be that stupid, would you?"

The curse of a good friend—they always knew what one was thinking. Nathan leaned back in the chair and crossed his arms in defiance. "I promised to avoid contact before we met for lunch today. I've kept that promise, but I didn't commit to anything more."

"And now you plan to just go waltzing into the park and get arrested in front of everyone for violating the restraining order?"

"Getting arrested isn't part of the plan." Nathan locked gazes, a test to see who would back down first, but he lost and dropped his eyes. "I'm not going into the park, so no one will know I'm there. I'm going to drive up to the Point and then wander down through the woods until I find a good place where I can watch the game without being seen."

Danny lifted his mug and sipped as he studied Nathan's face. With a sigh, he settled the glass back on the table, a thin streak of beer foam on his upper lip. "Then no one will smell your breath either, so having a beer wouldn't matter."

Nathan's body slumped into his chair as his arms unfolded and fell into his lap. He looked down at the table and shook his head, cursing under his breath. Of course Danny would figure out what he was planning.

"Don't screw this up, Nathan. No contact means no contact. You need to be a good boy."

"The Point. I promise. They won't see me."

Danny drummed his fingers on the table, his eyes continuing to reflect doubt. After a while, he shrugged his shoulders. "Make sure they don't."

Nathan reached for the pitcher and poured beer into the mug, the foam bubbling up and over the side of the glass. He sipped it, determined to have just the one. He was eager to find out what Danny had learned and then get to the game before the first pitch. "Did you see Donna?"

"Yes." Danny relaxed in his chair. "We had a good talk."

"So Hank wasn't there?"

"He was in the house, but he stayed out of the way so we could chat. She didn't say it, but I got the impression she had asked him to give us room. He didn't look too happy about it."

"Good for her. And I don't care how unhappy he was." Nathan chewed his lip. "Have they told Jacob anything yet?"

"She talked to him on the phone last night but didn't tell him anything about your issues. She plans to talk to him later about that."

"Just Donna?"

"Yes. She was adamant about that. Hank won't be there."

Nathan sipped the cold beer, feeling the liquid flow down his throat. He wasn't sure which was more satisfying—the taste of the drink or the knowledge that Donna was managing Hank.

After settling the mug back onto the table, he ran his finger along the ridge of his nose, feeling the same bone that was broken in Hank. "How did he look?"

Danny's serious look was shattered by a wry smile. "Like you knocked the crap out of him."

"Good." He studied the wood grain on the table, his finger tracing the puddles of liquid. "And Donna? How bad is she hurt?"

Danny's smile faded as he shook his head. "She winced when she moved too quick and kept an arm wrapped around her chest. She tried to hide it, but I could tell she was in pain."

Nathan's fingers hooked around the handle of the mug, and he rocked the bottom of the glass on the table, the liquid sloshing and foaming inside. He felt physically sick at the thought of having hurt his wife. "I feel horrible about that. I never meant to harm her."

"She knows that. She was more resigned to everything that was happening than mad about the fight. And she feels guilty you found out about them the way you did. She kept saying she should have told you." Danny motioned to the jacket hanging off the chair at the end of the table. "Despite the pain from her ribs, she got up early this morning to pack your clothes in your duffel bag. She even washed your jacket. Said she was worried you might need it on chilly mornings. If she didn't still care, she might have stuffed your clothes in the bag or even thrown them out on the lawn."

"But she still wants a divorce, right?"

"She packed your clothes. She didn't hang them in the closet, waiting for you to come home." Danny flicked a piece of ice off the side of his mug and watched it melt on the table. "Besides, after knowing about Hank, would you really want to go back?"

"Probably not. I would only go back if we decided staying together was best for Jacob." Nathan drew beads of water around the table with his finger. "Did she say anything about custody?"

"We didn't talk a lot about details, but she seems sure she will end up with custody."

Nathan's voice raised. "But I caught her in bed with Hank."

Sammy and the two guys sitting at the bar glanced over. He glared at them, daring anyone to comment. They shifted their attention back to the sports announcers on the TVs over the bar.

Danny leaned across the table and spoke quietly. "Yeah, and you broke his nose and Donna's ribs. Call it a draw. You don't play the adultery card, and they don't play the domestic-violence card. I'm not even sure her cheating on you would have any impact on custody nowadays. But the good news is she wants to work this out so Jacob doesn't have to hear all the dirt."

Nathan grimaced. "So he doesn't find out his mom was having an affair, but he'll know I hurt his mom?"

"You really want him to know about the affair?"

"No, of course not. But if you could see she was in pain, why won't he? And how else is she going to explain it?"

"She just said she's hoping she doesn't have to tell him."

"She'd do that?"

Danny shrugged. "She's going to try, but I don't see how she can. She doesn't want to make you out to be the bad guy. Not sure if that's for you or for Jacob. Maybe it's for both of you."

"Can she hide it at the game today? Or isn't she going?"

"No, she'll definitely be there though she isn't skulking through the woods to watch the game." Danny rolled his eyes. "Matt and Colette are bringing a picnic lunch, and they're all going to sit together. Her plan is to sit real still in a chair and hope he doesn't notice."

Nathan's head popped up. "So Hank will be with them? How does Jacob not figure things out from that?"

"The boys will just think of him as Luke's uncle. Nothing else." Danny waited to see Nathan nod agreement before continuing softly, "She'll tell Jacob he gets to spend another night with Luke and then come home Sunday afternoon. That'll give her time to plan out what to say. She'll call me tonight or tomorrow morning with details before she does anything. After she talks to him, she'll have him call you to give you time with him. She wants to make sure you both are telling him the same thing."

"That's fair." Nathan hung his head. "This whole thing sucks, but I understand how she's handling it. You don't know how much it hurts not to be able to see him, to talk to him."

"No, you're right—I don't have a clue. But I can tell, sitting there and talking to her, Donna really wants this to work out as well as it can. Whatever that means."

Sammy delivered a platter of Nachos Deluxe, the same gastroabomination they had eaten the previous afternoon. Nathan thought about his pledge to eat better and lose a little weight but decided he had bigger issues to face first. With a shrug, he scooped a nacho full of cheese and beans from the plate and chased it down with a sip of beer. "So you didn't get a chance to talk specifics about custody? Guess maybe he stays with me on weekends and with her during the week? Maybe I stop by and pick him up for school? Poor kid, having to bounce between two homes."

Danny's hand paused in midair, his reach for the food frozen. He slumped back in his chair and sighed. "That's where things went south."

Nathan paused with a chip in his hand, cheese dripping off and landing on the table. "What did she say?"

"Not her." Danny hesitated and chewed his lip. "Hank."

"What does he have to do with it? I thought he wasn't part of the conversation."

"Just relax and listen a second." Danny took a big gulp of beer and swallowed hard. He leaned forward and propped his elbows on the table. "This was after. I thought everything was good, and I was getting into the van. Donna went back inside, but Hank came around the house and caught me before I drove off."

"Spill it. What did he say?"

Another big sigh. "Right after the school year ends, they're moving with him to Atlanta."

Numbness spread from Nathan's chest into his arms and legs. The sound of the TV blaring behind the bar disappeared into a buzzing in his head. "Why can't Hank move here?"

"He works there for that security company. He can't do that from here."

"What about Jacob's friends? And baseball?"

"He's young. He'll make new friends down there. And the school he'll go to has a great baseball program. Hank said it was one of the best in Georgia."

Nathan's body tensed, and his blood pressure rose. His hands around the beer mug trembled. "So, what does that mean? How often will I see Jacob?"

"He didn't say. I was so stunned because none of this came up when I was talking to Donna. But let's be real: Jacob isn't going to travel up here every week. He isn't going to want to. He'll be a teenager and want to hang out with his friends on weekends. So I'd guess maybe a weekend a month. A couple of weeks in the summer."

In a measured voice, Nathan whispered, "They aren't taking my son away from me. I won't let them. I'll fight it."

"With what? If you take it to court, they'll press the domestic violence charges and paint you as dangerous. Then, not only will you not have custody, but you won't even have visitation rights."

Nathan stared at the table and fumed, his hands gripped tightly around the glass. "So, what are you saying? I just let them take him?"

"No." Danny studied the tabled for several minutes. "Let me talk to Donna again. I'm missing something. I walked out of the house feeling good about everything, and then Hank threw me that curveball. I should have just gone back in right then and confronted her, but I didn't know what to say. That's on me."

Nathan raised his head and opened his mouth to reply, but they were interrupted as the four guys who had been playing pool walked past the table.

One of them smiled and said, "The Fearsome Foursome."

Though they looked up, startled, and started to shoo him away, he didn't give them a chance. "You're Nathan Thomas, and you're Danny Morgan, right?" As they nodded, he continued to babble. "I'm Chet Everswood. Went to Millerton High two years behind Matt Saunders, so I guess that was three years behind you, but I got to play football with him his senior year. I watched you guys beat Roosevelt High your last game. That was one mean hit you put on Ricky Ward that last play. Never forget that night."

Nathan and Danny exchanged glances. "Neither will we."

Chet's face reddened as he realized the significance of that date. "Oh, yeah, sorry. I forgot, that was the night that Charlie Mills died, wasn't it?"

Danny leaned back in his wheelchair and stared at Chet, whose face reddened even more.

The man's eyes roamed across the table, anywhere to avoid looking at the wheelchair as he stammered, "Anyway, Matt's older brother, Hank, was the fourth, right?" As they exchanged glances, Chet babbled on. "Did you hear about what happened to him?"

Nathan squinted his eyes. "Hear what?"

"He got lucky."

Nathan's face reddened, and he locked eyes with the interloper. His voice came out in a deep-throated growl. "What do you mean *lucky*?"

Chet took a step back, confusion spreading on his face at Nathan's menace. "The lottery. He's the big winner."

Nathan sat stunned for several seconds until his anger mushroomed. He rose to his feet and glared at Chet. "You're saying *Hank Saunders* had the winning ticket? The one bought at Abe's Market?"

Chet took another step back and glanced toward the bar. Sammy wasn't leaning anymore but standing and watching the exchange, ready to intervene.

Chet licked his lips and said, "Man, I'm sorry. Thought you would be happy for him."

"You sure he won?"

"Yeah, I just got off the phone with Matt. Hank didn't even think to check his tickets until just a bit ago. Can you imagine? With the news floating around town that someone local won everything, and he didn't even look. Must be good money in that security job to not check the ticket right away, or he was really distracted this morning. What kind of idiot doesn't check? I was looking at mine first thing this morning. Anyway, he saw he won and called Matt."

Nathan's face flushed as he collapsed back into his chair. Chet spread his hands wide as he stood awkwardly at the end of the table, confusion etched into his face. He backed away from the table, shaking his head, turned, and walked out the door with his friends.

The closing door blotted out the sun as it banged shut. They sat in stunned silence, neither able to speak, until Nathan exploded in movement. He reached across the table and grabbed his jacket. He dragged it across the table, jostling beer out of his glass, and shoved his hand in the front pocket. Empty. He checked the other pockets. Empty.

He looked at Danny. "The coat's clean."

Danny had been startled at the sudden movement and grabbed a napkin to mop up the spilled beer. "Yeah. Donna said she cleaned it. So what?"

"They stole it."

Danny stopped wiping and stared at Nathan, beer dripping from the soaked napkin. "Who stole what?"

Nathan's face flushed as he shook his jacket. "My lottery ticket was in here. She cleaned it. So she found the ticket. And she gave it to him."

Danny's mouth gaped open, and his eyes widened. "Nathan, you don't know that. Maybe she washed it. How would she even know you had a lottery ticket? You never buy the things."

"Donna does everything just so. You've seen our house." Nathan crumpled the jacket in the empty chair beside him. "She always empties the pockets before washing to protect her washer from all the crap Jacob lugs home, so she would have found my lottery ticket. They figured out it was the winner and kept it."

Danny reached out from his chair and wrapped his hand around Nathan's arm. "Calm down. You don't know that."

Nathan's body quivered. "I know a lot of things. Hank lives in Atlanta, so why would he buy lottery tickets at Abe's? And I know *my* lottery ticket was in *my* jacket I left at *my* house when I found them boning each other. And my wife tells you she cleans my jacket, so she admits she had it. And, amazingly, that thief who already stole my wife and is trying to steal my son calls his brother and tells him he won the lottery. I think I know exactly what happened."

"That's a whole bunch of assumptions, so hold on and calm down."

"How much more am I supposed to let him take from me?"

"Think, Nathan. Donna wouldn't do that to you even if Hank would." He motioned toward the parking lot. "Let's go out to the van and check the duffel. My bet is she put it in there with your clothes."

Nathan stood, grabbed his jacket, and walked toward the door. As he rolled outside, Danny waved his hand at Sammy, an indication he would be right back inside. No one risked being banned from one of the few bars in town by stiffing an unpaid bill.

Out in the parking lot, Danny pulled open the van doors to reveal the large canvas duffel. Nathan opened the bag and removed neatly folded clothing, at first slowly but then with increasing franticness. Halfway through, he picked up the bag in frustration and dumped the contents on the van floor. He rifled through the clothes without success.

Defeated, he sat down on the bumper and faced his friend. "Told you. Not here." The anger he had felt melted from his body, replaced with an aching emptiness. "He steals my wife. Makes it so I can't go to my own house. He's taking my kid to Atlanta so I'll never see him. And now he pockets my lottery winnings." His voice faded off. He half-heartedly kicked a pebble on the asphalt.

Danny watched the rock bounce across the lot. "So, what do you want to do?"

Barely above a whisper, Nathan said, "I don't know if I have any fight left."

Danny rolled close, bumping his knees into Nathan's and forcing him to look up. "You're not a quitter. Never have been. So don't you dare give up on me."

A faint smile crossed his face. "Yes, Coach." He stared at

his boots and mumbled, "But I need a timeout. I need to think."

They sat for several minutes, neither speaking, before Nathan stood, sucked in a deep breath, and picked up a shirt. Without any attempt to fold it, he stuffed it into the duffel. Danny watched until all the clothes were jammed into the bag. "So does this mean you want to go back inside and make a plan?"

"Nope. I've got something to do first. Let's catch up over dinner."

"What could possibly be more important?"

"I have a game to watch. I want to see my son play while I still can."

18

Nathan planned to drive straight to the Point, but his house was just a couple of blocks off the main route, a short diversion that wouldn't make him late for the ball game. Donna and Hank should already have been at the park, enjoying a picnic lunch with Matt, Colette, and the boys, so the house would be empty.

And if not—if they were still home—he would just keep driving. No harm, no foul.

He didn't want to go inside. He didn't even want to get out of the truck. He just wanted to see the house, the place that held so many happy memories—watching Jacob ride a bike without training wheels on the short driveway, playing catch in the backyard and quitting only when it became too dark to see the ball, teaching him to use tools as they worked on projects together around the house.

As the house came into view, he could see no one was home. He relaxed and parked the truck, engine idling, just down the block.

The driveway was empty. A small oil stain marked where Donna's Ford Fiesta normally parked. Despite his best efforts,

Nathan couldn't keep the car from aging. Every time he fixed one problem, another cropped up. But he'd kept it running, saving them from having to replace it and add debt.

Could Hank fix it? Would he even try? When Abe had shown the boys how to fix something on a car, Hank would wander off through the garage, bored and inattentive. Danny, Charlie, and Nathan would have parts spread across the shop floor, figuring something out, and Hank would be sitting on a stool, regaling them with stories they had heard a hundred times.

Besides, with all that lottery money, he wouldn't have a need to fix it. He could buy her a brand-new one, never driven by anyone, something shiny and fancy like his Dodge Charger.

Or Donna would talk him into a sleek, little convertible. Bright red. Nathan smiled despite himself at the thought of her driving down the road, hair whipping in the wind. If he had the money rather than Hank, he would buy her something like that.

As the thoughts of those winnings weaved themselves through his head, he also envisioned building her her own bathroom in a wing off the house. It would have a fancy spa tub with wide shelves for candles. She could create the private getaway she had always wanted inside their house while he and Jacob watched baseball on a brand-new wide-screen television.

He shook his head and laughed at himself, realizing he still wasn't thinking big enough. With those winnings, they wouldn't stay in this little house. He could build her the fanciest house ever with a private master suite. It would have a big garage to park that fancy sports car along with his brand-new pickup.

But the smile faded as quickly as his vision. Their problems wouldn't be solved with fancy cars and houses. Their problems couldn't be addressed with a big pile of cash.

Deep in his heart, Nathan knew they had been drifting for years. Jacob was their anchor, the passion they shared. In a few years, when he struck out on his own, nothing would be left for them. What was happening now was inevitable and probably had been inevitable from their early days of dating. If not for the pregnancy, they would have never married, just another couple breaking apart in high school.

Sobered by the thought, Nathan took a last look around. The house was tidy, well maintained through countless hours of weekend projects. It might have been small and lacking any elegance, but they had always taken pride in it.

The grass needed its weekly mowing, a task that Jacob handled under supervision. The boy was pretty good with his chores, doing most of them without nagging. Sure, he forgot sometimes—*don't all kids?*—but he got them done. Doing household chores taught responsibility and contribution, lessons Nathan believed in deeply, lessons he had learned himself from his own father and then from Ronnie.

Would Hank teach Jacob those things? Show him that hard work was the key to success? Or did lucky Hank, slide-through-life Hank, wink-and-a-smile Hank even understand it? Nathan worried he couldn't impart those lessons in just a few measly days of visitation a month.

His gaze settled on Jacob's bicycle, leaned against the side of the house. The bicycle was old, but the chain was freshly oiled, the gears adjusted. A father-son team worked together to keep it in good shape. He'd taught Jacob how to do those repairs, how to make things work. Nathan fretted he would never find the time to teach him those necessary skills.

He hung his head as he realized he was fooling himself. Jacob would move with them to Atlanta. He would become a teenager interested in girls and sports and friends and not in hanging out with his father. He certainly wouldn't have time for a father in some dying little town miles away when Atlanta would offer so much more than Millerton ever could. *Why would Jacob want to come back here?*

He gripped the steering wheel until his knuckles turned white, silently cursing the unfairness. Hank hadn't changed diapers. Or hovered over a sick child hot with a fever. Or sat at a dining room table, helping to solve inscrutable homework problems. Or patched up a skinned knee and wiped tears off his son's face.

Fighting to control his emotions, Nathan shook the thoughts off. He reached down to put the truck back into gear before a voice stopped him.

"Yo, Mr. Thomas."

He turned to see Josh, the neighbor teenage pothead, walking across his front yard. The boy was shirtless, showing off his skinny arms and hairless chest. His baggy jeans hung below his butt and exposed his yellow-smiley-face boxer shorts. His hair was mussed as though he had just crawled out of bed, and his eyes were bloodshot.

He was a likable enough boy but aimless and drifting toward trouble. His own father had never been in the picture. A stepfather had moved in a few years before, just as the boy entered the teenage years, but they never seemed to connect. Nathan tried some guidance—the boy craved it—but could do only so much in a handful of interactions. He'd been more concerned about keeping the older teen's influence away from Jacob.

Josh leaned through the window of the truck. "I heard I missed the party yesterday." He stretched the word party out long—parrrr-teeeee—emphasizing the last syllable as he giggled. Seeing Nathan's confused look, he continued, "You know, the main event. The championship fight."

Nathan shrugged, not wanting to discuss his marital problems with this kid. Undeterred, Josh rambled on. "I got home, and the whole neighborhood was buzzing about it." He giggled again at the word "buzzing."

Nathan tried to smile to match his neighbor's amusement

but could only bring himself to mumble an apology. "Sorry about all that."

"Heard the cops were here and everything."

"I guess one of the neighbors called them."

"Nah, man, I asked around. None of them called. They never would."

Nathan didn't want to argue about it. It didn't really matter who had called. Josh was probably just happy he wasn't sitting stoned on the front porch when the police had arrived, drawing unwanted attention to himself.

Though Nathan shifted the truck into gear, the boy remained, leaning through the window and babbling. "Was it over that dude with the badass car? Man, that thing is sweet."

"Just an argument." He pointed down the street. "I have to get on over to the park to see Jacob's game."

"Game day—awesome. Super-sport Jake will be slugging homers today."

"I sure hope so." Nathan rolled forward but stopped and looked at his neighbor. "Josh?"

"Yeah, Mr. T?"

"Do me a favor? Don't tell Donna I was here. I was supposed to go straight to the park, and she'll think I forgot."

"No worries. I forget stuff all the time. Occupational hazard and all that, you know. So I'll just forget that you forgot." He chuckled again, continuing to amuse himself with his own wit.

Nathan drove off, more determined that his own son would not drift down the same path Josh was on.

19

After leaving the neighborhood—and kicking himself for having driven by the house and risking the addle-brained teen telling Donna—Nathan drove to the last intersection of town, the dull traffic lights hanging from the wire marking the entrance to the industrial park.

Abe's Market sat on the corner, the parking lot still crowded with hopeful idiots spending money they couldn't afford on lottery tickets that would never win—or, if lightning struck twice and they did win, former friends and unfaithful wives would steal.

Several cars turned to the right, the entry to the town park. The grass around the faded entrance sign was neatly trimmed, and fresh spring flowers bloomed. Volunteers worked on Saturday mornings to handle the maintenance the town couldn't afford. The parking lot was cluttered with cars, their occupants sitting on folding chairs or blankets and enjoying a warm spring afternoon. The younger kids' game had just ended, and the eleven- and twelve-year-old teams were warming up on the field.

Nathan needed to find a place to watch the game before it

started, but rather than heading into the park, he turned left, taking the twisting two-lane road up the hill into the forests and away from town. The timber companies still owned much of the land, so only a few sparse houses dotted the road, most barely visible through the dense trees. The ridge at the top marked the county line, the rural farmlands beyond belonging to an even poorer county, as hard as that was to imagine.

His pickup truck strained on the incline as he searched for the opening to the fire roads crisscrossing above the town through the former timberland, a turn he had taken dozens of times as a teen but rarely as an adult. Spying the two faded No Trespassing signs nailed to trees, barely visible and largely ignored, he flipped on his signal, slowed, and eased the truck onto the dirt road.

The woods were dense and his path overgrown with weeds that brushed against the undercarriage though the road was still passable. The truck's radio antenna swung back and forth as tree limbs clipped it. The tires slipped through the ruts, bouncing against loose boulders and rough potholes. Three deer bounded across the road in front of him, startled by his intrusion on their quiet world.

The farther he went from the main road, the thicker the trees grew, blocking the sun from the ground. He bounced over a fallen tree, its trunk crushed by previous visitors. At each fork, he instinctively took the turns memorized in carefree high school days.

Light returned as the trees thinned to reveal a gurgling creek hemming in a sharp curve in the road. Giant boulders jutted out of the ground, covered with graffiti from high school kids.

Andy + Maria 4Ever
Gravity Is False. The Earth Sucks.
Hannah Gives Great Head

Tammy had been replaced in this generation by Hannah, whoever she was. No doubt, the current Hank of the high school had spray-painted her claim to fame on the granite, whether she wanted the reputation or not.

Nathan hoped Andy and Maria would find longer happiness than he and Donna had. And, with his present problems, he agreed with the anonymous muse's thoughts on the earth though even his weak grades in high school science didn't prevent him from understanding gravity was quite real.

Though he intended to drive straight out to the Point, he brought the truck to a stop instead and stared at a specific large boulder that loomed in his memory. A large scar was gouged out of its face from the force of a violent impact, a reminder for generations to come. A single tag spray-painted across the top had faded over the years but was still visible:

Charlie Mills R.I.P.

Graffiti on other boulders had been marked out and painted over many times, but not this one. Even though the present-day visitors to this area had been toddlers when the accident happened—the youngest might not have even been born—they honored the memory. Nathan grimaced as he realized they probably even made up ghost stories about this area being haunted by a drowned high schooler.

Torn between wanting to see the opening of his son's game and a desire to linger in this sacred site, he reluctantly pushed open the door and stepped out into the shaded clearing. Birds whistled in the trees. Limbs swayed in the breeze. The creek sang its bubbling song. The peaceful sounds were much as they had been that night so many years before though the air was much warmer and more comforting.

As the memories flooded back, he ran his hand along the streaks carved deep into the rock face high above the ground.

The screech of metal filled his ears. The helpless feeling as the car rolled over into these woods. The agony of breaking bones. The stench of spilled fuel. The distant splash as a body landed in the midst of the flowing water.

Tears filled his eyes as he carefully stepped over the tangle of rock to the tree, its bark still bearing the scars where the car had come to rest. He stared at the spot where he had lain in the dirt, holding Danny's hand as Charlie drowned just a few feet away.

He had always been haunted by his inability to reach his best friend. The further the memory of his own pain receded, the more convinced he became that he should have been able to ford the water. He hadn't needed the strength to pull Charlie to safety, just to hold his head above the current.

He stared at the boulder in the middle of the stream, the rock that had been Charlie's pillow, as the bubbling waters flowed around it. In the bright light of an April day, the creek didn't look as intimidating as it had seemed that cold November night. The current wasn't as swift, the water not as cold or deep. His doubts about his own efforts swirled through his mind.

He sat down on the bank, picked up a small rock, and bounced it across the surface of the stream with a flick of his wrist. The ripples disappeared quickly in the rolling water. He glanced around, sure he was alone but confirming it anyway, and said aloud, "Charlie? Can we talk? Like old times?"

The weeks and months after the accident had been some of the loneliest times in Nathan's life. Isolated from everyone else by grief, he had no one to talk to about his empty feelings.

Once discharged from the hospital, Nathan found home life quiet and depressing. His own room wasn't a comfort because it had been Charlie's room first. The posters on the wall heralded music never to be heard again and movies never to be seen. The bookshelf overflowed with novels, reminders of his friend's passion for reading. The closet door hid all the clothes hanging, waiting to be worn. But the worst was the empty bed across the room, neatly made and horribly vacant.

Still, Nathan stayed in his room as long as possible before school to avoid facing Ronnie. Only once he heard him leave for work each day would he venture into the rest of the house.

And at the end of the day, Ronnie picked at his dinner then sat in the dark den, staring at nothing, no TV or music playing. As bad as the weekdays were, the weekends were much worse, nearly interminable, hours of deafening silence.

They tried to talk, but Ronnie was so overcome with grief —and Nathan with guilt—that they found connecting nearly impossible.

School, despite the normalcy of its routine, was equally awkward. Friends treated him like damaged goods, scared to laugh and joke in case it intruded on his mourning. They tried to include him. People invited him to parties, but if he went, the mood would quiet when he arrived as people put down their drinks and drifted away. He stopped going, not wanting to kill everyone else's fun.

The reality was that his classmates had their own best friends, forged over years. That wasn't going to change over the few months remaining of his school life.

The few times he stopped by Abe's Market were no better. Abe removed all the beer from the coolers before reopening after Charlie's funeral, but he couldn't bring himself to work in the garage again. He sat on the stool behind the register while Martha stayed back in the deli, neither their usual gregarious selves when customers walked in. They struggled between supporting their son as he worked his way through the court system and feeling ashamed and guilty for what had happened.

And the three surviving friends who were closest to him before the accident—Danny, Donna, and Hank—were of little help after.

Danny spent months recovering in a hospital from his injuries then sat in a jail cell serving a sentence for manslaughter and drunk driving. Nathan tried to see him several times, but Danny refused the visits.

Donna was absorbed with doctor's visits and baby plans. Nathan tried to help and be supportive, but he always felt awkward and out of step. Grieving for his friend consumed him and made coming to terms with unexpected fatherhood much more difficult. Celebrating the pending arrival of a new life felt wrong when he was still grieving for the one lost.

Hank was the worst. He had shared the horrific experience and was the only person who could truly understand it, but he refused to talk about the night at all. With the season over, they no longer shared football practice and found they had little to talk about. In the last months of their senior year, he avoided Nathan in the halls at school and never came over to visit the house. He only grudgingly attended their wedding the day after graduation but then left the next day for boot camp.

With nowhere else to turn and deep in grief, Nathan resumed conversations with his best friend. Charlie had always been a good listener, and his being dead didn't change that.

At first, Nathan visited the cemetery several times after leaving the hospital. He talked to the headstone that marked the grave or the outline of sod over the casket, but he didn't feel as if Charlie was there. Besides, he felt self-conscious talking out loud where others might see him.

In desperation and loneliness one night, Nathan returned to the river. He sat on the very rock he was sitting on today and sensed his friend in the trees, the running water, the soft breezes. Comforted by that feeling, he began making regular treks to sit and talk in the spot where Charlie had breathed his last.

Their conversations were as wide ranging as they had been when Charlie was alive. Nathan talked about being behind in studies, the pressure of a pregnant girlfriend, and the job waiting for him under Ronnie.

And he cried—a lot—something he never felt comfortable doing with anyone else. Hank wouldn't even acknowledge the grief. Donna didn't want to be reminded. Ronnie would join too quickly. Abe and Martha were ashamed that they had raised the cause of the pain. And nobody else at school knew how to react.

The visits became more frequent, daily by the end of the school year. But as summer came and Jacob was born, he couldn't disappear as easily. And he had less reason because the birth became the impetus for reconciliation. Ronnie came alive again and doted on the infant. Abe and Martha welcomed the newborn into the store. Friends dropped by for visits.

Most importantly, Nathan felt alive again, holding the wriggling bundle. He saw hope and a future in those gorgeous blue eyes. He might not have fully healed, but the wound scabbed over.

Thus, the daily chats with Charlie became weekly and then monthly. In the last few years, he came only on the annual date of the accident, Charlie's birthday, or holidays. In fact, he realized he had not sat in this spot in months, since the last anniversary of the accident the previous November.

Despite the length of time since their last chat, Nathan settled quickly into the comfortable routine of talking to his deceased friend, telling the story of the last two days in detail. He described the humiliation of being arrested, the horror that he had hurt Donna, the anger at Hank's betrayal, and the fear of losing his son. He talked until he was exhausted and the story ended.

He picked at the pebbles on the ground before raising his head. His voice cracked as he spoke. "I can't lose Jacob." He chewed on his lip as he considered his words. "I know that's selfish of me. I should be thinking of what's best for him, not for me, but I can't lose anyone else. I don't think I can take any more."

He stared at the boulder, watching the water twist around it. The sounds of the forest filled the void until he spoke again. "I wonder every day what you would have become. Would you be teaching here in the high school? Inspiring other kids like me to read a little Shakespeare and think it's cool? You could have me laughing at your stories of stupid things your students would do while we watched our kids playing together.

"Or maybe your own novels would be bestsellers by now. We would be standing at the grill, cooking burgers while I ask you what you meant by some chapter you wrote. And after dinner, you would tell some of your funny, made-up stories. What I would give to hear another one."

He picked up a stick from the ground and twirled it in his fingers. Gripping it with both hands, he broke it cleanly in two. "Instead, all I hear is you trying to breathe. Coughing and gagging from the water. Choking to death while I lay right there, doing nothing."

Charlie's jersey hung in the trophy case in the front hall of the high school. Above it, his smiling face beamed from a photograph, a memorial to a beloved student, a warning of the dangers of drinking and driving. Yet everyone believed his death was instantaneous and painless.

Even Ronnie. The police had told him Charlie hadn't suffered—he had died on impact or, at least, was unconscious, never knowing pain.

That trooper had told Nathan the same lie about his own dad. They always told the family that.

He didn't suffer. He never knew what happened.

But Nathan knew. And Danny and Hank knew. They never discussed it after the accident. All were too busy and absorbed in their own problems to talk about Charlie's suffering.

They certainly told no one else that Charlie had still been

alive after the crash. Not a soul. Not even Ronnie. Not once. Nathan had let him believe the lie of instant death because it was easier than telling the truth. He saw how Ronnie blamed Danny, hating him for taking his son.

If Nathan told him the truth, that Charlie had been alive and might have been saved, maybe Ronnie would look at him with the same disgust. That was something he just couldn't handle.

But the fact was Charlie was alive that night, for at least an hour, and they could have saved him.

Danny couldn't—he was trapped in the wreckage.

And Nathan, despite all his doubts over the years, knew he couldn't—he was too injured to go into the water. But...

Nathan's eyes blurred as he watched the white foam bounce and splash over the spot where his friend had died. He tossed the stick with a sudden fury and screamed the deepest secret of that night. "Why didn't Hank drag you out? He was right there with you. He propped your head up and then just left you there. If he had gotten you to the bank, I could have stayed with you. Talked to you. Kept you alive. But he didn't give me the chance."

Tears flowed down his face as he sobbed, his chest heaving. The sun flashed in his eyes as the trees vacillated in the breeze. He collapsed backward onto the ground, stared up at the leaves, and whispered, "Why didn't he save you?"

20

A s the tears dried up, exhaustion crept over his body. Numbness replaced the flood of emotions from the last two days. He needed a couple of hours of release, and nothing worked better than watching his son play baseball.

Nathan stood and brushed the dirt from his clothes. With a whispered word of thanks to Charlie, he climbed back into the truck and continued through the dense woods toward the Point.

Around a final bend, the forest abruptly ended and opened into a small field. The grass was beaten down and rutted from high schoolers' cars. A pile of beer cans gleamed in the sunlight at the end of the open area. A close inspection of the overgrown grass along the edge of the field would reveal thousands of cigarette butts and more than a few used condoms.

Little had changed at the Point over the last generation. As the darkness descended, particularly on weekend nights, teenagers drifted in. Made out. Drank beer and liquor. Smoked weed and cigarettes. Got laid or blown. Or just hung out and talked with friends.

But in the light of a Saturday afternoon, much too early in

the day for the inevitable gathering of adolescents, the lot was empty.

Directly below, the park spread out on the flat ground between the factories and the rise of the mountains.

Years earlier, during the strong manufacturing economy of the time, the owners of the mills had donated money to build a sprawling park in the shadows of the plants. Even after jobs fled overseas, the park remained a source of civic pride.

Special events were held there throughout the year. The Millerton High School Orchestra and Choir performed in the band shell. Local churches came together and hosted Easter sunrise services. The local manufacturers association—those that were left—continued to sponsor an ever-smaller fireworks show for the Fourth of July. For Memorial Day and Veterans Day, VFW members planted rows of American flags to represent fallen soldiers, including to the consternation of a few, casualties on the Confederate side of the Civil War.

Young couples married under the shade trees and later pushed strollers along the paths. Children explored the faded informational signs on the nature trail winding through the forest on the perimeter. The basketball courts hosted shirts-versus-skins games. Pop Warner football drew crowds in the fall while Little League baseball and softball games did the same in the spring.

On this sunny spring day, the parking lots overflowed as families gathered. Young teenagers, clad in safety helmets and kneepads, practiced tricks on their skateboards. Bicyclers and joggers shared the paved paths. A group of teens played soccer. Dogs ran inside the fenced dog park.

But Nathan's focus was the group of uniformed Little Leaguers suited up for baseball on the lined fields. The boys were finishing warm-ups as he walked to the edge of the Point.

The trees on the hill below him cluttered his view, and he

was too far away to see clearly. He needed to get closer to enjoy the game, but he wanted to remain out of sight.

He scanned the crowds around the field until he spotted Donna. She sat stiffly on a folding chair, perhaps being careful to protect her injured ribs. A blanket was spread at her feet, the fixings of a picnic lunch scattered about. Matt and Colette sprawled on the ground beside her, chatting as they waited for the start of the game. They looked tranquil and happy. Nathan ached to sit with them and enjoy the sunny afternoon.

But Nathan wondered why Hank wasn't sitting with them. True, Donna had said they would try to hide their affair, especially from Jacob since they hadn't told him, but Danny was right—he could sit with his brother and sister-in-law without raising suspicions.

Maybe he had returned to Atlanta, called back for work. Security for bigwigs wasn't a Monday-through-Friday job. It didn't matter. He wasn't there, and that was one fewer set of eyes that could spot Nathan sneaking through the woods.

Knowing where Donna was made his choice of direction easier. He wanted to be sure to stay the proper distance away from her and hidden from view but still close enough to watch the game. He worked his way down the hill and through the trees on the opposite side of the outfield from where she sat.

After ten minutes of fighting his way through the dense forest, he emerged onto the nature trail. Walking on the finely ground mulch of the trail was easier and quieter than crashing through the woods but still hidden from the ball fields by the trees. The trail terminated near the Nature Center at the lower parking lot, but well before that, it crossed through the woods just beyond the left outfield fence. He would be able to veer off into the thicket of trees between the trail and ball field and find a quiet, hidden place to watch the game.

A young boy came skipping around the corner of the trail, laughing and licking an ice-cream cone. Steps behind him, a little girl clutched her dad's hand and sang some inane Disney song from yet another inane Disney movie. He nodded at the dad as they passed.

Hold on tight to them, Dad. They can slip away from you fast.

Rounding another bend, Nathan slowed his steps. The light from the open field filtered through the tree leaves. He could see the fence and painted lines. This wasn't as good as a seat closer to home base, but he would have a clear view of the game yet remain secluded from view. He slipped off the trail and found an old stump to serve as a seat, confident he was hidden.

A team of boys wearing blue T-shirts played defense. Their outfield was backing up in respect for the batter stepping out of the dugout. The closest defender was backed almost to the fence just beyond the tree line, mere yards from Nathan's hiding spot.

The batter walked to home plate, taking smooth practice swings. His jersey glowed in the sun. The lettering for Abe's Market was clear even from Nathan's vantage point, the red leaping from the crisp whiteness.

This early in the game, the boy hadn't yet streaked it with dirt and grass, but he would. He always did. He would dive for balls, roll in the grass, and pop the glove over his head, high in the air so that the umpire could see his catch. After a hit, he would slide for a base if the throw was close. His mother worked hard after each game to get that jersey clean.

Nathan's pride swelled as the boy held his hand out to keep the umpire from allowing the throw as he knocked the bat against his feet, loosening any caked-on dirt. He kicked his feet into the batter's box and dug in his cleats for grip, just like the pros he admired so much on television. Positioned and ready, he gripped the bat with both hands. The tip bounced over his shoulder.

Jacob was at bat.

WHEN HE WAS six years old, Jacob had begged to go to a soccer day camp at the park. He had played in an organized town league ever since. The tryout date for Middleton Middle School was already circled on the summer calendar.

Playing soccer in the autumns meant Jacob wouldn't follow in his dad's football footsteps, a decision that thrilled Donna since he would avoid the inevitable football injuries. As much as Nathan had loved the sport as a kid, he was quietly relieved too.

In the winter, Jacob and his buddies played basketball until they couldn't see the net in the dark. Sometimes, after a good game in the neighborhood, he would talk about trying out for the school team, but Nathan could never tell if he really wanted to or not.

But baseball was Jacob's passion. He and Nathan could spend hours in the backyard, tossing the ball back and forth in a nearly endless game of catch. Every spring, he'd played for the town Little League teams, starting with tee ball at four years old. This was his last Little League year, and the middle-school coaches were eager for him to join their team the next spring.

They didn't know he might be in Atlanta by summer and not playing for Millerton Middle. Of course, Jacob didn't know that yet either. He stood at the plate, not knowing that his world had already been shattered.

When he wasn't playing baseball, Jacob was watching it on TV. They traveled down to Asheville several times each season for games of the minor league Tourists, a Class-A farm team for the Colorado Rockies. Jacob always insisted on getting there early so he could watch the players warm up, and he had snatched quite a few autographs that way.

The past summer, Nathan had spent some of their hard-earned savings on a family weekend in Atlanta. Jacob was luke-warm about going, not wanting to be away from his friends, until he learned his dad had scored tickets to not one but two Braves games from a salesman visiting the plant. He still talked about that weekend and how awesome being in that huge stadium was.

In a few months, he would be living in that giant city. That security company probably even had access to tickets so that Hank could take him often. The mere thought of not being able to see Jacob's smile in those stands crushed Nathan.

The boy stood still for the first three pitches, challenging the pitcher to give him a good throw. The count stood at two balls and one strike, a good situation for a hitter. He bounced the tip of the bat in his hand, his knees bent and body ready to fly. The pitcher reared back and released a fastball low and to the center, a dangerous pitch against a strong hitter. Jacob didn't pass the gift up, his swing smooth and true. *Crack!* The ball rose high into the air as it raced for the far end of the field. The outfielder backed as far as he could, but he never stood a chance. The ball sailed far over the left-field fence and bounced into the woods not far from Nathan. He froze, hoping to remain hidden.

Two little kids raced after the ball, the winner getting to toss the ball back onto the field—the Little League budget wasn't big enough to allow the fans to keep errant balls. They were so focused on beating each other that they never noticed Nathan among the trees. One of them snagged the ball and ran to toss it to an umpire as Jacob jogged around the bases. He didn't gloat or brag, but the bounce in his step signified his elation.

The crowd, scattered among blankets and folding chairs on both sides of foul territory, cheered his success. Whoops and hollers of congratulations floated through the air, but one familiar whoop pierced through them all. Donna, despite her pain, cheered from the other side of the field while Matt whistled and Colette clapped.

The crowd quieted down as the boys' celebration ended and they trotted back to their dugout. Luke approached the plate for his at bat. He connected with his first swing but sent the ball into foul territory. Families dodged the ball as it bounced off one folding chair. A laughing dad caught it and tossed it back toward the umpires, high school baseball players who volunteered their Saturdays to be back on the field with the Little Leaguers.

The next pitch dropped and curved, forcing Luke to reach for it. He sent the ball high in the air, over the heads of the fans, deep into foul territory to Nathan's right. It bounced and rolled to the tree line.

A man stepped from under the shade of the trees lining the edge of the field, scooped up the ball, and tossed it back. "Way to go, Luke!" he shouted.

The voice chilled Nathan as he watched Hank walk back under the trees to a split-rail fence running along the edge of the field. Parallel to the third-base line, it separated the grass from the forest beyond. He leaned against the top rail and watched the game from behind his dark sunglasses. He still wore the brace protecting his broken nose.

Conflicting emotions coursed through Nathan as he stared at his former friend. Anger, disgust, and betrayal made him want to confront Hank, but the consequences of doing so were too steep. Any chance he had of a healthy relationship with Jacob depended on his actions. He hunkered down in the woods, determined to remain camouflaged, and seethed.

Another crack of the bat drew his attention back to the field. The ball arced high and dropped just behind the baseline between first and second, an easy pop fly for the second baseman to field. With a thwack of ball in glove, the inning was over.

As the teams switched sides, Nathan glanced toward his nemesis and continued to struggle with the rage inside himself. That man had once been a friend, someone he trusted. But he was taking his wife, his son, and his money. He was stealing every chance of happiness Nathan had. He squeezed his fists together and struggled to remain calm.

Salvation came in the form of Jacob trotting out to left field with his old glove in hand. The coach had rotated him through several positions, including pitching and shortstop, but today had him playing outfield. The variety was good for him at this age, learning the various positions. Unfortunately, that also put him only feet from where Nathan was hiding in the forest, much closer than the restraining order allowed.

Should I leave? Just slink away before anyone sees me? Better to stay put and not draw attention by moving from my cover. No one knows I'm here. Besides, all I'm doing is watching a game.

The defense tossed the baseball around while waiting for the batter to get ready. Jacob fielded the ball cleanly and fired it to the center fielder. His too-long hair stuck out from under the cap. His blue eyes glistened in the sun. His white teeth flashed as he smiled and joked with his teammates.

I can't walk away when he is so close.

The umpire called for the inning to start. Nathan smiled as he realized the ump was Carlos Estrella, the high school pitching star that had thrown to his son. The boy was volunteering to umpire a kid's game on a weekend day rather than goofing off like so many other teenagers—a good role model for Jacob to admire.

The first pitch sailed through the air and smacked into the catcher's glove. Strike one. A smattering of applause and shouts of encouragement came from the fans. Jacob popped his glove with his fist and rocked on his feet, chattering to his teammates in an endless string of encouragement.

The next pitch sailed past the batter. The umpire called

ball. The crowd groaned. Jacob stretched and settled back into position, ready for action.

The next pitch slammed into the catcher's glove with a pop. The umpire's voice carried across the field: "Striiike." The crowd applauded. Jacob shifted in the field, drifting closer behind the third baseman as he called out to the others on the field—a natural leader, confident in his skills.

Pitch. A crack of the bat. The ball streaked through the air just over the third baseman's stretched glove. A solid, hard, fast line drive to Jacob's right but within fair territory. If it got past him, the runner had an easy double.

Jacob sprinted and leapt into the air, stretching his body and reaching out with his left hand. He neatly wrapped the glove around the racing ball and tucked it against his body as he curled and rolled on the ground. He bounced to his feet and held the glove high, the ball visible as the crowd roared its approval.

Despite her injuries, Donna stood in front of her chair and whooped again in celebration. Colette was laughing with her while Matt cupped his hands and yelled encouragement. Nathan bit his tongue to keep from joining the celebration and revealing his presence.

As the cheers subsided and the crowd settled back to their seats, Hank's voice floated across the field. "Way to go, Jake."

Jacob looked a few yards to Nathan's right and smiled. "Thanks, Hank!"

21

F orgetting his need to remain hidden, Nathan stood and stared at Hank, who clapped his hands and cheered. The anger he had kept in check coursed through his body. The familiarity that his son and his enemy showed each other bothered him more than anything else.

But he needed to be rational. Of course they knew each other. With all the sleepovers and after-school time and doing homework and playing sports, Jacob would know anyone at Luke's house. While Nathan hadn't realized how often Hank was coming to town, he wasn't surprised that he was there sometimes when the boys were.

Yet the little exchange, the friendliness of it, grated on him.

As he fought to get his emotions under control, Nathan failed to react as Hank turned around to head back to his place along the fence. Hank's eyes narrowed as he spied him standing among the trees.

They stood glaring at each other for a minute before Hank jerked his head toward the nature trail, beckoning Nathan to join him. They could talk out of sight of the game and of Donna if she happened to look across the field. Still, Nathan was wary of any confrontation as he edged his way cautiously through the woods. He emerged onto the nature trail and approached Hank but stopped several feet away, out of reach.

Hank glared at him and asked through clenched teeth, "What are you doing here, Nate?"

"I just wanted to see Jacob play baseball."

"You can't be here. We have a restraining order."

"I can't be within a hundred feet. Donna's on the other side of the field, so I came over here to be far enough away."

Hank glanced out to Jacob's back. "Jake's closer than a hundred feet."

"I didn't know that when I sat down. I had no idea he would be playing left field. When I saw, I started to leave, but I knew he couldn't see me. I didn't try to talk to him at all."

"Doesn't matter, Nate. You're too close. I could have you so busted for this."

Nathan waved his arm toward Jacob and opened his mouth to protest but then cocked his head. He watched Donna sitting on the far side of the field, laughing with Matt and Colette. "Wait a minute. Why are you over here? Shouldn't you and Donna be celebrating your big lottery win?"

Hank looked startled. "Where did you hear about that?"

"Sammy's. Chet Everswood said Matt told him."

Hank sighed and shook his head. "I shouldn't have told Matty but didn't think he would go blabbing it around town."

"Did you tell him you stole my ticket?"

Hank's eyes widened, and he busted out laughing. "Is that going to be your game? First thing from every one of you is how you want your hands on my winnings. Matty just assumes Luke's college is paid for and he didn't have to worry about it anymore. Donna balked at a prenup and got all pissy with me. And now you come along with a crazy story about a stolen ticket. Bunch of Millerton leeches."

"It's my ticket, and you know it."

Hank threw his arms up in the air. "Good luck with that one. Hire a lawyer and sue me. The guy will tell you lottery tickets belong to whoever has them. The ticket is in my hands, so you can't prove a thing. Just get over it."

Nathan shook with rage. "Get over it? You steal *my* wife, kick me out of *my* house, try to move *my* son to Atlanta, and now you steal *my* lottery ticket—and I'm just supposed to get over it?"

A few people along the fence glanced over their shoulders at the two men arguing.

Hank rolled his eyes and turned to walk away. "Nate, I'm done. You're within a hundred feet of Jake, so you're breaking the restraining order. Go away, or I'll call the cops right now."

Nathan glared at his back as he marched toward the fence and shouted, "My name is Nathan, not Nate! And my son's name is Jacob, not Jake!"

Hank stopped and turned around slowly, a perplexed look on his face. He paused for a moment before a smile crept across his face. He returned to Nathan and leaned in close. "Okay, *Nathan*. I'll call him *Jacob*. But I got big news for you. He ain't your kid."

STARTLED, Nathan stepped backward. He tried to read Hank's face to understand what he had just said, but the protective mask for his broken nose and dark sunglasses covering his eyes made that impossible. He asked in a shaking voice, "What do you mean he's not my kid?"

Hank smiled and straightened himself to full height. "I'm telling you I'm Jacob's father."

"Just because you marry Donna doesn't mean you're his father. That makes you a stepfather."

Hank's grin broadened. "I'm his father because I'm the one who got Donna pregnant."

Nathan held his breath as his brain buzzed in confusion. "What? No, that's impossible. You couldn't be Jacob's father unless…" Numbness spread from his chest through his body. His vision narrowed and focused on Hank. The sounds from the park disappeared into a hum of background noise. "You slept with Donna in high school? While she dated me?"

The smile broadened across Hank's smug face. "Yep."

Nathan shook his head, trying to focus his mind. His body felt as if he was submerged in quicksand. "When? I was with you every day at football practice and with her every evening doing homework."

"At night after you had to be home because of Ronnie and his stupid curfews. She and her mom were always fighting about stuff, and she would leave her house, but she couldn't go to you because you were scared to get Ronnie mad. Worried social workers would find out and stick you in some foster home or orphanage or something. But my mom worked third shift, so she could come hang out all night. At first, we just talked. I would hold her as she cried. But after a while, it became more."

Nathan tried to fight off the feelings of loss overwhelming him. "The house wasn't empty. Matt was there. How did you keep it from him?"

"We didn't. Matty knew. He always knew. Go ahead. Go ask him. He almost told you the night of the accident."

Nathan thought back to the banter when they were sitting in the car after the game, Matt threatening to expose his brother and Hank warning him not to. "He threatened to tell who you were sleeping with. We all thought how weird for you to hide that. You always bragged about girls you were with." He scrunched his face, trying to think through the overflow of information. "Why would he keep your secret?

Not like you two didn't fight every other day over something."

"Blackmail is a funny thing. It works both ways. Donna wasn't the only girl sneaking into our house at night. Colette came over as often as she could. Matty didn't want Danny knowing that his little sister was spending the night. So if he told what I was doing, I would break open *his* little secret."

Nathan slumped against a tree beside the trail. "So Matt is in his room getting his girlfriend pregnant, and you're in your room getting my girlfriend pregnant. Did you two idiots not pay attention in sex ed?" His mind raced, struggling to comprehend everything. "But why sneak around? If she wanted to be with you, why didn't she just break up with me?"

"Our stupid code. The Fearsome Foursome never stole each other's girlfriends."

"Not that it ever stopped you before."

Hank shrugged and grinned. "I wasn't worried about it, but she was. She didn't want you to get mad at me during the season and screw up our team. We had games to win."

Nathan shook his head slowly in disbelief. "She didn't want to break up because she thought it would affect football? We weren't even that good."

"Hey, a cheerleader has to think of those things." He chuckled before continuing, "I got her convinced to tell you right after the Roosevelt game. Season would be over, and it wouldn't matter anymore. But then she found out earlier that week that she was pregnant. Didn't see that coming, but it still would have worked out except the accident happened. I kept trying to get her to tell you, but she didn't want to do that to you while you were in the hospital for weeks and going through all that physical therapy."

"How thoughtful."

"Think whatever you want, but it really was thoughtful. She felt horrible with everything going on. The problem was that she started showing, and people started figuring out she was pregnant. What was she going to do then? So she told everyone the baby was yours. So I thought, *Screw her—plenty of other girls out there.* I left for the Marines after graduation. Put her out of my mind until I ran into her last fall."

Nathan puzzled through what he had heard. "Even if what you're saying is true—"

"Ask her. Ask Matty."

"Not that. I believe that you two were screwing around behind my back. Wasn't the first time you went after a girl I was dating." He waved it off. "What I meant was she told everyone Jacob was mine. And we were sleeping together, so why couldn't he be my son?"

"I thought the same thing. Wondered sometimes but figured she knew somehow. Then I got proof he was mine."

"How?"

"You know those genealogy DNA kits you can buy on the internet?"

"Yeah, so?"

"I took one years ago. Lady I was dating at the time was all into researching family trees and was curious about mine. I thought I knew all about our family, but the test revealed a surprise. I'm part Russian."

"Big deal. What does that have to do with Jacob?"

"Like every old-time family in Millerton, our ancestors were Scotch-Irish. They all came over here in the 1700s and started farming. Your family is probably like that. Donna's is, Danny's, everyone except for people who have moved here recently, and there ain't too many of them. The whole Appalachian mountains are like that, settled by Scotch-Irish. Except I'm not. I'm half Russian. That meant my dad was Russian."

"That's nonsense. Your dad's from here, and he ain't Russian."

"Well, see, that was the surprise. Matty's dad is from here. Turns out we're half brothers. His dad is my stepdad. Apparently, my mother had her own secrets. Guess it runs in the family. But it does explain why Matty is wiry and fast and I'm big and slow." Hank stuck his hands in his pockets. "I confronted Mom with the test results. She confessed that my dad was a sailor in the Navy, some guy she dated for a while—an American citizen, but a Russian by birth."

Dread crept through Nathan as he grasped for straws to disprove the story. "How does a Navy sailor come to Millerton?"

"When she was young, she took off for Charleston just to live somewhere other than here. She had a secretarial job at the shipyard and met this hunky sailor. They had fun, but they both knew the relationship wasn't really that serious. After he took off on his next tour, she found out she was pregnant. Surprise. She came back here to have me and started dating Matt's dad. Everyone assumed he was father to both of us. Including me. He sure acted like my dad, even ran off without saying goodbye, just like my real dad. No one would have ever told me different if I hadn't taken that stupid test."

Nathan really didn't want to ask the question, but the need to know was impossible to ignore. "What does this have to do with Jacob?"

"Donna saw the ads for these tests and told me about an old family rumor that she had some Cherokee in her. I saw my chance, so I got Donna one of those test kits for Christmas. I couldn't give her jewelry or anything you would notice, right?"

"She got me one of those for Christmas too." Nathan's mouth gaped open as Hank's eyebrow shot up. "I'm such an idiot. She got it to cover that you had bought her one too."

"Actually, *I* got it for you. Guess you owe me a Christmas present." He waved Nathan's objection away with a flip of his hand. "Partially, I got you one for cover. At least, that's what I told Donna. But, really, I needed to know your background. Another piece of the puzzle. You remember your results?"

"Mostly Scotch-Irish and some from Britain. Donna's was pretty much the same. No Cherokee. She was disappointed." He dismissed the talk, motioning to move the conversation along. "But doesn't matter because we don't know what Jacob is."

"Yeah, we do."

Nathan legs went weak, and his knees nearly buckled. "He never took the test. He would have told me."

"He didn't know. I got Jacob and Luke into a spitting contest one day over at Matt's house. Convinced Jacob to spit into the little test tube. He thought it was funny."

"You tricked our son into taking a DNA test?" Anger flared briefly but was quickly replaced by an aching fear as his stomach roiled. "And you're saying he's a fourth Russian?"

"You got it."

"That still proves nothing."

"Well, since we know Donna's heritage and that she's the mom, it proves that his dad is half Russian. Someone like me. And not someone like you."

A cheer erupted from the crowd, drawing their attention through the trees to the game. The fight drained out of Nathan, replaced by a sinking feeling of despair. This crazy story couldn't be true. "So you plan to prove that you're his father?"

Hank turned back to him with a slight smile on his lips. "Nope. Provided you make things easy on Donna, I'll leave it alone."

"Meaning what?"

"Don't contest the divorce. Don't fight over custody."

"What do I get?"

"Visitation. A weekend a month. A week in the summer.

And the boy never knows the truth. See how nice a guy I can be?"

Nathan's mouth gaped open as his body tensed. "That's not enough time with him. I'd have to fight that."

"No, you won't. Because then you'll force me to prove he's my son."

"No court will accept a stupid genealogy test bought off the internet as proof."

"Maybe not, but they will accept a paternity test."

"I won't take one. You can't make me."

A smile spread across Hank's face. "You don't get it. I don't need you to take one. I'll take it. And it will prove I'm the father."

Desperation flared. "I won't let Jacob take it."

The smile spread further, and Hank's blue eyes grew icy cold. "You won't have a say. Donna will get temporary custody for sure, thanks to your stunt yesterday. And she'll authorize it. No court would agree to not find out the truth anyway. Face it —you can't stop it. Once those test results are back, it's over. Done. You're out. No claim to him at all."

"No. No way. I raised him. You didn't do anything all those years."

"No one told me I was the father. As soon as the test proves I am, then I have rights. And you won't."

"But I raised him. The court has to see that."

Hank poked a finger in Nathan's chest, jabbing between his ribs. "All the court will see is a guy convicted of assault and domestic violence, who can't even pay attention to a restraining order. Caught sneaking up near his wife and the boy—my boy —during a peaceful day at the park and hiding in the woods. One call from me, and they'll know you're a danger to him. And then, while you sit in a jail cell, I'll prove you're not even a blood relative. You'll be nothing."

"I thought you weren't going to press charges."

"Donna doesn't want to. But I will. Unless, of course, you agree to Donna having full custody. And her moving to Atlanta with Jacob. If you agree to that, the boy never has to know that his father isn't his father. It'll be our little secret."

"And what prevents you from just waiting and taking the paternity test later?"

"Nothing. You just have to trust me."

"Trust you?" Nathan felt the anger rising in him again. "How can I trust you?"

"Because you have no choice." Hank pulled out his cell phone and started dialing. "Agree right now, or I call the police and tell them you're violating the restraining order. The cops will arrest you right here, in front of your kid." He grinned. "I mean my kid."

"Stop. Please don't call."

Hank pressed his thumb against a button to cancel the call and held the phone high in the air. "Then we have a deal?"

Panic crept through Nathan's quivering body as he struggled with the best answer. He could accept a deal that felt patently unfair and was based on details he had never known but at least gave him an option to remain in Jacob's life, or he could choose to fight and risk losing the boy who was the focus of his life.

He wanted to get away, to have time to think, but Hank was forcing him into a corner. Distraction came via the sound of footsteps in the woods, interrupting them. He turned to see Donna coming toward them.

She waved at the two of them and asked, "What are you doing?"

Seeing his estranged wife approach, his panic exploded. She could back up Hank's story to the police, and Jacob would see him led away in handcuffs. The whole town would.

Nathan backed up the nature trail. "I'm leaving, I swear."

She cocked her head and looked at him. "Why are you two back here in the woods?"

"I'm sorry. I wasn't trying to violate the restraining order. I just wanted to see Jacob's game." He waved his hands at the two of them. "Finding out about you two, getting arrested, having my lottery ticket stolen… and now I don't even have a son. It's just too much." He turned and ran up the nature trail, leaving Hank and Donna to watch him disappear.

22

Nathan ran as hard as he could up the nature trail, fear and anger powering his strides. His work boots pounded the ground. He raced past a young woman on the trail, fear etched on her face as she grabbed her daughter and pulled her to safety, away from the crazy man.

At the point the trail looped and started heading back downhill, he plunged into the woods toward the Point and scrambled over fallen trees and hidden rocks. Branches slapped his face as he stumbled through the dense forest. The thorns of a blackberry bush raked the exposed skin of his arm, digging deep and drawing blood.

His foot sank deep in a hole covered by a thick layer of leaves, which twisted his ankle and threw him forward. To break his fall, he grabbed a tree trunk, the rough bark scraping his palm. Wincing in pain, he extracted his foot and shook off the dirt.

Slowing his breathing and fighting to gain control of his emotions, he pushed aside a branch to continue his march. A startled bird flitted away, squawking its displeasure at the interruption. Ignoring its protests, he scrambled up the slope. When the grade became too steep, he dropped to his hands and knees and crawled.

Finally, he broke through the last of the trees to the clearing. His legs burning from the exertion, he stumbled toward his truck and leaned on the hood, panting to catch his breath. Sweat dripped down his face as he turned and looked over the park below.

The ballgame continued, the boys blissfully unaware of the chaos around them. Donna walked swiftly back to Matt and Colette, who were standing to meet her. She had her arms wrapped around her chest as Hank, a few steps behind her, waved his arms in an animated conversation.

Are they calling the police? Am I going back to jail? Have I screwed my last chance to be with my son?

But Jacob isn't my son. Hank didn't even leave me that.

No police car was entering the parking lot, but Nathan wasn't going to wait for one to arrive. He pushed off the truck and stumbled to the driver's door. As he climbed inside, he dropped the keys to the floor. Cursing, he picked them up, fumbled through the ring until he found the right one, and jabbed it into the ignition. He pumped the gas and turned the key. The engine sputtered and died. He tried again before it roared to life.

Throwing the truck into gear, he stomped on the accelerator. Dirt sprayed from behind his spinning tires as he circled the vehicle through the clearing and drove into the darkness of the forest. The truck bounced and rattled as he pushed it faster and faster, branches slapping against his windshield.

He marveled how everything had fallen apart so fast. Jacob had sat right beside him in this truck just the morning before, back when they both thought the worst thing possible was to have a birds-and-bees talk. Now, he might never get to have a father-son moment ever again.

The sharp curve at the creek came into view. The scarred

boulder loomed just beyond the turn. The turn Danny hadn't slowed down for that cost so much. If he wrecked now, no one would even know he was here. He might lie in the mud for hours before some hapless teenager headed to the Point stumbled across his body trapped in the wreckage.

Maybe he would be thrown through the windshield and land in the creek, gasping in the water as Charlie had done—a fitting end as the cold mountain water filled his lungs.

Jacob's face flashed through his mind. Lost. Alone. His father ripped away from him. Nathan knew that pain too.

He slammed on the brakes, and the truck skidded across the ruts and shuddered to a stop, the engine stalling in protest. He slumped his head against the steering wheel and let the tears flow as frustration overwhelmed him.

The fleeting thought of ending everything scared him to the core. He knew loss, more than maybe most people his age —tragedy, anguish—but he had never given up, never even toyed with the idea.

This was not going to be the first time.

He sucked in deep breaths to clear his mind. He leaned back against the seat and closed his eyes until his body stopped shaking. He listened as the water splashed, flowing down the stream. A gentle breeze rustled the treetops. Birds whistled their tunes as they protected their nests and fed their hatchlings.

Nathan paced his breathing to match the serenity of nature around him and opened his eyes. He watched a squirrel dart across the forest floor, scamper up a tree, and disappear into a hole in the trunk. He imagined a nest of baby squirrels tucked in the warmth and safety.

A deer stepped cautiously into the clearing. She sniffed the air and turned her head, searching for threats. She gingerly stepped to the edge of the bank, lowered her snout, and lapped fresh water. A spotted fawn stumbled after her, its legs unsure.

The doe turned and nuzzled the youngster, pushing it back into the brush for protection. The baby was supposed to stay hidden, safe to grow until it was strong enough and old enough to take care of itself.

Nathan watched without moving, not wanting to spook them. After they had disappeared, he listened to the symphony of the forest and smiled as a calmness settled over him.

He reached for his cell phone and dialed. Danny sensed trouble and asked right away if everything was okay.

"I ran into Hank and Donna at the ballgame."

"Thought you were going to watch from the Point."

"I got closer so I could see better. Hid in the woods."

"Not well enough, I'm guessing."

"No," Nathan admitted. "I think they're going to report me for violating the restraining order."

"I was afraid of that. What happened?"

"Nothing. I swear. I left the second Donna walked up. But before she came over, Hank told me some stuff. Some crazy stuff. Listen…" He relayed the conversation, the revelation of the high school affair, the shock of the genetic test, and the reality of Jacob's parentage. Once he finished the story, he sat quietly, phone to his ear, waiting for Danny to absorb it all.

"So now what?" Danny asked.

"I'm not ready to give up. I almost did… for a second." He shuddered as he gazed at the boulder in front of his bumper. "As crazy as it sounds, I want to fight for Jacob and for what's right for him. He needs me in his life. There has to be a way that's fair for Donna that's also good for him."

Though he expected Danny to explain why it wouldn't work, he instead replied, "Then let's figure it out. Come to the trailer, and I'll make dinner when I get home."

"I better not. If they call the cops, we'll have good ol' Officer Carrington knocking at the door again."

"You can't run from that."

"I'm not running. I'm just delaying. They'll keep me there until Monday morning no matter when they find me, so no reason to start that any earlier than I have to."

"Fair enough. Where do you want to meet?"

"At the Point?"

"It's Saturday. High school kids will start showing up there soon. We're a little old for that."

Nathan stared into the forest as he thought. "What about Jared Hampton's old place? It's abandoned, and no one would have any reason to think I would be there."

"Better than the trailer. I haven't seen it in years. I'll get dinner and meet you out there as soon as I finish up here."

"You still at Sammy's?"

"No, I'm..." Danny paused. "I'll explain when I see you. Give me a little time. I'll be there by five."

23

A t the end of the fire road, Nathan turned away from town and drove his truck up the curvy road deeper into the mountains. Within a few miles, an old crumbling rock wall appeared on the left and outlined an overgrown drive diverging through the woods. He inched through brush as tall as the hood of his truck as he navigated through the trees of the dense forest, praying that no trees had fallen across the road and no giant rocks were hidden from view.

After several hundred yards, the trees abruptly yielded to an open, rolling field. The mountains were dotted with farms carved into the hillsides by the settlers in the 1700s. The Hampton farm was one of the oldest in the Millerton region, passed from generation to generation, and belonged to Jared Hampton, an old classmate. As children, they had played together in these fields, hiding in the rows of tall summer corn.

When they were in the eighth grade, Jared's father suffered a massive heart attack and died among the rows of plants. His son found him when he came home from school and headed out to the fields for his daily chores.

Knowing the pressure of keeping a family farm going, many expected the boy to drop out of school, as so many sons of farmers had through the ages. But Jared already knew enough about the struggles of earning a living growing crops and managing a small herd of cattle, so he had other plans. Or maybe he'd never intended to take over the farm even if his father had lived.

He doubled down on his studies, worked on homework long after the sun set and his chores were done, and earned a scholarship to college. Like many children of Millerton, he left to find a life away from farming and manufacturing.

Today, he lived in Charlotte, Atlanta, or Nashville—Nathan couldn't remember which since they were all just big cities with traffic and crime—doing some job that required a tie around his neck. Nathan couldn't fathom how that was better than calluses on your hands and being at the mercy of the weather, but Jared must have thought so because he rarely returned to Millerton.

The last return trip was a decade before, after the old family home was struck by lightning and burned to the ground. The land had been for sale off and on over the years, with a faded sheet of plywood giving a phone number posted by the main road, but no buyers saw value. The farm was just another large tract of land, too far from town on a remote road to build manufacturing, too little demand for housing, and not high enough in the mountains to attract the millionaires to build their monstrous second homes.

Nathan maneuvered his truck past the stone foundation of the old farmhouse. The fireplace's stonework rose over the charred wood like a headstone marking a grave.

He parked in front of a large wooden barn, its paint long faded from decades in the sun and wind, and admired the scenery. Acres of overgrown grasses and weeds swayed in the breeze, the scent of wildflowers wafting through the air. Silence descended as he killed the motor, only the ticking of the hot engine in his ears.

Sitting in the truck, absorbing the warm afternoon sunshine, he found his mind drifting back to pleasant memories of his own childhood. He surprised himself when he realized he was speaking out loud. "Dad. I need some help here."

He felt his father's arms wrap around his shoulders and sensed his ears attuned to his words. A calmness descended over him. "I can handle a lot. You've taught me that. But this… it's too much. I don't know how you handled everything so well.

"I remember that day you picked me up from school and told me about getting laid off from the plant. A man's first responsibility, you said, was to his family, so you were going to drive that semi and be gone for days at a time. To give me what I needed, you had to leave me for long stretches. I was confused we had to be separated so you could take care of me. I wanted to ride in the truck with you so we could be together, but you said it didn't work that way."

He stared out the window and watched clouds drift across the peaceful skies. "You said I would be okay while you were gone because Ronnie would look out for me. He would treat me just like he did Charlie. And he did. Made me do chores and my homework. Listened to me and gave me advice.

"I don't think you imagined never coming home, but Ronnie took me in without question after your wreck. Living with him wasn't the same as having you around, but it was the next best thing. He wasn't my father—he'd never replace you and never tried to—but it felt like I still had a dad."

A hawk sailed across the sky, gliding in the wind drafts, effortlessly floating. "So does that mean to take care of Jacob, I need to be away from him? Would he be better off in Atlanta?

Have more opportunities? Make a better life? Am I being selfish trying to keep him here with me?"

He sighed and gripped the steering wheel. "But is Hank a good man? Can I trust him? Do I even have a choice if he's Jacob's father?"

The hawk dove toward the ground and disappeared into the grasses. A second later, she reappeared, wings flapping hard as her talons gripped a field mouse. She flew toward the trees, taking her meal with her.

"You never stopped trying for me, did you? Sure, we were separated, but you came home over and over. You didn't abandon me. You were taken from me." He paused and looked around. "Maybe I'm like Ronnie—not his dad by blood but his dad in every other way."

Nathan nodded, understanding flowing through him. "So that's what I have to do, isn't it? Never quit trying for Jacob. Whether he is my child or not, I'm responsible for making sure that the best thing possible for him happens, whatever that is."

He felt exhaustion settle over him. The last two days had been filled with conflict, trauma, and grief. He needed to take advantage of the peace and quiet of the farm to focus his mind. And nothing was like soaking up the spring sunshine to help a person relax.

He stepped out of the truck, stretched, and walked into the barn. Empty stalls covered one side, a wooden feed bin on the exterior wall. Old tractor implements sat abandoned in the rear, the tractor and more valuable parts long ago sold or stolen. Initials were carved in the leaning support beams. The smell of rotting hay drifted through the air.

He gathered the cleanest of the straw from deep in the shadows of the barn and spread it across the bed of his pickup truck. Satisfied with its inviting comfort, he stretched out on top of it. He closed his eyes and felt the warmth of the sun hitting his body. Slowing his racing thoughts, he organized his mountain of troubles, intending to focus on them one at a time. But within minutes, his eyes grew heavy, and he drifted to sleep.

24

Nathan woke with a start, swatting away a fly buzzing around his face. The sky outside had morphed into a deep purple of dusk. Darkness cloaked the corners of the barn. He spied an owl perched high in the shadows of a rafter, eyeing the unwelcome intruder to the abandoned barn.

Deep in the woods beyond the field, tires crunched on gravel, announcing an approaching vehicle. Nathan sat up, stretched, and yawned as the headlights bounced off the trees lining the narrow driveway. Danny's van emerged from the woods and passed the old house on its trek across the field. He parked beside Nathan's truck and extinguished his lights, dropping the barn back into shadows.

The side door of the van opened, and the wheelchair descended on the lift. Danny reached back inside and lifted a heavy box, settling it into his lap. The smell of fried chicken floated through the air, making Nathan's mouth water.

Together, they unpacked the box onto the open tailgate of the truck, a makeshift picnic table for their buffet. Potato salad, slaw, green beans, and a large jug of iced tea joined the chicken in the tantalizing spread of food.

Nathan realized how little he had eaten since the breakfast early that morning. A few nachos at Sammy's had done little to satisfy his hunger. He searched the barn for a seat before emerging with an old milking stool and settling down beside Danny's wheelchair. "Did you make all this?"

Danny shook his head and slid a loaded plate in front of his friend. "All my mom's home cooking here."

Nathan lifted a piece of chicken and inhaled deeply. "You asked your mom to make us dinner?"

"Nope. She offered as soon as she found out I was coming here to meet you."

He bit into the chicken, savoring the juices as he watched Danny's face. "How did she know?"

"Because I was talking to her when you called."

"You were at the store?" Nathan cocked his head and chewed the food. "What brought that on? You almost never go there."

Danny sighed and looked across the darkening field. "She called me just as I was going back into Sammy's. Asked how our lunch was—which meant she knew we were having lunch, so I figured you'd stopped by there earlier today. Seems the two of you did some talking about me."

Nathan grinned sheepishly. "I should have mentioned it, and I didn't tell her about our conversation this morning. But we did talk about the store and you."

"It's cool. I'm glad you did." Danny set a chicken leg down on his plate and wiped his fingers with a napkin. "I know they've been ashamed of me, so it's hard to go over there."

"Ashamed? Come on…"

Danny raised his hand to stop him. "It's okay. I don't blame them. I've been ashamed of myself. And I don't mean just the accident. Yeah, sure, that was it at first, but then it's what I did *after* the accident. I didn't want to be seen around town, knowing that everyone knew what I had done. And looking at me in this chair. So I just gave up."

"Danny…"

"It's true. I gave up. I sat in that stupid trailer every day, drank beer, and watched TV. I quit life. Stayed away from the store and everyone else. And the longer I stayed away, the harder it became to go back."

"You didn't stay away from me."

"You've got that backwards. You kept coming by and calling. Would hang out in the trailer and watch TV. Fixed up that van for me and taught me how to drive it with the hand controls. Convinced me to go to Sammy's and have a beer rather than hide in the trailer."

"Come on. That's what friends do. Nothing special."

"But that's the thing. It is special. It means everything to me. And it made me want to start living again." Danny leaned back in his chair and smiled. "So I was thinking about what you said as you left Sammy's, about not being sure if you had any fight left. And I realized what an utter lie that is. You've been knocked around more than anyone I know. And yet, every single time, you just get back up and start fighting."

Nathan shrugged. "What else can you do? That's life."

"That's my point. Some of us just quit, but you don't. Just took me a little longer than you, but I decided I'm tired of being a loser."

"You're not a loser."

"You're right. Not anymore. I'm ready to stop being a loser. And the fastest way back is to go back to work in the store. After all these years of avoiding it. That's what I need to do. I was trying to figure out how to tell my parents when you forged the path for me."

"They'd love to have you there."

"I know that now, thanks to you. Mom called and asked me to return. I said yes. I start Monday."

, Nathan couldn't help himself. He jumped to his feet and wrapped his friend in a bear hug. "That's awesome!"

Danny untangled himself from Nathan's arms and laughed. "Glad you feel that way because I'm going back to the store—with or without you. But I'm hoping it's with you. We need that garage open."

As DARKNESS CONTINUED TO GATHER, they ate and chatted about Danny's plans for the store and, mostly, the deli. They talked about ways to expand seating and reconfigure the kitchen area by knocking down the side wall and adding some additional room.

Once they were both full and picking at the remains, Danny reached into the box and pulled out a homemade strawberry pie. The early spring berries had been picked from Abe's garden just that morning and converted to dessert by Martha. As he cut generous slices, he grew serious. "While I was at the store, I asked if Hank had come into the store and bought lottery tickets. Since we know that's where the winning ticket was sold, if he didn't buy them there, then we would know he stole yours."

"Please tell me he wasn't there."

"Sorry. Dad said he came in around nine thirty Friday morning and plunked a twenty-dollar bill down. Spent it all on the lottery."

Nathan swatted away a fly. "So maybe he did buy tickets, but it doesn't prove mine wasn't the winner."

"True. All it proves is that he *might* have bought the winner, but it *is* a possibility." Danny licked strawberry juice off his fingers. "But I'm wondering something else too. You said you told Donna about Hal's job offer yesterday morning."

"Yeah, she didn't like that very much."

"But why not?"

Nathan held up his hand and counted off the three reasons. "First, she said fixing broken down trucks on the side of the interstate was too dangerous. And second, that it would cause me to miss Jacob's ballgames. And finally, she wanted to get her old job back at McDonald's and would be working nights and weekends. She needed me to take care of him."

"That's what confuses me." Danny popped another bite of pie into his mouth and chewed. After swallowing, he asked, "Why would she worry about you missing his ballgames? And why try to get her old job back? Why would any of that matter if she was planning to move to Atlanta?"

Nathan scrunched his face as he traced his finger along the edge of the tailgate. "I don't know. She was already seeing Hank, so she must have been thinking about moving."

"Maybe thinking about it, sure, but not like she had a time-line planned out. The only thing that makes sense to me is she wasn't really planning for Atlanta Friday morning."

"You're saying my catching them made that happen? Or that him winning the lottery did that?"

"Not winning the lottery. When he told me about Atlanta, that was before he knew about the money, remember? So maybe catching them started everything. But she still had to realize everything was going to come out sooner or later."

"They were planning it because they had already talked to a divorce attorney."

"Yeah, but that's weird too. Why would Hank go with her for that? That's pretty ballsy, taking your lover to meet your divorce attorney."

Nathan flinched at the use of the word *lover*. "Well, Hank's always been ballsy."

"Exactly, that's my point." Danny saw Nathan's quizzical look and smiled faintly. "Hank, yes, but Donna? She has never been the one to push things like that. As you said, she didn't want to break up with you in high school because she didn't want to hurt you. She says she always wanted to leave Millerton, but she never did. She didn't tell you for months that she was seeing Hank again. And she met with a divorce attorney and never told you. So why is she suddenly willing to make all these changes, hurt you, and tear Jacob away from here?"

"Because she's mad I caught them?"

Danny shook his head. "But that's not the way she acted when I talked to her this morning. She's *embarrassed* you caught them, not angry about it. And, yeah, I think it's a relief, too, because it forces her to make the changes she wants, but that's very different than just leaving and never looking back."

Nathan pushed pie crumbs around his paper plate with the fork. "So you think Hank is driving everything? He's pushing her to move to Atlanta?"

"Yeah, I do."

"Because he wants Donna so much? And Jacob?"

Danny leaned back in his chair and stared at the sky. "That's the part I really struggle with. He stayed away for a dozen years. Never tried to get in touch. Never tried to claim Jacob. But suddenly, he is trying to take them both away."

"He didn't know until he took that DNA test."

"And how long ago?"

"I don't know. He didn't say."

"But he said he discussed it with his mother, right?"

Nathan's head shot up, and he snapped his fingers. "She died five years ago."

"Exactly. So that wasn't the spark."

Nathan slumped on the stool. "Of course not. He didn't make the connection until he saw Donna over at Matt's house."

"Come on. A girl in high school you're sleeping with gets pregnant but marries someone else. You don't wonder if the kid is yours again until you see her years later?"

Nathan nodded and chewed his lip. "Maybe he meets Jacob, gets to know what a great kid he is, and that starts bugging him. He figures out that his weird genetic result could be a way to find out. And once he finds out, now he starts thinking of Jacob as his son."

"Yeah, maybe. I thought about that. But it doesn't make sense to me that he just recently met Jacob since he and Luke have been best friends since they were in diapers. So in all those years, especially the years after Hank knew his unique ancestory, he never wondered. He only tested once he started seeing Donna again."

Nathan sat in silence before looking up. "So he falls for Donna and then starts wondering about Jacob. There isn't any other reason unless you think he's trying to hurt me."

"I've thought this through all day long, and that's exactly what I'm wondering."

Nathan froze on the stool and held his breath. When he spoke, his voice was tense. "But why? What did I ever do to him?"

"He's always been jealous of you." Danny laughed and waved his arm. "He was jealous of all of us."

"Jealous? Of what? We were all a bunch of dirt-poor kids. What did any of us have that he didn't?"

Danny paused and let the quiet of the night settle around them before speaking softly. "We were a foursome, but really, we were two pairs of best friends. You and Charlie were thick as thieves, and Hank and I ran together. He was different when you guys were around, but when we were alone, I heard all his rants. His dad—I guess he was Matt's dad and his stepdad though Hank didn't know that then—left when they were little, but our dads were around. His mom had to work nights and was never home, but we didn't go home to empty houses. And even Matt, who lived in the same house, was way better in football. The way he saw it, everyone led better lives."

"It's not like the rest of us were living perfect lives. We were all missing things."

"Hank could only see what others had that he didn't. He was always ragging me that I had it made. Both my parents were around. I could take over my dad's store when I got out of school. Life was set. When I tried to point out I had to work weekends and after school whether I wanted to or not, he would wave it off."

"That's crazy." Nathan continued, "And your parents may have been around, but neither Charlie or I had our moms around."

"But Charlie was great at school. Was going to college. His dad's job was steady."

"Jesus." Nathan squeezed his hands together. "What delusions did he come up with about me?"

Danny interlaced his fingers and stretched as he exhaled. "He was more jealous of you than anyone."

"For what? My dad raised me alone. I didn't have a store to go run. And I wasn't a genius in school. And then my dad died. Who thinks an orphan is better off?"

"That's just it. Everyone always rallied around you."

Nathan's mouth dropped open. "He's jealous because of my bad luck?"

"Your mom dies. What happens? Nora acts as mom to you and Charlie. Your dad loses his job, and Ronnie steps in with a place for you to stay so your dad can drive the truck. And when your dad died, he gives you a permanent home rather than let the state ship you off to a foster home or an orphanage. And in Hank's mind, you did have a store to go to after school. Two of them. Ronnie wanted you to work for him at the plant, and I always talked about you working in the shop when I got back from the Marines."

Nathan could only slowly shake his head. "That is so warped."

"Yeah, very warped." Danny stared out at the dark trees beyond the field before continuing softly. "The thing he really hated about you? You always had a girlfriend."

"Oh, come on, he had way more girlfriends than I ever did."

Danny smiled sadly. "No, he had way more girls but not a lot of girlfriends. You would date the same girl for months. Do homework together. Go to the movies. Just hang out."

"That is total insanity."

"It's the way he thought back then." Danny rubbed his hands across his face. "And I'm wondering if maybe it's the way he still thinks."

"What can he be jealous of now? He's down in Atlanta with this great job, making lots of money, and driving a brand-new car. I'm covered in grease every day and driving my dad's old pickup."

"Think like him. You have to look at what you have he doesn't." Danny held up fingers as he counted off reasons. "You're in your hometown surrounded by people who care for you and, until he appeared, a wife and kid. You're doing exactly what you always said you wanted to do—fix things. You didn't want to go to college or be in the military or even leave Millerton. You wanted to work with your hands."

"So what? Hank did what he wanted too."

Danny smiled. "Exactly. Did. Past tense. He wanted to be a Marine. That's all he ever wanted to be. Sure, he got to do that for a few years, but now what? He drives rich jerks around and escorts them in and out of buildings. That can't come close to being a big, bad Marine. He's had a string of girls but no real relationships I know of. And he sure isn't raising a family."

Nathan felt a weight settle in his stomach. "You think he did all this on purpose?"

"On purpose?" Danny swirled the plastic cup of tea, the ice plunking against the sides. "No, I don't think he ever schemed for ways to hurt us. I just think he reacts that way. Remember back in high school—Matt would have a great practice and the coach's praise, so Hank would pick a fight with him. Some girl he never paid attention to would start dating one of us, and *bam*, Hank would start chatting her up. I think he just reacts to what he sees."

Nathan stared off across the field, processing what Danny was saying. "So you think he took Donna not because of some long-lost love but because she was with me?"

"Maybe he does care for Donna. I don't know. But I think he pursued her because she was with you."

"And Jacob?"

Danny shrugged and looked off over the field. "I don't know if that's any different to him."

DARKNESS CLOAKED the field as they sat in silence, listening to the crickets and frogs singing in the night. They each mulled over their conversation, picking at it in their minds.

Nathan could barely see the outline of his friend beside him though he could hear him sucking on an ice cube. "So what? What am I going to do about it?"

Danny started and shifted in his chair. "What do you mean?"

"If everything you just said is true, so what do I do? It doesn't change the fact that he can prove Jacob is his son and Donna is moving with him to Atlanta."

"I think it changes everything."

"How?"

"We've been assuming he and Donna are in full agreement."

"I caught them in bed together. They sure agreed on that."

"That doesn't mean they agree on what's best for Jacob. And it doesn't mean they agree on cutting you out of his life."

"So, what do we do?"

"Two things. First, you get an attorney. A good one. And figure out what your options are. If Hank is going to try to take Jacob from you, you have nothing to lose anyway."

"Visitation."

"I don't think so because I can't see Donna forbidding Jacob from seeing you."

"How do we know?"

"That's the second thing. I'm going to go talk to Donna again. I need to find out how much she agrees with Hank's little plan."

"You think she'll tell you?"

"Yes, I do, as long as Hank isn't around. She was open with me this morning, but I wasn't thinking about this the way I am now, so I didn't ask the right questions. If she refuses to talk to me, that tells us a lot too, but I think she will."

Nathan chewed on his lip. "Just one little problem with your two-step plan."

"What?"

"I've got no money for a lawyer."

"Borrow it."

"With what?" Nathan slapped his hand on the tailgate and listened to the ring of metal. "My truck is collateral for my bail money. The house is mortgaged. I don't even have my ring to hock. I don't think a duffel bag of clothes will convince anyone to loan me money."

"Ask Ronnie."

Nathan sucked in his breath. "I can't do that."

"Would you pay him back?"

"Every penny. Plus interest."

"Does he know that?" As Nathan nodded, Danny continued, "He would do anything for you and anything for Jacob.

And I think he would be mad if you didn't ask for his help when you needed it."

Nathan wrung his hands and rocked on the stool. "I hate it, but I'll ask."

"Good. You go do that, and I'll see if I can meet Donna. I'll call you when I know more."

They packed up their dinner and drove back into town.

25

Nathan parked his truck at the curb in front of Ronnie's house. A light was on in the den, and the glow from the TV flickered through the window. He walked up to the dark porch and knocked on the door. The porch lights came on, and Ronnie peeked through the curtain covering the glass. He opened the door and ushered Nathan into the small den. "What brings you here on a Saturday night? Anything wrong?"

"I want to catch you up on my day and then ask a couple of favors."

Without hesitation, Ronnie waved his hand at the couch as he shifted a TV tray out of the way. "Sit."

"Frozen dinner?" Nathan spotted the familiar packaging, a long-running joke about Ronnie's lack of kitchen skills. He and Charlie had learned some basic meals and cooked dinners growing up out of sheer necessity.

"My favorite recipe. A microwave is all a man needs." He picked up the remote and turned the TV off as he settled onto the couch.

Nathan filled him in on the events of the day, including the story of Hank's genetic testing. Ronnie listened attentively, asked an occasional question, and nodded at Danny's theories. After Nathan finished the tale, the two sat in the dim light of the den.

Ronnie rubbed his chin and asked, "So you need a good attorney?"

"Yes, sir."

"I could suggest a couple that I've dealt with from work. Not sure if they handle divorces or not, but they can guide you to the right person. But something tells me you are here for more than a name."

"Yes, sir. I hate to ask, but..." Nathan licked his lips before plunging ahead. "I don't have the money for one."

"So you need to borrow some money? Of course. That's easy. Whatever you need."

"I promise to pay you back."

"Of course you will. I can't imagine you not."

Nathan paused and studied Ronnie's face for any sign of hesitation or resentment. "I feel bad asking."

"Son, it's okay. In all the years I've known you, you've never asked to borrow money from me once. Not ever. So you wouldn't ask if you didn't really need it."

"I know things are tough at the plant and you could lose your job, so I don't want to put you in a bind."

"I've known for a long time the plant was going to close, so I've been saving for years. Why do you think I eat those things?" He waved his hand at the congealing dinner.

"Because you can't cook?"

Ronnie ignored the comment and continued, "And I still have the money saved to help pay for Charlie's college."

"I don't know how I can ever thank you enough."

"Easy. I don't care what Hank's genetic test says or even the fact that you and I aren't related, I think of that boy as my grandson. So work out something good and bring him around here when you can."

"Yes, sir."

With a flick of his hand, Ronnie dismissed the topic and moved on. "You said 'a couple of favors.' What else?"

"No, I couldn't. Not after asking to borrow money."

"What is it?"

Nathan paused and swallowed. "Danny's going back to work at his family's store. They want me to reopen Abe's old garage."

"That's terrific news. I've really missed that place, and it would be great for the town for it to be open again."

"But that would mean leaving the plant."

"I get that, and it makes it even better news. You deserve the opportunity."

Nathan looked down. "But I would be leaving you when you really need the help at the plant."

"Son, you aren't leaving me. I'll see you all the time because you'll be bringing Jacob around. And I'll finally have someone I can trust to keep that old Buick running. I expect a family discount, of course." His eyes twinkled with mirth before he continued, "I'll call Carl tomorrow and see if he wants to come back. He'll jump at the chance so he can be home with his family again."

A loud knock at the front door interrupted them. Ronnie joked, "More company than I've had in years," before opening the door to reveal Donna and Matt standing under the porch light.

Seeing them, Nathan leapt to his feet, fearing the worst. "Is Jacob okay?"

Matt assured him, "He's fine. Colette is back at the house with him. He and Luke were sprawled on the den floor, watching a baseball game when I left."

Donna stepped through the doorway. "Danny told me all about today, which connected some dots for me. He suggested we get together tomorrow, but I didn't want to wait. I mean, if you're willing to talk to me after all I've done."

Nathan stepped forward and offered his hand. "Of course. Let's go find somewhere to talk and let Ronnie have his house back."

"Stop it," Ronnie protested. "It's not like I have a bedtime or something. Y'all come right in here and talk."

He started pushing the door closed when Donna stopped him. She pointed outside. "We can't leave him out there."

Ronnie stepped out onto the front porch and spied Danny as he sat in his chair at the base of the front-porch steps.

Danny raised his hands. "It's okay. I brought them here to talk to Nathan. I'll wait in the van."

"Danny—" Ronnie began.

"No, it's fine, Mr. Mills. I'm the last person you want in your house."

Ronnie studied him for a second and called back over his shoulder. "Matt? Nathan? Come out here and grab that chair. Lift it up on the porch so he can come inside. No guest of mine is waiting outside."

Nathan and Matt walked down the steps and lifted the chair.

Danny whispered, "This is a really bad idea. I should have called you and met somewhere else."

Nathan replied, "You're here. And I'm not telling him no right after he helped me out, so you're going inside that house. Deal with it."

They settled the chair on the front porch. Nathan held open the front door and waved his arm in a dramatic welcoming fashion. Danny rolled his eyes and pushed through the doorway into the den. Ronnie carried in kitchen chairs to create enough seating in the small den.

Donna settled into one of the chairs and looked around. Her eyes were red and puffy from crying. Matt sat in the other chair, looking around more nervously than even Danny. An uncomfortable silence filled the room.

———————

DANNY CLEARED HIS THROAT. "I guess I get to direct traffic since I've heard all the pieces. So first things first, Donna has already called the police department to ask about lifting the restraining order. It's not quite as easy to do as you would think, but she's making it happen. I'm just saying she understands the problem with being in the same room with you but wanted to come anyway."

Donna looked into Nathan's eyes. "I'm so sorry about the whole restraining order. You were never a threat to me and certainly never to Jacob, so I wouldn't have asked for one."

"You didn't request it?"

"No. The doctors had given me some strong pain meds, so when we got home from the hospital Friday, I went straight to sleep. I had no clue that Hank had called the police and told them about you showing up at the hospital. He convinced them to issue the order and promised I would come in Monday to give my statement. But when I found out about it, I decided to tell them the whole thing was unnecessary, but I couldn't do anything until Monday. It didn't even cross my mind when I came up to you at the park today."

Nathan swallowed and looked around the room. "So where is Hank?"

Donna shrugged. "Back in Atlanta, I guess. I told him to leave after Jacob's ballgame. I was furious at him."

"Furious?"

"We had a fight before the game, but I really lost it with what you said at the park. I tried to stop you and ask about it, but you took off running before I could open my mouth. I didn't understand what you meant about a stolen lottery ticket.

And that comment about not having a son hurt so bad, and I had no clue what it meant. I was so confused and demanded Hank tell me everything. He told me enough to infuriate me, so I told him to go away. Danny filled in the rest after he left, or I might have punched him in the nose myself."

Donna reached into the pocket of her sweater, extracted a small sheet of paper, and handed it to Nathan. "That's your lottery ticket. I got up this morning before Hank and started doing chores. I picked up your jacket to wash it and went through the pockets. Found the lottery ticket and laid it with your clean clothes. Later, when Danny called, I packed everything in your duffel but never thought about the ticket. First time it ever crossed my mind was when you said it was stolen. I confronted Hank about it, and he just reached into his pocket and handed it to me."

He looked down at the sheet of paper. "This is the winner?"

Donna chuckled and shook her head. "No. It's worthless."

"You're sure it's mine?"

"Look at the time stamp. I know it's not Hank's because, well, he was with me then."

The printout showed the ticket was purchased at the time Nathan was in the store. "But you didn't know it wasn't the winner when you put it with my clothes?"

"No, we hadn't even heard someone had won until after Danny picked up your clothes. I was more surprised you had bought one. But even if I had realized the ticket was the winner, I still would have given it to you." She looked at everyone's bemused smiles. "Oh, please. Don't make me out as some saint. I still would have gotten half in a divorce."

The chuckles around the room relieved some of the tension.

Nathan stared at the paper and said, "But I thought he won."

"He did. I saw the ticket myself. Bought at nine fifteen Friday morning, just like all his other tickets. He showed it to me to prove he hadn't stolen it from you. But I pointed out that he still had your ticket. A thief is a thief. And a stupid thief because he stole it long before we even knew a winner was out there, so he didn't know if it won or not."

"So you told him to go home because he stole a worthless lottery ticket?"

Donna wrung her hands. "No, if it had just been that... I couldn't figure out what you meant about not having a son. Hank wouldn't tell me, and I knew he was keeping secrets. I didn't find that out until Danny came over."

She looked up. "I'm getting ahead of myself. Something happened even before I found out he stole your lottery ticket."

As they all watched, she took a deep, shaky breath. She dabbed her eyes with a tissue and began, "Right after Danny left with your clothes this morning, Hank heard on the radio that a lottery winner was sold from Abe's. He gets all excited and starts rooting through his suitcase. He comes up with the tickets and compares the numbers and started yelling and screaming. He's jumping up and down and hugging me and shows me the ticket. I can't believe it. It's the winner. I see it with my own eyes. All that money. And then..."

Tears flowed down her face, and she tried to mop them up with the tissue, but it was too soaked and worn. Nathan reached into his pocket and pulled out a handkerchief, neatly ironed by Donna after the last laundry.

She nodded her thanks and continued, "We're dancing around the room, celebrating, and he says, 'We've got to amend the prenup for this, don't we?' and then races out of the room to call Matt."

The room had gone totally silent. Donna's voice grew very quiet, but her words were clear. "It had bothered me before that he wanted one. I mean, you and I argued about money sometimes, but neither of us thought, *This is my money, and that's your money*. We were in it together. But he said a prenup was just normal and expected. But for that to be the first thing he thinks of after finding out he won all this money... the first thing." She sank her head into her hands. "It made me realize how utterly selfish he is. So unlike you."

Nathan reached over and held her hands as she cried. Only as her tears slowed did he ask, "So does that mean it's over with him?"

She wiped her eyes and grimaced through her tears. "God help me, but I love him. I don't like him very much, and I think he's an ass for everything he's done, but it still hurts that he's gone."

"So, what are you going to do?"

"Figure out how to stop loving him. Or how to live with the fact that I do love him, but I can't be with him because of the type of person he is." She patted Nathan's hand. "It's not fair, I know. You're a good man, but I don't love you. At least not in the way I need to for us to be a couple. I'm really sorry for that."

Nathan grimaced but left his hand in hers. "So where does that leave us?"

"Friends, but not married. I mean, if you'll have me as a friend. I know that might be too awkward, but we were always great friends."

"We can try."

"I think what I need right now is to live on my own. Try to be my own person. I've never done that. Can you deal with that?"

"Yeah, I can." Nathan nodded, with tears in his own eyes. "So does that mean you're going to stay in Millerton?"

"Oh, I never told you." She smiled through her tears. "Right after you left for work Friday morning, I called over to the McDonald's. They were ecstatic I wanted to come back and gave me the job on the spot. I start back next week as an assistant manager. If you can help me by watching Jacob while I'm working, of course, because I have to work weekends and nights."

Relief poured through Nathan, and his tense muscles relaxed. "You bet I can help."

Ronnie piped up. "And anytime he can't, Jacob can hang out here."

Matt added, "Or with us. Luke loves it when he's there."

Everyone bubbled with conversation, but Nathan sat silently, thinking through the day. He raised his hand to quiet everyone. "But that still leaves Hank as Jacob's father. He could petition for custody."

Donna pointed toward Matt. "I seriously doubt that, but this is Matt's part to tell."

―――――――――

MATT SIGHED. "Before I start, let me be clear I love my brother. I agree with Donna—he's an ass sometimes, but he's still my family."

Nathan squinted his eyes. "Please tell me the Russian story is made up."

"Oh, no. It's true. Absolutely rocked his world when he found out." Matt took a deep breath and continued, "Mom was already in the hospital by this point, and we knew she wasn't going to be around much longer. Hank comes racing in with these printouts, throws them on her bed, and demands to know what they mean. I'm trying to get him calmed down— you know how hard that is to do—and we suddenly realize that Mom is just staring at them. She just looks up and says, 'I'm sorry.'

"You can only imagine how stunned we were. We knew our old man—well, I guess it's my old man—was a piece of work.

Ran off with another woman when I was in third grade and Hank in fourth. After that, he never sent money, never called, nothing. But still, to find out that he wasn't even Hank's dad… that sent me reeling. You can only imagine what it did to Hank.

"You know what he was worried about? The first thing he thought of? He was scared they were going to find out at his work that his dad was Russian. The owners of the security company are two Green Berets who were in Vietnam. They rant about communists all the time, and so in Hank's mind, being half Russian was just like being a commie. Mom kept trying to tell him the guy was American, just from Russia, but Hank went nuts about it."

Matt stared at the ceiling as he thought for a minute. "Guess he finally figured out a way to turn it into an advantage."

"So Jacob is his kid." Nathan slumped in the couch and leaned his head back against the cushions.

"Maybe. Maybe not."

"But the test?"

"I wonder about that. When he got his own DNA test results back, he couldn't stop talking about it. But never said a word about Jacob's."

Donna interjected. "Not to me either. First I heard about testing Jacob was when Danny told me the story a little while ago."

"You think Jacob's test shows he doesn't have Russian blood?"

"I don't think he's ever been tested at all. It's just the type of stupid story Hank would tell." Matt smiled sheepishly and continued, "Remember, I heard this for the first time tonight when Danny told Donna. It just sounded really weird, so I went outside where the boys were tossing a Frisbee around under our floodlights and challenged them to a spitting contest. They laughed like it was the silliest thing they had ever heard.

Colette thought I had lost my mind. She's probably still wondering what I was up to.

"Anyway, I had them going for distance first. Had a tape measure and everything. Then I pulled out a jar and said we had to go for accuracy. They were giggling, and I said, 'What? You've never spit in a jar before?' They both howled with laughter and screamed, 'No!' Jacob never said a word about a spitting contest with Hank. Don't you think a twelve-year-old would remember that?"

Nathan felt a weight lift off him, and he relaxed. But the more he thought about Jacob not having taken the test, the more the pressure came crashing back down. "Without a test, we really don't know whose son he is. It's still possible Jacob is his kid, right?"

Donna took his hand. "I wish I could tell you for sure, but I can't. I'm so sorry for that."

Nathan held her gaze. "Don't we owe it to him to find out? Doesn't Jacob deserve to know?"

She sat looking at him then slowly nodded. "Someday, maybe. But I don't see a rush. He's already going to have to deal with his parents living apart. That's a lot to take in. And I think he needs both his mom and dad to be there for him through this. I mean the dad who has been there every day of his life. Later, we can find out who fathered him."

"But what if Hank forces the issue? Can't he insist on a paternity test? I'll always worry he will come take him away."

"Fat chance," Matt said and busted out laughing. "He'll never push for it."

Donna and Nathan exchanged puzzled glances. "Why not?" they asked in unison.

"How often do you play catch with Jacob? Or shoot hoops? Or go fishing? Or even just sit and help him with his homework."

"As often as I can."

"Same with me and Luke. I'm even getting halfway decent on the Xbox, playing games with both of them."

"So?"

"Why do you do it?"

Nathan shrugged. "Because it's a lot of fun to hang out. He's a cool kid."

"Hank's different. Sure, he buys Luke presents for Christmas and all that, but he never just plays with him. He doesn't sit on the floor playing video games or hang out in the yard tossing a ball around. I think the only reason he was interested in Jacob was because he was interested in Donna."

Donna spoke up. "Even if he tried, all he would get is some visitation rights. There's no question I'm the mother, and I'm going to make sure he spends time with you, Nathan."

Matt shook his head. "What I'm saying is it will never get there. It's actually the other way around. At some point *you're* going to want to try and prove that Hank is the dad."

Donna and Nathan both shouted in shock, "Why?"

Matt tsked. "Because he just won the lottery, folks. All you have to do is threaten to have him tested, and Hank'll be itching to settle. Jacob's college fund is totally covered. "

26

The conversation slowly petered out as exhaustion from the day settled on everyone. After a period of extended silence, Danny spoke up. "Colette's going to wonder if I kidnapped her husband, so I should get him home. Ronnie, sorry we invaded your house. I appreciate you letting us hang out for a bit, but we should get out of your way."

The group moved out onto the expansive front porch with its rocking chairs and porch swing. The twin lights on either side of the door brightened only a portion of the front yard. Their cars were but dark shadows lining the curb.

As they all chattered, Donna grabbed the porch railing and took a first step down the stairs when she froze, her foot dangling in midair and her eyes widening as she stared into the darkness. Nathan followed her gaze and spotted a tiny orange dot—the end of a cigarette glowing.

A man shouted from the darkness, "You going back to him?"

Hank emerged from the shadows and tossed the cigarette onto the cracked sidewalk, scattering sparks. He slammed his foot down on it and twisted, extinguishing the lit tobacco. He walked forward until he was blocking their path down the front walk with his menacing stance.

Nathan descended the steps and stood protectively in front of Donna as she slowly shook her head.

She spoke quietly, her voice just above a whisper. "No."

"You'll go back to him. Just like you did before. Scampering back to the golden child."

"Not this time." Her voice was firmer, more confident, despite the threat in Hank's voice.

"Prove it. Get in the car. Let's go to Atlanta right now. Leave all this crap behind."

"No."

"Why not?"

"Jacob."

Hank stood glaring from the shadows, anger oozing off him. He clenched his fists and took two steps forward. "If it hadn't been for that boy, you would have come with me after high school. Your life would be totally different today."

Donna stepped around Nathan, her hand gentle on his elbow, and nodded. Her voice soft, she said, "Yes, but I wouldn't have 'that boy.' And Jacob is the world to me. It would be less rich without him."

Hank continued to stare for several seconds before his head dropped and his hands slowly unclenched. He matched her drop in volume. "He might be mine. Maybe the three of us could have gone off back then. Been our own family."

She continued advancing until she touched his hand with her fingers. "Maybe. But it's not the way things happened. We can't change the past. And you really don't know who the father is, do you?"

He stood still for several seconds before reluctantly shaking his head.

"Jacob never took the DNA test, did he?"

The shake of his head was almost imperceptible as he mumbled, "No."

"So why such a crazy lie?"

His head snapped up, and he glared at Nathan. "Because I knew you wouldn't move to Atlanta without Jacob. And no way would you take him away from his father. So I thought if I could convince him I was the father, he would just let us go."

"Oh, Hank." She tsked and shook her head. "I wouldn't take my son away from Millerton and the only father he's ever known, because that's what's best for him. It's not about what you want or what Nathan wants or even what I want. And it's certainly not about which one of you fathered him years ago. The only thing that matters to me is what Jacob needs. Once he's in college or working and he doesn't need me around as much, I might have moved with you." She shrugged. "I still might though we would have a lot of things to work out first. But no matter what, not before Jacob is ready to stand on his own, even if you are the father."

Hank reached under his jacket and withdrew a cellophane pack and tapped the box against his hand. A cigarette extended itself, and he offered it to Donna. She eyed it but shook her head in refusal. "They're bad for me" is all she said.

He sighed and extracted the cigarette, placed it in his mouth, cupped his hands, and lit it with a flick of his lighter. After inhaling deeply, he blew a large cloud of smoke into the air and looked over the group. "It's just high school days all over again. I got tired of competing against him then and am tired of it now."

Jolted, Nathan protested. "I never knew we were competing."

"Sure we were. We've always competed. Since the day we met. Who's faster? Who's stronger? Who gets the girl?"

Donna looked at the two of them. "So I was a prize?"

Hank paused and scratched his chin. "I hate to admit it,

but at first, yeah. I know that sounds horrible—it is horrible—but then I really started to like hanging around you. Talking to you. Being with you. Those nights at my house were some of the best of my life."

Donna started to walk away, but Hank called after her, "I don't mean the sex. Yeah, that was great, but you were the first girl I ever saw a future with. I loved you." He paused and drew in another lungful of smoke. "I still do." As Donna turned to look at him, he continued, "When you wouldn't break up with him back then, it broke my heart. I realized I cared for you more than you cared for me. That had never happened to me before. I was always supposed to be the one who could just walk away."

He turned his back on the group and looked out at the dark street. "I couldn't hang around with you two and watch you together. It ate me up inside. I couldn't wait for school to be over so I could just leave and forget you. The worst day of my life was watching you get married to him."

He turned back toward Donna and took a hesitant step toward her. "I had tried so hard to forget, but I couldn't. Did you know I kept a picture of you in my locker during the Marines? Told all the guys in my platoon that you were my girlfriend. And the more I thought of you"—he turned to look at Nathan—"and you being with him, the more it hurt. Even when I was discharged, I made excuses not to come back and see Matty because I was scared to run into you. And then I did, and the feelings just exploded again."

Donna mumbled, "At Matt's house before Halloween."

"Yes." Hank looked away, his moist eyes glistening in the porch light. "Talking to you that day, I could tell you weren't happy. Not with Nathan. Not with your life. I thought maybe I had a chance."

"You did."

"But Jake…" He glanced over at Nathan. "Jacob. As much

as I had a chance with you, you would never tear Jacob away from Nathan. All of our time together, all she talked about was Jacob this and Jacob that, and that was cool because he's a good kid, but she also said Jacob and Nathan too much. And so I thought, maybe, if I could drive a big enough wedge between you and Nathan, maybe I had a chance. I hated that he hurt you, but I saw my chance to break you up for good. And then when I saw him hiding in the woods, watching the baseball game—"

Nathan smiled wanly. "I didn't want to miss his game."

"But, you see, I knew right then—I didn't stand a chance. You love that kid too much. You love him enough to hide in the woods so you can watch him play a game. It's painted all over your face, just like it's painted all over hers. So I panicked and told that stupid DNA-test story."

"Thinking I would let him go if he wasn't my son?"

Hank nodded and shrugged.

Nathan said, "I don't care what any test says. He's my son."

"I get that now. What I did was a desperate and crazy thing." Hank turned and took several steps toward his car before turning back. "You know she was going to break up with you back in high school."

"Danny told me. After the Roosevelt game."

"Yeah." Hank took another drag on his cigarette. "Have you ever wondered about how things would have been different?"

"No. I didn't know you two were, well, together back then. So I haven't had time to think about it."

"I don't mean just your happy little family." Hank chewed on his lip. "I mean about everything. The weird little things that happen and change everything. If she hadn't gotten pregnant, she would have broken up with you that night. Don't you see how different everything would be?"

"Yeah."

"I don't think you do. What would have happened?"

"We probably would have gotten into a big fight."

"Exactly. And if we would have done that, we would never have gone together to the Point. You and Charlie would probably have gone home and Danny and I to my house. We would have made up a few days later, but either way, that would have meant Charlie would still be alive."

Hank's voice grew quiet as he looked down the street. "All those little twists of fate, just like Charlie was always trying to get us to see in Shakespeare. If you hadn't tackled Ricky Ward, he would have scored, and we wouldn't have wanted to celebrate. Or if Matty had told you that I was sleeping with Donna while we were sitting in the car, we would have brawled right there. Or if it hadn't been raining, others would have gone to the Point, and we wouldn't have needed to get back to my house."

"Just the way things went."

"But that's my point. A whole bunch of random things happened, and there we were in a wrecked car up by the Point. Stupid, horrible luck."

Hank's eyes were filled with tears when he turned back to face them. "And worst of all, the one that will haunt me forever —what if I had been the one hurt rather than you? You wouldn't have left him there in the river. You would have pulled him out."

When Nathan took a step forward, Hank waved him off with his hands. "If I hadn't been so drunk or so scared of the trouble we were in or so stupid, I would have got him out of there. But you weren't that drunk or scared or stupid. You were just hurt." His voice breaking, he struggled through his words. "How's that for the worst luck of them all? Charlie needed one friend to not let him drown."

Nathan closed the gap between them and put his hands on Hank's shoulders. He opened his mouth to protest but was stopped by Ronnie's booming voice cutting through the night.

"Is that what y'all think? That Charlie died because you didn't get him out of the water?"

Hank replied, "They said it in court. He drowned."

"Yeah, he did. But that doesn't mean he was going to live if you got him out." Ronnie looked up at the starlit sky and sighed. "I can't ever get that autopsy report out of my head. The whole thing. His skull was crushed. Massive internal bleeding. Shattered bones. Organ damage. He was never going to wake up. The water just got him before something else did. He drowned only because it was the quickest path."

Hank stood in stunned silence before speaking. "So you're saying it didn't matter what we did?"

"Being drunk mattered." Ronnie looked sternly over at Danny. "Driving drunk mattered."

Danny dropped his gaze to the ground as Ronnie turned back to Hank. "I'm saying you did everything you could to save the ones that could be saved. You ran to get help, and it got there in time to save these two." He turned his eyes to Nathan's face. "And you kept Danny alive by talking to him, keeping him conscious." He reached out and put a hand on the back of Hank's and Nathan's necks and pulled them close. "Neither one of you could have saved Charlie. It was too late. He was killed the instant the accident happened. It just took a little while to be over."

———

THEY STOOD awkwardly in the front yard trying to talk, but the bonds of friendship had long since frayed. Hank muttered his goodbyes, looked longingly at Donna, and climbed into his car. They watched Hank's taillights disappear down the street.

As they stood quietly in a huddle, Danny's voice reached them from the front porch.

"If I could get a little help, I need to get back down to yard level without doing a kamikaze down the steps."

They all chuckled at the visual. Matt and Nathan lifted Danny's wheelchair from the porch and gently placed it and its occupant on the front sidewalk.

As they moved toward their vehicles, Ronnie's voice carried through the night. "Can I ask a favor?"

They answered in unison and without the slightest hesitation, "Sure."

"I have a carpentry project that needs to get done. I could sure use some help."

Nathan scanned around the house, always on the lookout for a loose gutter or rotting trim work. "Glad to help with anything. What do you need?"

Ronnie walked down to the sidewalk and motioned behind him. "These steps are great for sitting on in the morning and sipping a cup of coffee. But I think they're wide enough that we would have plenty of room to build a ramp on one side. That would make the porch more accessible."

The older man paused and nodded toward Danny sitting in his wheelchair. "If Nathan is going to come over here and bring Jacob, then you should feel comfortable coming and going without asking for help. I want to have my boys hanging out on the porch again. It's not right you can't get up there without help."

Shock spread on Danny's face as he opened his mouth to speak, but he could only stutter. Ronnie got down on a knee so that he could look Danny in the eyes. "It's been long enough. I miss Charlie and will never stop missing him, but I've been holding on to my hurt and anger too much. I hope you can forgive me for that."

"Forgive you? I'm the one who needs the forgiveness."

Ronnie extended his hand for a shake. "I can see what a good person you are. How you've been there for Nathan. Any friend of his is welcome in my house, so I'd like you to feel free to come around anytime you want."

Danny gripped the offered hand firmly and shook. "I'd like that. More than you'll ever know."

"Good." Ronnie stood and addressed all of them. "Why don't y'all come around tomorrow, and I'll fix lunch? We can map out a plan so I can get the lumber we need."

"And which frozen dinner are you microwaving for us?" Nathan asked with a sly smile.

Ronnie tried to protest, but Danny interrupted. "I've got a better idea. I have a restaurant to open, so I need to practice cooking for lots of people. The store is closed on Sundays, so why don't *y'all* come down *there* for a big lunch. Matt, you bring Colette and Luke. We'll have a big celebration lunch and then come out here and build a ramp."

PART IV

SUNDAY

27

The garage bay doors stood open, a cloud of dust hanging in the air as Matt swept the floors. Abe and Ronnie sat in swivel office chairs and watched the work, telling stories of their own youthful days and laughing at long-forgotten antics.

Nathan half listened to them as he organized tools in drawers and tested equipment. Over a decade of inactivity had taken its toll on the machinery, but his adept hands were bringing them to life one by one.

He focused first on the compressor. After only a few minutes of tinkering, it came to life with a roar of air building in the tanks. He found the old basketball, deflated from years of neglect, in a dusty corner and filled it.

Luke and Jacob promptly started a game of Horse. At first, they took turns performing layups and short jump shots, but the game progressed to a more difficult and challenging level. As he giggled, Luke hopped on one leg and took a hook shot with his eyes closed. To everyone's amazement, the ball swished through the rotting net—Nathan made a mental note to buy a new one—and Jacob was attempting to recreate it or risk scoring an *R*. Their infectious laughter echoed off the wall of the shop.

Donna and Colette supervised the game with amusement as they sat in lawn chairs in some shade off to one side of the parking lot. They chatted and laughed, comparing notes on the exploits of their sons.

When Colette went inside to refill their iced tea, Donna waved Nathan over. "Thanks again for coming over this morning."

He settled into the chair beside her. "He deserved to hear it from both of us."

"Yes, but I meant more than that. Not telling him about… the affair."

"No need for him to know that. He needs his mother. I'm not taking her away from him."

"He needs us both." She sighed. "I'm surprised he's taking it as well as he is."

Nathan watched his son swish a long-distance one-handed shot. "Maybe Hank was right—half of his friends' parents are divorced. Or maybe he could just sense things at home. Or maybe he's just hiding his feelings. I don't know."

"When you pick him up for school tomorrow, talk to him. See how he's feeling."

He reached out and patted her hand. "I'll call you after I drop him off. Let you know what he says."

Martha emerged from the house behind the store, two pies balanced in her hands. She placed them on the long folding table beside arrangements of fresh flowers as she admonished the boys to leave them until after their meal. The second she disappeared through the back door of the store, they raced over and hung over the table, drooling.

A few minutes later, Martha reappeared through the door, carrying the first of many trays of food. Donna and Colette called their boys to come help, and the four of them joined Martha in hauling the feast out to the tables.

Danny had been cooking since early in the morning, when he had fired up the ovens in the deli. A clipboard rested in the kitchen, filled with a list of equipment and ingredients he wanted to add. The Liar's Table, empty of its regulars on a Sunday morning, was covered with drawings that Abe and Nathan had sketched that morning of an expansion for the building, adding seating and a separate restaurant entrance.

The meal was exquisite, the taste amplified by the warm spring air and jovial gathering of friends. Everyone returned to the buffet for seconds—the boys for thirds—before Martha sliced pies despite people's protests of being too full. The boys wanted to taste each flavor and, to the amazement of the adults, succeeded in doing so before racing off to resume their basketball game.

Full from the meal, Nathan sat in the shade, watching his son play basketball with his best friend. He couldn't help but smile as they bantered with each other.

Martha crossed the lot and settled into a chair beside him. She watched the chaotic game for several minutes before reaching over and patting his hand. "They're good kids."

"Yeah, they are. Every day, I want so much for them it hurts."

Martha glanced over at Danny talking with his father. The two men laughed and talked as they pored over the expansion sketches spread before them.

"Any parent does," she said. "It's natural. Just like your dad wanted everything for you."

They enjoyed the quiet of each other's company for a few moments before Martha stood to join her family. Before walking away, she turned and faced Nathan. "You know he's proud of you, right? He would be so happy to see how you turned out."

Nathan didn't trust himself to speak and could only nod. His eyes teared up so that he almost didn't see Matt approach.

"We need to expand this game and teach those boys how basketball is really played," Matt said. "Come on."

Nathan strolled onto the court, tousling his son's hair as he walked past. They played as the afternoon waned. No one kept score.

Get *Alone Together* Free!

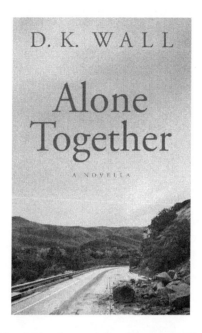

A simple pebble trickles down a hill, a hint of the disaster about to plummet to the highway below. A heroic decision saves lives, but forever alters the path of young Nathan Thomas. *Alone Together* takes you back, before *The Lottery*, before the football game against Roosevelt High, and tells you how Nathan came to live in the Mills' house.

Sign up for my newsletter—a monthly update plus the occasional short story—and I will send you the short story absolutely free.

You can unsubscribe at any time and keep the short story without further obligation.

For more information, visit the link below:

dkwall.com/subscribe

ACKNOWLEDGMENTS

Writing may be a lonely pursuit, but publishing a novel requires a team. I have been blessed to be surrounded by incredible people and *The Lottery* would never have been printed without their effort.

Editors are the silent partners in the background, prodding the author with thoughts and questions. Lynn McNamee's team at Red Adept Editing was invaluable and I particularly want to thank Sara Gardiner, Kelly Reed, and Amanda Kruse.

Sara patiently worked with the early drafts—asking questions, making suggestions, and challenging my tale. Her input and guidance strengthened the story, helping Nathan and friends come alive.

Kelly's sharp eye shaped and structured sentences and her questions helped tighten the story. Amanda wrangled every errant comma, apostrophe and quotation mark.

In just a few sentences, I greatly understate how valuable their efforts were and look forward to working with the Red Adept team on *Lost and Found*.

Glendon Haddix of Streetlight Graphics captured the spirit

of *The Lottery* beautifully with the gorgeous cover. It took my breath away the very first time I saw it.

And a shout out to Bryan Cohen and the team at Best Page Forward for the book description and marketing materials to help *The Lottery* reach the widest audience possible.

One of the most pleasant aspects of my journey to a debut novel has been the incredible warmth and support I have received from so many authors. The writing community is incredibly generous and I continue to be pleasantly surprised how helpful everyone is. Whenever I had a question or worry as a rookie, an experienced author always took the time to help me. I can never express my gratitude enough.

I also want to thank all of the people who have read my short stories over the years and encouraged me to write a book. Your friendship and support means the world to me.

Finally, none of this would have been possible without the cheerleading and coaching from Todd Fulbright. From the beginning, he told me I could do this and encouraged me every step of the way.

Don't worry, readers, he is already asking when the next book will be ready for you. *Jaxon With An X* will hit stores summer 2020!

D.K. Wall

ABOUT THE AUTHOR

D.K. Wall has spent his entire life in Tennessee and the Carolinas, from the edge of the Great Smoky Mountains in Maggie Valley to industrial towns of Gastonia and Hickory and the financial center of Charlotte. He shares stories of this area through his writing and photography.

He is married and shares his home on the salt marsh of Murrells Inlet with a family of rescued Siberian Huskies known as The Thundering Herd. With their never-ending help, he is hard at work on his next novel.

For more information and to enjoy his short stories and photographs, please visit the author's website:

dkwall.com

FOLLOW D.K. WALL ON SOCIAL MEDIA

facebook.com/DKWallAuthor

twitter.com/DKWallAuthor

instagram.com/d.k.wall

pinterest.com/dkirkwall

Made in the USA
Las Vegas, NV
21 November 2020